McKnight

McKnight

A NOVEL

For Melissa + Kinsey,
God Bless you guys.

DAVID WEHR

TATE PUBLISHING
AND ENTERPRISES, LLC

Published by Tate Publishing & Enterprises, LLC
127 E. Trade Center Terrace | Mustang, Oklahoma 73064 USA
1.888.361.9473 | www.tatepublishing.com

Tate Publishing is committed to excellence in the publishing industry. The company reflects the philosophy established by the founders, based on Psalm 68:11,
"The Lord gave the word and great was the company of those who published it."

Published in the United States of America

ISBN: 978-1-62024-486-9
1. Fiction / General
2. Fiction / Christian / Western
12.06.07

To Christina, my courageous Oregon girl.

Distant rifle fire woke him. He had been sleeping hard after the good food. It was early spring. The night was clear and cold with a half moon. He came up on his feet, right hand full of .44. Two miles below him, on the valley floor, the farmhouse was on fire. Ewell was striking the family he had just eaten with. Ewell and his crew of renegades had been raiding this country for the past year. Everywhere they went they left a trail of burned-out farms, dead menfolk, and tortured women and children. More rifle and shotgun fire. The farmer and his ten-year-old boy were fighting back.

No time. No time, he thought. Sam had to force himself to take the time to grab his fighting gear. Only a fool goes into battle unprepared. He pulled on his boots and saddled Buck as fast as he could. Slipping on his leather gloves, he buckled on his .44. Sam drew his spare .44 from the concealed holster built into the underside of his saddlebag. Hat and coat were forgotten in the need to rescue. He swung onto Buck and gave the big chestnut his head.

"Yah!" Sam leaned into his horse, and Buck began to eat up the distance. Sam made no attempt to guide the big horse; he just encouraged him to move. Buck sensed the need and strained hard to please his master.

Sam thought back on the family he had eaten with that day as branches rushed past him. He had ridden into the neat, little farmyard on his way up to the high country. The farm was isolated. It was a good, two days' ride to the nearest town.

A one-story, white farmhouse stood on the east end of the farmyard with a sturdy barn just to the south of it. A great oak grew to the north of the house. *In the summer, the tree must shade the whole yard,* Sam had thought. The cool, spring air was filled with the smell of warm cornbread. He could almost taste it.

He called, "Hello!" to the house. A boy about four years old stepped out on the porch. He was black and as cute as a new colt. To the right of Sam, the barn door swung open, and out came Big Brother. He was pointing a 12-gauge shotgun at Sam. The gun was almost as big as the boy. *Eight,* Sam thought.

"You git yo'self back inside. 'Member what Daddy told you," Big Brother said.

"Yes." Little Brother's eyes grew wide, and he ran inside calling, "Mama, Mama! Come quick!"

Sam leaned forward in his saddle. "I don't think they get much company, Buck."

"Who you talkin' to?"

"My horse, Buck, of course." Sam smiled. Buck looked at the big brother.

"You crazy, mister," the boy said, shaking his head.

"No, I'm a US marshal, son. You can put down the scattergun." The gun didn't move.

A lovely, young woman stepped out on the porch. "May I hep you?" she said. Sam pulled off his broad-brimmed, Texas-style hat revealing his dark, short hair. "Good afternoon, ma'am. Name's Sam McKnight, US Marshal. I'm on the trail of Tom Ewell and his bunch."

"In that case, you is welcome, Marshal. My name is Sally Webster, and this is my youngest, Daniel. My guard over there is David." She looked at Big Brother. "David, put that gun down. The marshal here has come to hep. Come on inside, Marshal. I hope you like venison stew and cornbread."

"Oh, yes, ma'am, I do."

As Sam was unsaddling his big chestnut, the husband came in from the fields. He was a giant of a man, six foot four, two hundred forty pounds, and he towered over Sam's smaller frame. Sam was only five foot ten and one hundred sixty pounds of bone and muscle. The husband was carrying a hoe and a Winchester repeating rifle. The rifle looked to be one of the first, and it was still in mint condition.

"This is one of the finest, little farms I have ever seen. Sir, you have done yourself and your family proud." Sam stuck out his hand. "Sam McKnight."

The giant's wary look changed to a cautious smile. He wrapped his huge hand around Sam's. "Nick Webster," he said, and the two men headed for the cornbread.

This family could eat! After a massive meal, Sam was invited to play horseshoes with Nick and the boys—Nick and Daniel against Sam and David. Sam's first shoe hit the pit and rolled six feet to the right. David knew they were in trouble. Nick's first shoe was a ringer. The look on Sam's face brought out a huge, bass laugh from Nick.

The afternoon turned out to be one of the most enjoyable Sam had ever spent as he relished watching this good man with his good family against a daunting backdrop. In the late afternoon, the boys begged him to stay. Sam explained to them he had to keep moving. He didn't want Ewell's trail to get cold. Nick shook Sam's hand, and Sally gave Sam a big hug. She whispered in his ear, "Thank you for bein' so good to my boys." She kissed him on the cheek.

◆◆◆◆ ━━━━ ◆ ━━━━ ◆◆◆◆

As he rounded the last bend, he realized the shooting had stopped. "Oh God, don't let me be too late." He reined up Buck. The roar of the fire was deafening. Sam and Buck couldn't be seen in the dark, but they could see the farmyard clearly. The farmhouse and barn were totally enveloped in flames. The corral fence was also starting to burn.

In the firelight he saw five outlaws sprawled on the ground. David and Nick had gotten their licks in. The Websters had been dragged to the center of their farmyard. With the flames dancing on it, the great oak looked like some demon from hell. Four men were holding Nick. His hands were tied behind his back. Ewell had given Nick's face quite a beating.

A righteous anger began to rise in Sam. It was a tangible feeling, moving up out of his chest into his scalp. His eyes glistened with bright fury.

A rope had been thrown over a limb of the monster oak and tied off at the trunk. A noose hung at its end. It took six of Ewell's eight remaining men to put Nick on a horse. One of the men placed the noose around Nick's neck. Little David broke free. He slammed Ewell in the gut.

"No, boy!" Nick yelled.

The doubled-over Ewell cussed the boy and came up suddenly. The butt of his repeater smashed into the side of the little boy's head. David's body fell like a rag doll to the ground.

"No!" Sam roared. The word filled the night air. The outlaws spun around to see where it came from. Suddenly, the warhorse and his knight exploded over the burning corral fence. A horrified outlaw caught both of Buck's hooves right in his chest and went straight to hell. Sam dropped the reins and pulled both .44s. Buck galloped straight for Nick. The outlaws reached for iron.

The fiery wrath of God poured out of McKnight's .44s. A crusty cuss with no hat and a beard stood twelve feet to Sam's right. Before No Hat could reach his gun, he took two .44 slugs in the belly. He flopped on his butt and began to scream.

To Sam's left, an outlaw wearing a buffalo coat and carrying Nick's Winchester rifle was moving to find cover by the burning house. Next to him stood a gunman wearing two .45s tied down and shiny, black boots. Sam swung both .44s on the pair. Buffalo Coat got off a shot from the Winchester. Sam felt the heat of a graze on his left shoulder. The graze pulled his aim left and high, so instead of hitting Black Boots in the chest, the slug blew off his cheek, ear, and the back of his head. The next slug hit Black Boots high in the chest, lifting him clean out of one boot.

Before Buffalo Coat could get off another shot, a .44 slug broke his right elbow. The slug that followed entered just above his heart and blew through his spine. Buffalo Coat slammed into the burning house and slid down to the dirt, leaving a burning, crimson trail on the wall.

The last two of Ewell's crew had now reached cover north of the oak. By this time, Mrs. Webster had picked up her limp boy and with her youngest in tow had run for cover.

Ewell was standing to the right of Nick's mount. Ewell locked eyes with Sam. The evil in this man dripped from him like sweat. He had a choice—run and try to save himself or kill one more innocent. Tom Ewell slapped Nick's horse on the rump. The horse bolted, and Nick swung.

Buck's chest crashed into Ewell at full speed. The impact lifted Ewell off the ground and threw him against the trunk of the monster oak. A small snag of a limb was driven right through Ewell's back and out his front. Overwhelmed by the pain of his broken body, Ewell could do nothing more than look down at the branch protruding from his chest and whimper.

Nick was still alive. To keep their heads down, Sam emptied his .44s at the remaining outlaws. Holstering his guns, he pulled his knife. He grabbed the rope and began to cut just as the slug hit him. The impact knocked Sam out of the saddle. He hit the ground, rolled, and came up on his boots.

The air was suddenly alive with bullets. Sam just had time to slap Buck and dive behind a trough. He could hear slugs hitting the porch rail, the trough, and the burning house.

I'm pinned down, the .44's are empty, and I'm losing blood fast, he thought. *Nick can't last for more than a minute. Lord, Sally and those boys need that man. I have nothing left. Give me what I need.*

Sam knew the hanging rope was tied off around the oak, just behind Ewell's body. Sam still had his knife. He got to his feet and began to run as hard as he could. Halfway there, his vision began to fade, and he stumbled. A hail of rifle fire burned the air around him. Sam could feel the bullets tugging at his shirt. *"Stay on your feet, boy."* Sam heard the voice of his granddaddy, one of the first Texas Rangers, in his head. *"Push through the pain. You kin do it."* Sam kept going. He reached Ewell's body, grabbed the rope, and cut it. Nick hit the ground hard. Ewell's dead face stared at Sam as he pulled the .45s from Ewell's gun belt and opened fire on the muzzle flashes in the darkness.

The remaining outlaws were silenced by Sam's sixth shot, but he kept firing. On the eleventh shot, he fell hard onto his back and fired the twelfth into the monster oak. The last thing Sam saw that night was Nick leaning over him, checking his wounds.

◆

The sound of hammers brought him slowly back from the darkness. He struggled to open his eyes, but the lids would not be moved.

"It's all right, darlin'. Open your eyes and I will fix you some soup."

Charlie, Sam thought. He forced his eyes open, and there she was. He could just see her dim outline. *It is her.* The hammering got louder, and light was getting brighter. It was morning.

"That's it, that's it. It's good ta see ya again, Mr. McKnight."

"Why are you...?" He swallowed and struggled to speak again. "Why are you calling me McKnight, Charlie?"

"Charlie? Why, Mr. McKnight, this is Sally. I'm Mrs. Webster, remember?"

Slowly, Charlie's sweet face faded until all he could see was Sally. "Mrs. Webster, how long has it been?"

"You've been out for three days. Nick said we was goin' to lose ya, but I told him a man who could keep on fightin' as hurt as you was wasn't goin' to let any bullet stop him." She wiped away a tear. "Oh, we have been prayin', and my Lord, He done pulled you through. Praise Jesus! Praise Jesus! Sam McKnight, He was watchin' over you and my family. I'm going to get you some soup. Now you stay still."

She stood up and pushed through the tent flap. The morning light poured in.

Sam tried to push himself up on one elbow, but his side was too torn up. He fell back on the cot. He peered through the flap. The boys were playing under the tree. David's head was bandaged, but he was alive, and that was all Sam cared about.

"Thank you, Father. Thank you," he said, nodding to the sky. He settled back with a sense of peace. The sun threw the shadowed outline of new oak leaves on the canvas tent top. Summer was coming.

A squirrel brought Sam back to the present. It raced up a tree and began scolding him. A smile broke out on Sam's face, a smile that came right from the center of his chest. Drifting on Buck, it was a good life—a life Sam had not had time to enjoy while recovering from being shot four months earlier. He loved this country and his part in it.

Buck was a big chestnut, the color of a fine, mahogany bar. He was a wonder to see, and he knew it. He was vain to a fault. It was a good thing there weren't any wild, young fillies around, or Buck would be showing off for sure.

Sam thought of Buck as a partner, one he could not do without. Buck was still in his prime, but Sam already worried about how he would replace him. In these past years as a US marshal, Sam had begun to think of Buck as one of those warhorses he had read about in Granddaddy's book, *The Arabian Nights*. Buck seemed to love the battle. He had proven he would kill to protect Sam. He was also the best watchdog Sam had ever had. If there was something out there, Buck's ears were up.

That's what got Sam's attention: Buck's ears were up, and he was looking forward. Someone or something was out in front of them. He pulled his new Winchester from the boot. It was filled to the top with .44s. The walnut forearm and butt felt good in his hands.

There was a small mountain lake just ahead. Two years before, he had spent a few weeks there. He had taken some lead teaching five outlaws that justice does come, sooner or later. After the fight, he had tried to make it back to the office in Salt Lake, but this lake was as far as he got. The time spent there renewed his spirit as well as his body.

It was surrounded by stands of ponderosas. Lush, waist-high grass was growing everywhere. A horse could live there for a year and never exhaust the feed.

It was his place. He had planned to spend two nights there preparing body and soul for his next assignment, which promised to be tough. Sam needed time to think, plan, and pray, but now his plans seemed to be fading.

He circled north to a small ridge overlooking the water. He stepped off of Buck and pulled out his army field glasses. At the east end of his lake, he saw that someone had put up a new, artfully built, little cabin. Each railing, every arch and post had been handpicked for the burls in them. This little nest was built by someone who had time and talent on their hands.

"This country is gettin' too damn crowded," he said to Buck. Sam thought Buck seemed to agree. "But it's a fine, little cabin." To the south of the cabin grazed a glossy, black mare. Sam looked back at Buck. "So that is why you had your ears up." Sam shook his head and smiled.

Movement at the water's edge caught Sam's attention. "What have we got here, boy?" Under a great ponderosa sat a woman.

She was running her hands through her short, blonde hair. It was still wet. Sam had rarely seen short hair on a white woman. It looked good on her. She must have just come out of the lake. Her white, cotton camisole clung to her still-wet body in a most delightful way. Sam found himself grateful for the powerful field glasses with which the Union had supplied him ten years ago. Bare feet stuck out from below her brown riding skirt. She leaned back against the tree and closed her eyes, letting the heat of the sun dry her off.

"I like her, Buck," he said softly. Buck just tossed his head.

Movement fifty yards to the south of the woman caught Sam's eye. A young punk was moving up on the woman, nice and easy. Sam scanned back to the lady. That is when he saw it: a doubled-barreled, sawed-off shotgun was leaning against the near side of the tree. "Well, I'll be damned," he said. Just to be safe, Sam lifted up the Winchester. Using the tree for stability, he sighted the punk in. He was wearing a misshapen hat; a ragged, blue shirt; and a new Colt .45, tied down.

"Who'd he back-shoot for that?" Sam wondered. The punk looked young, about sixteen. The .45 was in his hand.

It had been Sam's misfortune to come upon the aftermath of this kind of scene once too often, when there was nothing to do for the poor girl—who had been raped and worse—except bury her. This time would be different. Sam eared back the hammer of the Winchester and took up the slack on the trigger.

Suddenly, the lady's head turned south. She eyed the punk and reached for the shotgun.

The crack of a rifle made Sam jump. A bullet slapped the tree just above the twelve-gauge. The lady froze. The bullet had come from the rifle of a second gunman. He stepped out from behind the cabin, strutting as if he had just won a turkey shoot. His black pants were tucked into high, black boots. His white shirt was dirty, and he hadn't seen a razor in at least a week. The .44 Henry in his hands looked well maintained. The gunman wore two .44s tied down and looked ready to go.

"Damn," Sam said to Buck, "well, let's see. The gunman is about one hundred yards out, the punk is around seventy-five, and the lady is at about sixty yards. Let's let them come in a little, just to be safe, boy." He had to play this right, or the lady would pay dearly.

The punk reached her first. He was young and filthy. The lady probably smelled him before she heard him. He pointed his .45 right at her face. He was giggling like an idiot.

As the gunman reached her, he leaned his Henry against the tree and pulled the 44s. He was half-covered by the big pine the lady was still leaning against. He said something to the punk, and they both had a good laugh at her expense. The lady now had three guns on her.

If she was afraid, she didn't show it. In fact, she was smiling.

The punk spewed pure filth at the lady through his rotting teeth, but Sam couldn't quite make out what he was saying. He slapped her hard, grabbed the front of her camisole, and tore it open. Sam McKnight's green eyes grew into dark, angry emeralds.

The lady's face came up with blood dripping from her broken lip. She wiped her mouth with the back her hand and smiled at the punk. Her nakedness did not shame her. Everything about her dared them to do their worst. The young punk was ready to oblige. He holstered his .45 and began to fumble with his belt and pants.

Sam was waiting for an opening, but he couldn't wait much longer. Like a rattlesnake strike, the lady smashed her fist into the punk's crotch. His scream bounced off the valley walls as he grabbed himself and fell to the ground. The gunman cussed the lady and raised one of his .44s to backhand her. As he made his move, he stepped into the open.

"Thank you, ma'am," McKnight whispered and squeezed the .44's trigger. The slug tore though the gunman's neck. The outlaw released his guns and dropped to his knees, both of his hands clasping his neck, trying to hold his life in. Sam had meant to hit him in the chest, but shooting downhill was always tricky.

McKnight swung on the punk, but there was no need. The lady rolled to the tree and came up with the scattergun. Filling the air with a fog of profanity that would make an old cowhand's eyes water, the punk got to his boots.

"I'll teach ya. No whore's goin' to do me like that!" he screamed and reached for iron. Before he could clear leather, the lady emptied one barrel of the 12-gauge into him. At that range, the buckshot nearly cut him in half. The punk lifted into the air and landed in shallow water. He looked down at what was left of his middle and said, "Oh lordy, no. Oh, Mama." His head fell back into the water, and he died. Sam put the rifle back in the boot and stepped onto Buck. "Let's see if we can help the lady clean up."

Buck worked his way down the ridge as Sam's heart rate began to slow. It didn't matter how many times it was needed; he disliked taking life. He could hear his granddaddy sitting in front of his offices saying, "Ya cain't take that on, boy. People, they make choices, and those choices have consequences. If some flat-evil hard case chooses to hurt folk, that's his choice, not yours, Sam. It's the law's job to limit the bad consequences, but we cain't stop the original choice. But if you are lucky, boy, your bullet gets to be the consequence that sends that evil outlaw straight to his daddy in hell."

As they approached, Sam saw the lady turn her attention to the gunman. The lady calmly broke the breach-loading shotgun open, replaced the spent shell, and with one eye on the gunman, swung the shotgun on Sam. Sam reined up Buck and said, "I'm friendly, ma'am."

"I have had just about enough of friendly men for today, thank you."

"Name's Sam McKnight, US Marshal." He reached for his saddlebags.

"Move very slowly, Marshal, or I will blow you out of the saddle." The lady was about five-seven, maybe a hundred twenty-five pounds and wearing nothing more than a torn, white camisole and riding skirt. Sam could see her upper body clearly. Like most ranch women, this lady was pure muscle from belly to strong shoulders.

Sam took a moment. *Yes, Lord, you do some fine work,* he thought. For the first time she became conscious of the fact that she was not wearing much more than a ragged, white vest. With both hands on the shotgun, there wasn't much she could do to cover up her small but delightful figure.

She glared at him. "Well, what will it be?"

Sam smiled and ever so slowly pulled one of his blue-bib Cavalry shirts from the saddlebag. The captain's bars had been carefully removed and put away. He held it out so she could see it was just a shirt.

"You see? No tricks, m'lady."

The glare slowly broke into a small smile, and she lowered the gun. She followed his eyes down to her freshly bathed skin. Out went one hand for the shirt. Sam tossed it to her. "Men," she said, sighing deeply. "I'd say 'thank you,' but I believe you have already received your reward." She turned her back to him, took the white rag off, and threw it aside.

The sights at his little lake were even more inspirational than he had remembered. The lady put on the shirt and rolled up the sleeves to just below her elbows. She stepped over to the tree, picked up her belt, and wrapped it around the outside of the shirt. After picking up a rag, she walked to the water's edge and washed the blood from her face.

"I'll check the gunfighter," Sam said. Swinging off Buck, Sam walked to the still-gurgling gunman.

"Mc…McKnight. Who sent you?"

"No one, Max. You just got lucky." McKnight kicked the .44s away. The light began to go out of the gunman's eyes. "Anyone I should notify, Max?"

Max looked at the lady. "Eli, Eli!" he said, and died.

"Well, Miss…ah…?"

"Beth."

"Well, Miss Beth, that is the best my shirt has ever looked." To Sam's surprise, she seemed a little embarrassed at the compliment.

"Thank you."

Beth turned and walked toward the cabin. Stopping, she looked back and said, "Supper will be waiting for you when you're done." She continued on to the cabin, but the mare stepped into her path and nudged her. Beth's hands went up to the black's face, and she leaned hard into the horse's neck. Sam could see she was struggling hard not to cry.

I was so stupid, she thought, *letting my guard down. What was I thinking? How long were those outlaws watching me?* She was almost certain Larson had sent them. She had seen the older one with Larson on the trail last spring. They had called her by name.

Did they follow me here from the ranch, or had they discovered the retreat some other way? she wondered. She looked into the eye of her beloved horse and whispered, "They would have raped me, girl, and killed me if that marshal hadn't…" She would not cry. Beth gave the mare a good hug and walked with purpose to the cabin porch.

On the porch, Beth stopped to look at McKnight. She was surprised to see he was still looking back at her—into her, it seemed. She could not break the gaze. An unfamiliar warmth was building in her chest. *Who is he? Where did he come from? This man gave me my life back wrapped in a shirt. His eyes devoured me from belly to mouth, but his actions honored me.* Her mind was a fog. Beth looked down. *Get control of yourself. He's just a saddle tramp with a badge,* she thought. She looked slowly up. He was still looking right at her. The feeling in her chest became a heat that moved up into her throat and behind her eyes. *No, there is definitely more to this one. He is dangerous,* she thought, *Move, girl.* She turned and walked into the cool cabin.

◆

Sam pulled off Buck's saddle and let him roll. The sun was still high, and the lake was calling him, but he had two outlaws to bury first. He took off his hat, a broad-brimmed, Texas- style hat he wore in honor of his granddaddy. Next, he unbuckled his gun belt from around his slim, hard waist. He wore one of Mr. Colt's .44s tied down. It was simple and deadly, blued, with walnut grips.

He was fast, one of the fastest, but he had done all he could to avoid the label "gunfighter." Sam's Colt could not be bought. It was sold out to his sense of honor and fair play, to what was right or should be. In the aftermath of the war, America was battling to find her better self. It was still not clear if she could win. He was glad to be in the fight, proud to wear the badge of a US marshal.

Next his shirt came off, revealing his well-defined frame. He was of average size, with dark hair and skin from the Blackfoot on his mama's side. His size concealed his wolf-like strength. Many a big man had found out too late what his sledgehammer fist felt like and how he could take a beating and keep coming.

He stepped to the water's edge and splashed himself with the cool water. He took off his neckerchief and soaked it. It was one of the bandanas his young wife had given him on the only birthday God had granted them together. Six years had passed since he lost her. He paused for a moment and looked at the old cloth. Even now it brought her memory back fresh to him. He put it back on.

++++———◆———++++

After dragging the two outlaws well away from the cabin, Sam went through their pockets. The gunman had a thick wad of greenbacks on him. Sam counted out $400, and the punk had $75. Either these two had just robbed a bank, or someone had paid them to kill the lady. Knowing Max's past of rape and murder, Sam was leaning toward "gun for hire," but why?

He put the greenbacks in his saddlebags. *Someone will need these on the trail, maybe Miss Beth,* he thought. The .45, .44s, and the Henry he bagged for later use.

The sun was starting to get low as he put the last shovelful on the punk. He was hungry and hot. Tomorrow he would look for their horses and set them loose. Maybe their saddlebags would tell him something about why they had come there. But right now, supper and one of the most intriguing women he had ever met were waiting for him in that little cabin. As he approached the cabin, he looked to the heavens and smiled. "God you are good to me."

Walking up to the rain barrel, he put his shirt and hat on the rail and plunged his whole head into the cool rainwater. Sam flipped his head back and let the water run down his shoulders, back, and chest.

++++———◆———++++

Beth cut smoked meat and sharp cheese. Her hands were shaking. *Stop it,* she thought. She glanced up and saw him through the window. The heat came rushing back. She could feel her ears begin to turn pink. She looked away. *You have seen men with far less on, Elizabeth. Get ahold of yourself,* she thought. Her eyes drifted back to his torso. She looked closer at his hard body. A still-pink scar from a bullet hole was low on his left side. She found two older bullet scars, one just below his right collarbone. She would have thought a bullet there would kill a man. Here and there on his waist and arms were scars from knife wounds. Her heart ached for this man. There was no doubt in her mind about how he had gotten those scars. That was the price he paid for helping others the way he had helped her today. Beth was overwhelmed by the desire to hold him.

Sam called Buck and the big chestnut walked slowly over, paying more attention to the mare than Sam. "Did I interrupt something?" he said, stroking the horse's neck. "Good work today. Oh, and watch yourself with that one. She looks like trouble."

The big horse threw his head, and Sam laughed.

Reaching into the saddlebag he pulled out a clean white shirt and put it on. He ran his hands through his hair, picked up his hat, and walked into the finest, little cabin he had ever seen.

Beth was standing with her back to him in a small, efficient kitchen in the far corner of the cabin. He noticed she was still wearing his shirt.

"Can I help?" Sam asked.

"No, thank you. Would you like some cool tea?"

"Yes, please."

Turning to the shelf, she pulled down a Mason jar and filled it with tea from a large pitcher.

"Sugar?" she asked, never looking at him.

"No, ma'am."

She handed him the jar, but as he took it, she didn't release it. "Thank you," she said, staring at his hands. Slowly, her face came up, and she looked directly into his eyes. "For everything."

Sam could see the bruise coming on the corner of her mouth. Her tan, freckled skin seemed to glow, and her blue-green eyes reminded him of the Gulf on a hot summer day.

Her eyes began to mist. "Please, sit. I'll bring supper over to you."

Sam slowly emerged from her gaze and looked for a place to sit. In the front, northeast corner of the cabin were an overstuffed, brown, leather couch and matching armchair. Sam chose the chair because it had a better view of the kitchen and the cook.

The inside of the cabin was as well crafted as the outside. It was a single room, twenty-five feet by twenty-five feet. A large loft, twenty-five by ten, extended over the kitchen and back half of the cabin. The pine logs had all been varnished and polished to a high gloss. There were two large, glass-paned windows that overlooked the lake and filled the place with light. *It must have been hell getting that glass up here*, Sam thought.

Two colorful quilts were hung on the walls like art. Sam had never seen such a thing. He liked it. One quilt was all light yellows, greens, and blues. There was a lightness to it, a breeze on the first warm day in June. The other was made up of dark reds, oranges, and gold. It was made of heavy cloth, the perfect thing to wrap up in on a late autumn afternoon.

Beth brought over a tray with the meat and cheese and some fresh bread and placed it on the coffee table. She stood for a moment not knowing where to light; finally she sat on the corner of the couch next to him.

He paused, closed his eyes, and bowed his head. Cocking her head, Beth stared and waited.

"What are you doing?" she asked.

"Praying."

Gently shaking her head she said, "Not two hours ago you killed a man as easy as brushing away a fly and now you're praying?"

"More often than not the two go hand in hand."

Sam started to fill his plate and after taking a moment she joined him. They were hungry. It had been quite a day.

Sam spoke first. "When did you build it?" he asked, gesturing to the cabin.

"Last summer."

"I have never seen anything like it. I have heard of such things being built on the east coast for robber barons, but not out here, and not so small. It is the most amazing place I've seen. "How did you manage it, Miss Beth? Must have taken a crew of forty good men to put a place like this up in a summer."

"No, sixty. And please, call me Beth."

"All right, Beth, and you call me Sam." He smiled. "Where did you get the idea?"

"Well, it certainly wasn't my idea. I saw a cabin this young Swede had designed three years ago. There seemed to be magic in it. I talked to him about my ideas for a retreat. He was intrigued. Last summer was the soonest he could get to me." Her eyes were sparkling. "I love this place. Being here is like having a treasured quilt your mother made for you as a child and wrapping it around you. The smell of her and the feel of her arms around you all come rushing back. Until today, I felt safe here." She looked down.

"How long has she been gone?"

Beth looked up at his green eyes. "Since I was six." Once again, she fought against the tears. Looking away she stood and walked to the green and yellow quilt. She ran her fingers along its cherished edge as she gathered herself. "I'm sorry. I never do this."

"Beth, I know what it feels like to lose a mama young. It's all right. How'd it happen?"

Sam watched her as she caressed the quilt's edge. This woman did not trust easy, but she wanted to trust him. Dropping her hand to her side, she turned to him, drew a deep breath and began. "They rode up to the ranch house just after Daddy and the men had left to tend the cattle. They must have been watching and waiting. Mama was out front, hanging up laundry with my big sister, Mary. I was playing out back with my twin brother. We heard two shotgun blasts and ran to the side of the house. A man wearing a hood made from a burlap bag lay dead in front of Mary. Mary was crying. Altogether there must have been a dozen faceless demons with horrible burlap heads. Two of the monsters were running to Mama. She was strug-gling to reload the shotgun. Just before they reached her, Mama saw us. Her eyes told me she loved me. She nodded toward the forest." Beth paused, struggling to keep control of her emotions.

"Since we were little, we had played a game called 'Fawns.' We would pretend we were twin fawns and hide in the forest until Mama came and got us. We knew what she wanted us to do, but we couldn't move. The devil himself stepped off of his horse and walked to her. As he reached her, she said, 'You can't hide from God. He knows who you are under that hood,' and she tore off his mask. My brother grabbed my hand and pushed me toward the trees. Bullets hit the dirt all around us, but my brother kept pushing me. He was the leader, and I was always the follower. We ran and ran. Finally, we hid in some thick deer brush. The next thing I remember is my daddy calling for us. It woke me up. It was dark, and I was scared. I ran to him, and he scooped me up in his arms. He had never held me so tight, but my brother was not with me. I struggled out of my daddy's arms and ran back to our hiding place. My brother still lay where I left him, cold and still. He had been hit as we ran, but he'd never said a word. He was such a brave little boy, but he was gone. Part of me died right along with him. My daddy was crying. I had never seen him cry, and I never would again. My life was set on another path from that day forward."

All Sam wanted to do was to take this hurting young woman in his arms and comfort her. Instead, he leaned forward and put his hand on hers. "You were a good girl. You did just what your mama had trained you to do. She wanted you to live, Beth. If you had stayed and tried to help, those cowards would have killed you too." He moved next to her. "You didn't do anything wrong."

Sam's words released something in Beth that had been dammed up for a long time. The girl in her began to cry. He pulled her into him. "There is evil in this world, and some folks choose to swim in it. They enjoy hurting people any way they can. Gossiping, cheating, stealing, raping, and murdering—it feels good to them. There is a power to it. In their dark souls, they believe their victim deserves it. Somehow, it was the victim's fault." He stroked her short hair, and her crying began to ease a little.

"These evil folks come in all shapes and sizes. We had our share in southeast Texas. About six hundred folks lived in our little town. When I was eight, I spent all my time playing with this little tomboy named Charlotte, but we called her Charlie. If you didn't, she'd beat the tar out of you. She wore her hair in two brown braids. Looking back, I realize she was a pretty, little thing. Whenever our chores were done, we'd play Arabian Knights at her mama's ranch." Beth's crying had subsided, so he let her go.

"I'm sorry, I don't cry like this."

"It's all right."

"So tell me more about Charlie and you."

"Well, if it was really hot, we'd sneak away and go skinny dipping in the creek. On one such occasion, we heard someone coming up to our secret swimming hole. In a flash, we realized Charlie was a girl, and I was a boy. Charlie always played the boy's part, so we just hadn't spent much time thinking about that. To our shock and horror, we both were naked." He could tell Beth was trying to hold in her laughter. "We swam for cover."

"As we peered toward the clearing onshore, we saw it was Charlie's mother and our town's only lawyer, Mr. Wynette. Charlie's mother was a beautiful, young widow struggling to hold on to her ranch. Since I was raised by my granddaddy after my folks died, I used to pretend that Charlie's mother was my mama. Mr. Wynette wore the same black suit day in and day out. It smelled something awful. He was a small, greasy man whose face was always sweaty and shiny. From where we were hiding, we could hear them clearly."

"'I have paid the back taxes on your ranch,'" Sam mimicked a nasal voice. Beth finally laughed out loud. "'Now you will marry me, or I will put you and your skinny brat out on the street.' I had to hold Charlie back."

"'I will marry you,' Mrs. Perkins said.

"'I expect you to perform your wifely duties, of course.' Wynette said, then he grabbed her around the waist and kissed her. She hated him, but he didn't care. He was flat evil. Mrs. Perkins's suffering was frosting on the cake for him. Charlie and I managed to get to our clothes and head back to town. I headed straight for the Texas Ranger's office and told my granddaddy what I had heard. I somehow forgot to mention the naked part though." Beth giggled. Sam continued. "Granddaddy was a Texas Ranger. He'd know what to do. He listened to my story and, without a word, put on his ten-gallon hat and started for Wynette's office. His boots pounded the boardwalk, and you could hear his Mexican-style spurs jingle with every step he took. Everyone in town knew something was up, and Granddaddy began to draw a crowd. By the time he got to Wynette's office, a crowd of fifty had gathered."

"We all waited on the street as Granddaddy went inside. 'Wynette, you crap-eatin' little cockroach. I want a word with ya on the street right now!'" Beth chuckled as she pictured the scene.

"Wynette said, 'I am busy right now. Maybe this afternoon, McKnight.'"

"'I said *now*, ya evil, little blood-sucker.' Before any of the ladies could be shocked by Granddaddy's profanity, the front window of the office exploded outward. Wynette sailed across the boardwalk and over the rail and landed on his face in some fresh horse apples. As Wynette stood up, Granddaddy strode out onto the street, pulled on his leather gloves, and said, 'Did you pay the back taxes on the Perkins place?'"

"Wynette began to say, 'That is none of your—' and Granddaddy slapped him so hard Wynette fell into the crowd. The crowd threw him right back at Granddaddy, who grabbed him by the front of the shirt and repeated slowly, 'Did you pay the back taxes on the Perkins place?'"

"'Yes, I did,' Wynette whimpered."

"'That is all I needed to know,' said Granddaddy. He reached into his pocket and pulled out a wad of greenbacks he had taken off a horse thief. 'Here's yer money back, ya greasy, little, blackmailin' pervert.'

"'You can't call me that. Why, I will see you in court!'

"'Oh no, ya won't. It's time for some Texas justice.' Granddaddy reached all the way back to the Gulf before he let his fist fly. It caught Wynette square on the nose, changing his look forever. Wynette sprawled into the dirt, and Granddaddy said, 'If I ever see ya again, I will send your rotten, woman-molestin' soul right to hell!' Granddaddy then kicked his butt all the way out of town."

Sam chuckled and then grew serious. "My granddaddy chose to stand in evil's path wherever he found it. It is a family tradition, and now the tradition has been handed down to me."

"Oh, Sam, I'd like to meet your grandfather," Beth said.

"And he is always ready to meet a pretty lady like you. He is still living in east Texas with his third wife. Granddaddy wears them out."

Light from the setting sun was spilling into the room through the kitchen window. The entire room was bathed in gold. The laughter slowed as they looked at each other. Sam slowly leaned in and gently kissed her bruised mouth. They both lingered there, hungry for each other.

"No, I can't." She pulled away.

"I'm sorry, Beth. I…"

"It's not you. It's me. I'm sorry." She began to cry, turned, and ran for the loft ladder.

Sam stepped outside to give her some privacy. The sun had just set, and the sky was a blaze in the glory of His artistry. *What just happened?* he wondered.

He walked to Buck and checked his tether. "You were right, boy. Nothing but trouble." Buck whinnied in agreement.

As dawn began to creep over the pines, Sam slipped out to spend some time with his Maker. He looked forward to this ritual. Some forty-five minutes later, as the sun began to climb through the ponderosas, Sam put his logbook and palm-sized Word back in the saddlebags.

The smell of midsummer was all around him. Sam drank in the almost sweet fragrance of the warm pine forest. He had known townsfolk who brought in pine boughs to try and capture that scent. He looked up at the morning sun. It showed through the leaves of the aspens that lined the lake. Once again, he was struck by the painting it created. The overlapping leaf patterns and shades of green created by them were a beauty he never tired of.

He pulled out a bar of soap he had bought during his last visit to his favorite general store and walked around to a small, secluded cove at the edge of the lake. After stripping down, he climbed up on a large rock and dove into the crystal clear water.

Cold, he thought, gliding close to the bottom. He broke surface with a shout that echoed across the lake. After a few minutes, the water felt good. The sun had now cleared the trees. The morning mountain coolness was fading, and the summer heat was returning.

Sam took his time swimming back to the rock. He thought about the woman still asleep in her retreat. The only thing he knew for sure about her was he wanted to spend more time with her, much more time. Reaching the rock, he pulled himself out to dry. His left side said hello to him, loud and clear. The bullet wound from last spring was not quite healed.

The pain brought back that terrible, cold night, four months past. For the hundredth time, he began to relive every moment.

++++ ———————◆——————— ++++

Beth sat astride Belle on the ridge overlooking the lake. Through her field glasses, she could see him clearly. Beth felt a twinge of shame as she watched him bathe, but she didn't stop looking. She wanted to be in the water with him. Sam was spending time just sitting, looking at the lake. Beth had lived her life in the world of men. None of the men she had known would have stopped working long enough to say "thank you" let alone notice the glory of the land around them.

Sam was now shaving. In a few moments, this man—who had reached into her and held her heart so gently—would be hurt by her actions. She wanted to ride to him, but she could not. Her path had been chosen. She did not choose it, she did not want it, but she had learned long ago that in this world her wants and desires did not matter. Things happened that couldn't be helped. The world had taught her that the strong survive, and she was going to survive. The retreat she had loved was a fool's notion, and it had almost killed her. Beth would not make that mistake again.

"Damn men," she said. Belle looked at her. Then she thought of how he had held her safe in his arms. The embrace had been selfless. It was like nothing she had ever felt before. He wasn't like the men her daddy had told her about, men who only wanted one thing from a woman. She had felt free to let her guard down with Sam. Beth had shown weakness to him, something she learned only fools did, but the fool in her did not regret it.

Her only regret was getting back onto the path of the real world and leaving Sam and the world that could never be behind. She turned Belle north. Her path and her duty were at the Running J.

• 33 •

She must stand against Larson and the colonel. The only question was how long she could stand.

◆

Sam stepped onto the porch, hoping to smell coffee and bacon. He leaned toward the door, expecting to hear a young woman at work. The air was silent except for the birds all around him. The only scent was coming from the mountain forest he was standing in. He put his hand on the Colt and pushed the door open.

"Hey, gal, it's time to get up. Sunrise was an hour ago." His voice echoed in the empty cabin. Sam glanced up at the bed in the loft. It was made. *She is probably off doing her own bathing,* he thought. Looking to the kitchen, he could see a coffee pot on the wood stove and on the counter a bag of coffee beans with a grinder. He walked to the coffee and got it started. Next to the coffee on a cutting board sat a slab of bacon. He looked out the kitchen window to see how Buck and his new gal were doing. The black was gone. It was then he noticed a Mason jar full of wildflowers on the small, kitchen table. Leaning against the jar was a note. Sam looked at the flowers and picked up the note and read:

> Dear Sam,
>
> I will treasure the gifts you gave me yesterday all my life. You rescued me like a knight of old from villains I may not have been able to get away from. You seemed to love my cabin almost as much as I do. Most men would think this place is pure foolishness, whimsy without purpose.
>
> You were kind to me without expecting something in return, and all I have done is run away. Know that it was not the kiss. I wanted to repay you with much more than a kiss.
>
> It is me, Sam. All I can tell you is that my life is impossibly complicated. It would be too much to ask anyone to join me in it, even you, my gallant knight, so I must go. Do not follow me, please. I am not strong enough to see you again.

In repayment for your courage and kindness, I give you the cabin and all its contents. I know you will care for it with love. I will never return to it.

Remembering you always, bright knight,

Elizabeth

The note struck him like a solid blow to the chest. Sam walked to the stove and got the fire going. *Snap out of it, Sam,* he thought to himself. He focused on making breakfast, trying not to think, but it was no use. *I have only known her half a day. If she doesn't want to see me, fine. I sure have plenty of other fish to fry.* A few minutes later, Sam stepped out onto the porch of this gift he could not accept. He ran his hand along the finely finished rail. This place was something special, like nothing he had ever seen before. He knew from this day forth he would judge all cabins by this little masterpiece. Then he realized the same was true of Beth.

He remembered what his granddaddy had often said: "When ya find something extraordinary, whether it be a horse, or a piece of land, or a woman, you'd be a fool to let it pass ya by." Sam had rarely gone wrong following Granddaddy's advice.

Sam stepped out into the grass and looked up at the sky. "God, you have many blessings for us in this life. I know that if Beth is meant to bless me, you will show me, one way or another. Obviously this girl has got dangerous trouble complicating her life, and there is nothing I'd like better than to simplify things for her. Put me in her path, Father." He smiled and drank from his coffee cup.

"You get a good head start, Miss Beth, while I check out those outlaws' horses."

◆◆◆◆——————◆——————◆◆◆◆

After resupplying his kit from the pantry, Sam spent some time making sure the cabin was shut up tight. He saddled Buck, and they followed Beth's trail up to a small pass that led north. Sam swung off Buck to take a closer look. "Now we have her direction, boy, and she is not hiding her trail."

Sam pulled his field glasses and scanned the lake. He had a good idea of where those horses would be. Sure enough, in a large meadow to the south of the lake, stood two saddled horses. Like most good horsemen, Sam's first thought was to tend to those animals, and secondly, he wanted to see those saddlebags.

Sam worked his way down to the mangy beasts. Max's camp was filthy. There was trash scattered everywhere. Sam could smell the camp before he reached it. By the look of the place, he figured the two outlaws had been waiting two or three days.

Both horses could use food and some care. He pulled off the saddles and let the horses roll and run. The scrawnier of the two horses had no more than a saddle and a foul-smelling bedroll. Sam figured the horse and gear belonged to Pimple Face. The second horse was most likely Max's.

Sam carefully went through Max's gear. In the bags he found a remarkably drawn map that started near the town of Smith in northern Utah and led straight to the lake. There were handwritten descriptions of all landmarks and the cabin. The script was precise, almost feminine. Max and Pimple Face were to pick up the trail at Smith. That was Carl Larson country, the Double L. It was in the heart of where Sam's next assignment was taking him.

Sam had never met Larson, but from what he had heard, he would be surprised if Larson could have drawn such a map. Larson had had little or no schooling. His two boys were known as rough bullies. Neither boy was reported to be the sharpest knife in the drawer. The sister was said to be a wild, redheaded beauty, determined to breed every saddle tramp north of Salt Lake. Sam had a hard time picturing anyone in this family creating the map before him.

"Well, they were waiting for her, Buck. Somebody, maybe Larson, wants her dead," he said. *She headed north straight into Larson country. She probably had a good idea of who would want her killed. Well, no harm in mixing business with pleasure.* Sam stepped onto Buck and turned north.

Sam followed Beth's trail all day. She stayed to the high country, just below the timberline. Sam was careful not to crowd her. She worked her way along the western edge of the Wasatch Range. Just before dusk she made camp in a mountain meadow. She built a small fire that would not draw attention and made herself some dinner. Sam stayed a good mile back. He couldn't see much more than the fire and a dim human figure through his field glasses. As darkness fell on the little valley, Beth laid her bedroll out by the fire. Next, she grabbed a second blanket and her rifle and walked about three hundred yards into the timber. *Smart girl,* he thought.

Sam made a cold camp, no fire. He unsaddled Buck and rubbed him down with some dry grass. After eating some jerky and drinking some water, he too picked up his bedroll and walked back into the woods, covering his trail as he went. He found a well-protected spot and laid out his bedroll. Sam put his head on his saddle and slept soundly all night.

This kept up for two days. From morning until night, Sam followed her, keeping well back. It was no trouble. Beth was making good time, and the country was a glory to behold. The forest was old and open, made up of hemlock and pine trees. Each bend in the road presented a breathtaking, new view of the Wasatch Range.

Spring comes late to the high country. When the grass is dry in Salt Lake, the mountain meadows are just coming into bloom. Red, yellow, and blue wildflowers covered every open piece of earth, and for every flower there seemed to be a little, blue butterfly. Crystal clear streams and beaver ponds cut the trail from time to time. Crossing them gave Sam and Buck a welcome reprieve from the heat.

By the third morning, they had reached the Bear River mountain range. Beth turned west. Now they were on the edge of the high desert country. They were riding the transition line between pine forest and juniper desert. There were deer, antelope, and elk sign everywhere. Sam and Buck were constantly walking upon wild herds grazing or bedded down from the heat.

The weather was good, and the sky was a deep, western blue. When Sam had fought in the war, he had missed the western sky. In the east, the sky was never really blue. The haze and humidity mixed to form what Sam thought of as milky blue. The sky west of the Rockies always overwhelmed a greenhorn, and for the first time in his life, he would understand what the phrase "big sky country" meant. Each night huge thunderheads would build over the mountains and roar in the afternoon sky, but rain never would fall.

On the fourth morning, Beth broke camp early. Sam lost her trail for a few hours. About noon, he picked it up again, but he was not sure of how far ahead she was. Coming up over a small ridge, he spotted her.

Sam was too close. He pulled quietly back and stepped off of Buck. Bellying up to the edge of the ridge, he took a look through his field glasses. Beth was sitting on a log next to a creek. Her back was to him. She was wearing boots, men's britches, and her camisole.

Her hair was wet, and she was looking into a small, plain mirror. "What is she doing, boy?" Buck paid no attention to him and kept grazing on a small patch of grass. "I'll be damned. She is cutting her hair." Sam shook his head, not knowing what to make of it. He was sure about one thing: he liked what he saw. Strong back, kissable neck, and that amazingly touchable, short hair, all set in God's creation. She would have made quite a painting.

It was time to move. He was too close. Sam swung onto Buck and rode south for a mile.

Two hours later, he was standing where Beth had cut her hair. Sam picked up a lock of it and rolled in between his fingers. He lifted it to his nose and drew in her scent. It was part of her, all right. He wanted to touch Beth's face and taste her mouth, and he wanted both things right then. The strength of his feelings surprised him. It made him take a step back. His granddaddy always said, "Feelin' are just feelin', boy. They ain't right or wrong. They are just there. Ya can't deny them, but don't put too much stock in them."

Sam pulled off his bandana and looked at it. *Charlotte, my sweet bride,* he thought. He recognized these feelings. They were the same ones he had had for his childhood friend Charlie when she became a woman. As a woman, Charlotte had all of the fire and playfulness of her youth, but it was all multiplied somehow with tenderness and grace to produce something magical in a long, brown braid. She never gave up the braid. Sam could not dwell on her memory or look at her face burned in his mind's eye without feeling the loss of her rise in his throat.

Sam looked to heaven. "Charlotte, it has been six years. I loved my life with you. I still love you, Charlie. I still love you, but without you, I'm not whole. I want to be whole again. I want to have something like the life we had. No woman could ever fill the hole you left in me darlin', but this gal is different. There is something about her. Please forgive me, Charlotte."

A soft breeze rose up from the creek. It was filled with the sweet sent of wild flowers and wet grass. Visions of their old swimming hole where they had played as children and made love as man and wife flooded him. A warm peace fell over him, and he smiled. "Thank you, my little Charlie." Sam turned Buck toward Beth.

++++ ——— ◆ ——— ++++

In the late afternoon, Beth rode into the small town of Smith, named for the founder of the Mormon Church, Joseph Smith. Smith had a large general store, barber shop, saloon, hotel, and two things unique to the Utah territory: a one-room schoolhouse and a Mormon meeting hall.

Beth tied Belle to the hitching rail and strode up to the desk. "I want my usual room, clean sheets, and, George, have your boy bring up the tub and fill it with hot water."

"Yes, sir, Mr. Kennedy. Can I get you anything else?"

"No thanks, George." Beth took the key for the front corner room and stomped up the stairs, spurs jingling. Once in the room, she threw her long duster and Stetson on the bed. Then she stepped to the window to check the view of the street. She always took this room because she could see anyone coming into or leaving town. It was perfect.

She pulled a thin cigar from the inside pocket of her leather vest, struck a match on the heel of her boot, and lit up. The flame of the match reflected in the window, and she saw herself. She was wearing Sam's shirt, sleeves rolled up, and tan britches tucked into her well-made, brown boots. The britches were one size too big, but her fine-tooled belt with silver accents and engraved buckle held them up just fine. Around her slim hips hung a gun belt and holster, and in the holster was the new model '72 colt in .36. Colt did not make the '72 in this caliber, but two years earlier, she had met a young genius in Ogden, Utah. He was seventeen, long, and thin, with just the hint of a mustache coming. He was just two years younger than Beth at the time, and he was working in his father's gunsmith shop. For fun he was making rifles of his own design out of scrap iron. She had seen his conversion work and asked if it could be done on the Frontier model '72 with a five-and-a-half-inch barrel. The young man asked her to come back in one month.

Beth returned a month later, and the '72 was a marvel. He had not just converted a stock pistol; he had made a piece of art. The finish, the velvet action, and the lighter weight and balance were something Mr. Colt could only dream of. Beth had only asked for one, but he had made two. She bought them both on the spot.

Beth felt the walnut grips now. She had used pistols all of her life, but young Mr. Browning had made this gun just for her. The .36 did not deliver the punch the .45 did, but in the right hands, it was just as deadly, and this gun was part of Beth's hand.

She pushed her hand back through her hair and looked into the reflected face. *Eli,* she thought, *because of you, I will never have a family, but I need you to do the things I can't. We are going to settle with Larson and Dunhill once and for all.*

Elizabeth had become Eli on the day after her twin had been murdered. Her father was obsessed with the need to protect her from the fate worse than death that had befallen her mother and sister. In his grief, the only solution he could come up with was to have Beth become her twin brother, Eli, and be raised as a boy. As the years went by, Beth's father treated her more and more as a son. He was determined to make her tough so she would not be wounded by men or by grief as he was. He never showed her tenderness or held her as she desperately wanted him to.

With all of her heart, she wanted to please, and so she did everything she could to make him proud of her. But no matter what she did or how well she did it, he never was quite satisfied. He always found something she could improve on. She knew he had loved her; she just wanted to hear him say it, and now it was too late.

By the time Beth was twelve, she had disappeared in her father's eyes, and all that remained was Eli, but Beth never let her feminine self vanish completely. She held Elizabeth safe inside. She never let go of her hopes and dreams of love, a husband, and children. The cabin had been a vain attempt to keep her dreams alive—a place she could be a woman, wear a dress, and pick flowers. Her plan was to escape to the cabin on her way to and from Salt Lake, maybe three or four times a year. It was her fairytale world of make-believe, and into her kingdom of dreams rode a knight.

Sam had been just a dream, a bittersweet dream. Her eyes began to well up, and she dropped into a rocker next to the window.

Sam rode up on a Mormon farm just east of town. He knew the family well. Jon Rockport was the patriarch of the clan. Jon and Sam had met while riding on a posse together three years earlier. Sam had immediately liked the man.

These Mormon families made Utah different from the other western territories. This was because Utah was filled with women. Single men populated most of the other territories. The lack of women made for some frustrated and mean, old boys. When these bachelors were not doing backbreaking work, they were looking for ways to blow off steam. This led to some wild and dangerous times in most of the West, but in Utah, there were women, and that meant families.

Utah loved its women. In 1870, Utah's men voted to give its women the vote, making Utah one of the first territories to do so. Some seventeen thousand women over the age of twenty voted in that first election. There were more white women in Utah between the ages of fourteen and thirty than in the rest of the territories combined. This one fact quieted most of Utah down, but the Idaho border country and the southern four-corner area were still untamed.

Like most Mormon men, Jon loved his women. Jon was all Mormon, six feet tall with broad shoulders. He had the stamina to plow fields all day and to keep one of five wives happy all night.

Jon is always smiling, and he has good reason, Sam thought; although, after meeting Jon's wives, Sam thought the plowing might be the easy part. Jon called them sister wives, but they were not sisters. Elma was Jon's first wife. She was a plain-looking woman, about thirty-five, with a long, brown braid hanging down her back. Elma was a hard-working wife who ran the farm like a general commanding an army, and in fact, she was. There were fourteen children on the place, four other wives, and half a dozen farmhands. Whenever Sam showed up, Elma always had a smile, a bear hug, and a strong cup of coffee waiting for him. Coffee was frowned upon by the church, but strong coffee was part of Elma's Dutch roots. No one was going to tell her she could not have her coffee.

Elma also was editor of the Smith weekly newspaper, so Sam could always catch up on the local happenings at her kitchen table. At the same time, Elma's reporter's heart was always looking for a story, and Sam usually had one.

The other four sister wives were busy working the farm or tending to the fourteen children Jon had sired. Sam did not know the other wives well, except for the youngest, Susannah.

When Sam had visited the farm last fall, Susannah had been just nineteen and ready to pop with her first child. She was a pretty, little thing, about five-two, with a long, blonde braid hanging down her back. Even though she had been in the family way, her looks had continued to be the topic of many conversations at the saloon.

It had been hot that fall, and Susannah had used the heat and her belly as an excuse to wear as little clothing as possible. Sam had to struggle to keep his eyes on her face. This little ball of pure femininity was his good friend's wife, and he did not want to let his mind go where his eyes wanted to. It seemed to Sam that it became a game for Susannah to get him to look just where he should not. Sam hoped during this visit Susannah would be too busy with her new baby to play games with him.

By the time Sam sat down at the kitchen table, the family had already eaten and was headed off to bed. Elma instructed Susannah to fry up a rib steak and some potatoes for Sam. While Susannah half-heartedly worked at the meal, Elma, Jon, and Sam got caught up.

"Sam, my friend, it is good to see you," the big man said with a broad smile. "What brings you up to our part of the territory this time?"

"I'll bet I know, but you just go ahead and prove me right, Samuel. I'm ready," Elma said as she shifted into reporter mode. She pulled out a notepad from the front pocket of her apron and prepared to take notes.

"Now, Elma, is this off the record?" Sam teased as he gave her a wink.

"Oh, Sam, ya handsome devil, ya know I wouldn't print anything without your say-so," she said, slapping him on the knee.

"Well, if I have the word of the best reporter this side of the Big Muddy, that is good enough for me." Sam gave her a kiss on the cheek.

"Oh, Sam." She chuckled, and both men laughed out loud.

The sound of flatware crashing off the hardwood floor brought the conversation to a halt. "Sorry, I didn't mean to interrupt." Susannah sounded like a sullen child.

"It's all right, darlin', just bring the man his food. I'm sure he's ready to eat up the table by now." Jon spoke as if he were speaking to a toddler.

"Comin' right up, Big Jon," Susannah purred. Jon blushed. Sam could see that this girl had "Big Jon" wrapped around her finger, and Elma was not liking it one bit. Elma poured Sam some more coffee as Susannah came from behind his left shoulder and set his plate down on the table. As she leaned over his back to put the steak down in front of him, she rubbed her uncorseted body against his shoulder, and gave him a look that caused him to sin then and there. Susannah's back was to Jon, so he could not see what she was doing, but Elma could. Elma jumped up, grabbed the lusty, little gal by the braid, and dragged her out of the room. From the kitchen door, Sam and Jon could hear a loud slap, crying, and quite a scolding in both Dutch and English.

"This one is trouble. The young ones usually are, but Elma will bring her along. Tonight will be a good lesson for her. Better to learn on somethin' small than on somethin' big." Jon smiled.

Sam laughed and slapped Jon on the back. "Jon, you are a regular sage."

Elma came back into the room looking stern but satisfied with a twinkle in her eye. Susannah was following right behind her, dress buttoned up, head down, and wearing a very red left cheek. "Go on," Elma prodded her.

Susannah spoke to Jon and Sam without raising her head. "I apologize for my behavior, Mr. McKnight. Will you forgive me?"

"Yes, Mrs. Rockport," Sam said.

"Husband, will you forgive me for dishonoring you and myself?" She lifted her eyes to look at him. He smiled and opened his arms, and she ran to him.

"I forgive you, darlin', but you got to stop this nonsense, you hear?" He kissed her on the forehead and slapped her behind as she turned to Elma.

Elma put her hands on her hips and said, "Now, you finish those dishes double quick, girl."

"Yes, ma'am."

Elma sat down at the table, smoothed back her hair, and poured more coffee into her cup. "Now, where were we?"

Sam leaned back in his chair. "I was about to say that I came up here to Smith to sort out this mess between Larson and Colonel Dunhill."

Elma slapped the table. "I knew it. It is about time Salt Lake sent someone to look into it. If it goes on much longer, there will be a full-out range war, and good people will get hurt."

Sam nodded. "My job is to help everyone here avoid that range war if possible, Elma, but I need your help."

Elma leaned in with an intense look. "Samuel, whatever you need, you just ask."

"I need information. Whatever you can tell me will help."

Elma took a deep breath. "This all started some thirty years back, Samuel, right after the Mexican-American War. Three friends were awarded a large land grant in northern Utah for their acts of bravery on the battlefield. Their names were Carl Larson, Martin Dunhill, and William Kennedy. The three men came out west with their families to tame the land. They ran off or killed the outlaws and fought the Indians to a stalemate. For a time, they worked the land together, and all went well."

"But it didn't last, did it?"

Elma shook her head. "No, Samuel, it did not. There was a falling out between Dunhill and Larson. No one seems to know what happened. Some say it was a struggle for power, and others say it was over a woman."

"It always is," Jon added.

"So the men decided to split the land into three large parcels. Kennedy had always been the peacemaker of the trio, so it was agreed that he would take the center spread. It was the smallest, but the Juniper River ran right through it. It had the only water in the area for three months of the year. Kennedy agreed to share the water with both men and to keep the peace as long as he lived. Larson and Dunhill both trusted Kennedy with their lives, so the deal was struck. Larson took the western spread and built the Double L. Dunhill took the eastern section and built the Seven-C. Both men have built empires with their land, running over whoever gets in their way."

"What about this Kennedy?" Sam asked.

"Oh, that is a sad one," Elma said, shaking her head. "Soon after the split, William Kennedy's wife and two daughters were killed by rustlers. William fell into a deep melancholy he could never climb out of, poor man. Kennedy's ranch, the Runnin' J, just got by year after year. Poor man didn't have the heart to run it or to take care of his little boy, Eli. Eli survived the rustlers' attack and from that day forward took care of his poor daddy.

"The war came, and Dunhill led the Utah volunteers into battle. He came back a Colonel and the title stuck. After the war, settlers started pouring in, and Smith sprung up. Larson and Dunhill started to feel crowded. Both men struggled to hold on to the empires they had built. They both became obsessed with controlling the water and forcing the other out, but William Kennedy stood in the way. Each of them tried buyin' him out, but he wouldn't budge. William's wife and daughters were buried on the Runnin' J, and he wouldn't leave 'em. Then four years ago, William fell from his horse while checkin' his stock. Eli and his crew looked for him for days. They found him on some rocks. The body was already pretty far gone, but it looked like the fall had broken William's neck."

Sam cocked his head and lifted his eyebrows. "He fell from his horse?"

"I know what you are thinkin'," she said, "but the sheriff called it an accident. The Runnin' J fell to Eli. He was only seventeen, but he had a good head on his shoulders and the heart to run the place. In four years, he has turned the Runnin' J into a gold mine, and he will fight to keep it. He is also considered the most eligible bachelor in northern Utah, I might add.

"Now, to get the Runnin' J, Larson and the colonel either have to kill Eli or marry their daughters off to him. Last week we got word that Miss Laurie Dunhill was returning from her eastern school accompanied by her milquetoast brother, Quentin. They should be comin' in on the stagecoach sometime this week. Dunhill is goin' to throw a big dance for her return, and of course, Eli will be invited."

"Don't forget Red, Mama," Jon interjected.

"Oh yes, Victoria Larson. That little slut has been prowlin' around Eli for a year, but he pays no attention to her. Miss Larson has never experienced male rejection before, and it has her madder than a wet hen."

Jon stood up and walked to the counter where Susannah was working hard. "Lordy, Mama, you could talk all night. Let me finish.

This winter things heated up, Sam. Fences got cut, livestock disappeared, and then young Jeff Amos got shot and killed movin' cattle
from the Running J high range to the valley. He was a good boy,
smart and handy. Find who killed him, and you'll find who's behind
the trouble."

"What did the sheriff discover?" Sam asked.

Elma laughed. "He discovered he wasn't cut out for the job.
Turned in his badge and headed for Oregon country. We're supposta
have a new election in September, but Colonel Dunhill convinced
the town council to leave the position out for now. So we are without
a peace officer, Samuel."

Jon sat back down. "It seems at least once a week the Double
L boys are mixing it up with the Seven C crew, and the Runnin' J
hands are right in the middle of it. Larson and the colonel have both
brought in hired guns. I'm beginnin' to fear for my family. Someone
is bound to get caught in the crossfire."

"The Running J hands, how are they?" Sam asked.

"Good cowboys," Jon said. "Totally loyal to the brand. They ain't
gun slicks, but they are ready to fight and die for young Kennedy.
He treats them more than fair and pays a good wage, but there is
somethin' more to it than just wages and treatment. The way he
runs that spread breeds a kind of loyalty like I have never seen. I just
can't explain it. He is quite a young man, Sam. I think you would
like him."

"A good word from you, old friend, is good enough for me. I look
forward to meeting him. Now Elma, you said Dunhill is throwing
a dance next week." Elma nodded. "I do believe I need a new suit if
I'm going to attend, don't you?"

"You always look good in black, Samuel." Elma smiled.

Beth sipped coffee made so good and strong she could almost drink
the aroma. George's wife, Maggie, was the cook for the hotel res-

taurant, and she had found her calling. The chicken was crisp and golden brown, young, and tender, and the biscuits were so light and moist that they literally melted in Beth's mouth.

After throwing down a coin that would cover the meal and more, Beth crossed the street to the saloon. As she walked, she lifted the thong off the hammer of her colt. Tied to the hitching post in front of the saloon were three horses bearing the Double L brand.

Beth smiled. *Time to play with Eli.*

Eli pushed through the bat wings and walked to the bar. At the far end of the mahogany bar stood three gun slicks from the Double L. They were visiting with one of the saloon's soiled doves and working on some home brew.

"What the…" Collin said. He was wearing a red bandana. "He's supposed to be gone all week." The gun slick was young, lean, and mean. He had a reputation for kicking dogs and beating working girls.

"Shut up, ya half-wit," Bass said, the oldest of the three. He was about twenty-six and wore a Texas rig, long bandana, and broad-brimmed hat. Around each wrist he wore a leather cuff. Bass's long-barreled .44s look like they had seen some action. He wore them tied low. Bass was the leader of the three, and Red Bandana knew enough not to cross him.

Eli turned to the barkeep. "I'll have a beer and a bottle of your good stuff, Jim."

"Yes sir, Eli." Jim filled a mug with beer and put it in front of Eli; then he reached low behind the bar and pulled out a dusty bottle. Smiling with admiration for a man who knew what he liked, Jim put the bottle and a glass next to the beer. Eli lifted the mug to his mouth and took a long drink. It tasted good. From the whiskey bottle, he poured himself a shot. He looked at the amber liquid and smiled then drank it, enjoying the burn of it going down.

For months Beth had been gracefully sidestepping the Double L crew and the 7C boys, trying to avoid bloodshed and keep the peace, just like her daddy before her. But after the attempt on her life, those days were over. These boys had crowded her before, and she knew they would again before the night was over.

A pretty but slightly worn brunette stood next to one of the three hard cases, Leach. He was a short square of a man, always trying to prove he was tall. His lack of success at the attempt caused him to wear a constant scowl. He had hated Eli from the moment he had laid eyes on him. Everything about Eli—his good looks, his brains, and his ability to lead men—was an affront to Leach. People like Leach saw others' gifts as a personal insult. They would do anything to tear the gifted person down.

The saloon girl had been trying to cheer Leach up with a few inexpensive suggestions, but when she saw Eli, she moved to greener pastures. As she slid up next to Eli, Leach's mood grew even darker.

"Eli, you promised you were going to come see me weeks ago, and I haven't seen hide nor hair of you." She pouted as she slipped her hand around his waist.

Eli turned to her, reached out his hand, and cupped her cheek. "I know I did, Jenny, and I will keep my promise to the best of my ability but not tonight. I have been riding hard for four days, and I'm done in. I'll tell you what. Let me buy you a drink, and we will just sit and talk for a while." Eli spoke to her like an uncle might speak to a beloved child.

He kissed her gently on the cheek. Eli grabbed a second glass and began to lead Jenny to a table.

At the far end of the bar, Leach exploded. "She is mine tonight, ya damn little dandy. Ya strut in here like ya own the place and the women. Well, I'm tired of it. Just because she reminds you of your mama don't mean you can just pick her up whenever you like." The saloon fell silent. In the west, a man could weather many insults and still walk away, but when you insulted his mother, you were calling him out.

"Jenny, you go to your room," Eli said, as he sent her toward the stairs. She got as far as the banister and turned back.

"My God, Leach. Y'all finally got Pretty Boy's attention." Bass laughed. "Hell, if I'd known all I had to do is bring up the fact that Pretty Boy's mama had a good poke from just about every old boy in northern Utah, I'd a done that months ago." All three laughed.

"I hear his big sister was a ripe piece too," Collin added as he broke into a hysterical laugh.

The rage burned red hot in Eli, and he let it take him completely. The image of the burlap monsters flashed before him again. Looking for cover, he other patrons of the bar fled their chairs as Leach and Collins reached for iron.

The double roar of the .36 deafened everyone in the room. Leach slammed into the back wall. He tried to pull his gun, but the top of his heart had been ripped loose. No heart, no muscle control. He fell on his face, breaking out his front teeth. Collin fell into Bass. "Tex, oh no, Tex!" Blood began to drip from his mouth. He slid down to his knees and fell on to his side. Bass watched his two partners die and slowly looked up at Eli.

All Bass could see was the mouth of Eli's .36 pointed right at his middle. Bass had no idea Kennedy was so fast. Eli had pulled, eared back the hammer, and fired with such grace of movement that the colt seemed to be part of his hand. The move was so fast, most of the patrons had not seen it. Bass was feeling something he hadn't felt in years: fear. He did not like it.

With fury still raging, Eli spoke in a quiet voice. "You were saying something about my sweet murdered sister and mama."

Bass could see he might be living his last minutes. "I'm sorry, Mr. Kennedy. We was just havin' some fun. I'm real sorry."

"I'm sure you are, but you started this game, not me. You spit on my mama and sister's graves. You enjoyed it. Well, your friends felt the consequence for their cruelty, now it's your turn." Eli slowly put the Colt back into its leather. "Make your play."

"You just made your bad choice, Pretty Boy. You should have killed me while you had the drop on me. Now you are going to meet

· 51 ·

your mama and little whore sister in hell!" Bass shouted, trying to build courage.

He was fast. His hands flashed to his .44s. Just as the long barrels cleared leather, he felt a grabbing pain in his chest. The pain wrenched his whole body. He took a step back and tried to lift his guns. Eli's second blast hit him in the belly. The pain was unbearable. Bass fell back into a chair.

"I didn't know. I did not know you were so fa…fast." Bass said through the taste of blood.

"Now you know. Anyone you want me to notify, Bass?"

"Go to hell."

"I probably will." Eli walked to his bottle, poured a drink, and drained it. His hand was as steady as steel.

Bass watched Eli's control and cursed as his own strength slipped away. "You are a devil, Kennedy." With all of the strength he had left, Bass raised his .44.

"Eli!" Jenny screamed.

Eli turned, dropped to one knee, and drew. Both guns boomed at the same time. Tex's slug broke the mirror behind Eli. Eli's slug caught Tex in the forehead. Eli slowly stood up, pushed out the empties, and reloaded.

He looked at the three men he had just killed. There would be no stepping back from this fight now. Eli grabbed his bottle from the table and headed for the bat wings. As he reached them, he turned back to Jenny. "Well? Are you coming? I believe we have some talking to finish."

"I thought you'd never ask." She ran to him.

Eli threw a gold coin on the bar. "This should cover the mirror, Jim. Go through their pockets for the burial and keep the rest."

"Yes, sir."

Eli took Jenny by the arm and walked out through the bat wings into the street.

Sam put his leather-bound Word back into his saddlebags before first light. When he stepped back into the farmhouse, Elma had four fried eggs, a half a pound of bacon, and a hot pot of coffee waiting for him. The food and the company were good, and Sam ate everything that was put in front of him.

Sam was waving good-bye to Jon, Elma, and the rest of the Rockport clan just as the sun rose over the Bear River Mountains. Buck seemed a little reluctant to go, and Sam knew why. Last night, the big chestnut had been walked, rubbed down, and brushed twice by the ten-year-old, twin boys who lived on the place. When Sam had come out to saddle him up, the twins had beaten him to it. Usually Buck came to Sam as soon as he saw him, but this morning, Buck had just stood in the stall and looked at Sam. Sam laughed, grabbed Buck's lead, and led him out. Now they were headed down the trail to Smith.

As Buck walked toward the sleepy town, Sam's mind was filled with Beth; her head resting on his shoulder, the sound of her voice, and the feel of the short hair at the back of her neck beneath his hand. He could not shake her. Perhaps today he would touch her again.

◆

The first golden shafts of morning glowed on Beth's freckled skin. Her blue eyes gazed at her young friend still sound asleep on the bed. Jenny was still wearing her bright-red dress. She had fallen asleep after a good cry, and now she looked so young and innocent. Her face was calm and peaceful.

Beth was in the rocker where she had been all night. Jenny had done most of the talking, and Beth had done the listening. She had always had women friends, but that is all they were. She had heard of women who "liked" other women, but she wanted a man. In fact, she had preferred the company of men for as long as she could remember. With her women friends, she would play the perfect gentlemen and let the rumors fly. But in the past year, the masquerade had become heavy. She wanted to be held by a man and to give herself to him completely. If she let herself be honest, she wanted a child. She felt empty. And then the marshal had ridden into her life. Maybe Sam could fill the void.

Beth mulled over what Jenny had said. She was a simple farm girl. Under the rouge, she was just seventeen. Her daddy came west after Lee's surrender. The South was finished, and he knew it. The Southerner brought his family to a piece of dirt he had bought in the Four Corners country. Jenny was ten. The farm never amounted to a hill of beans, but the family owned it and worked it hard. Jenny thought of those two years as full of joy.

In the fall of '68, cholera hit the family, and her mama and two little bothers took sick. Jenny nursed and nursed them, but it did no good. First her two sweet brothers died and then her mama. She begged her mama not to go. The memory of her mother dying in her arms was burned into her mind.

Jenny's daddy had to blame someone, so he blamed her. He became bitter and mean. To deaden the pain, he turned to drink, but it just made him meaner. One night, while drunk, he decided to use Jenny to dull the pain. Jenny hated the things he made her do, but at least he was paying attention to her. Like all little girls, she just wanted him to love her, and if she pleased him, maybe he would forgive her. This went on for a year.

On her thirteenth birthday, her daddy took her to town. He had remembered her birthday, and she was so pleased. Jenny had to put on one of her mama's blue gingham dresses because she had grown out of all of hers. She looked in the mirror and liked what she saw. She was a woman—a pretty, young woman, just like her mama had been when they had come West.

Her daddy took her to the hotel restaurant for dinner. She had only been to a restaurant once before, when she was a little girl back in Georgia. She tried her best to act like a lady. She wanted to make her daddy proud, but he seemed somehow embarrassed and barely said a word to her. He was treating her better than he had since her mama died, so Jenny wanted to believe things were about to take a turn for the better.

She remembered the meal as being so fancy, and when they finished, they walked over to the saloon. The place was full of men and a few women. Cigar smoke filled the air. Jenny liked the smell. A piano played out of tune in the corner. Her memories were filled with red curtains and wood trim. She had never seen such a place. It had seemed like a castle.

Jenny's daddy introduced her to an older woman wearing rouge and the fanciest dress she had ever seen. Jenny knew this woman must have been an important lady.

The lady said, "She is a pretty thing. You say she is willing?"

"Oh yes," her daddy had said. "I caught her with a neighbor boy last week. She was taking him for a ride."

"I didn't know what he was talkin' about," she had said to Eli. "I didn't know the meanin' of the words. There were no boys within fifty miles of our place, and if there were, I would not have gone riding with them. I was so naïve, but I knew better than to question my daddy in front of others."

Tears began to softly fall down Jenny's powdered cheeks, but she went on. "The lady said, 'I'll give you forty-five dollars credit for her, Reb. She ain't proven yet.'"

"'She don't need provin' for this hole, Miss LuAnn. One hundred dollars and not a penny less.'"

"'Done.'

"The two of us walked to a table where men were playing cards." Jenny's chin began to tremble as she brought back the details of that night. "Daddy sat at the table and began to play. He ordered us both a drink. I did not like the way it tasted, but I liked the way it made me feel. I began to enjoy myself. Daddy was winning, so he was happy. All of my daddy's friends seemed to like me and kept buying me drinks. What a fool I was.

"As the night wore on, my daddy began to lose, and his mood grew dark. His friends began to put their hands on me. I looked around at the other women. They were all being touched in the same way, so I played along. I was so young.

"I heard the clock chime one." Jenny began to cry in earnest now.

"Go on, Jenny. It's all right. I'm listening," Beth had said.

"I remember my daddy slapping down his cards and standing up. He grabbed me by the elbow and yanked me to my feet. I could barely walk. He marched me over to Miss LuAnn. 'I'm out' he said. 'She's yours now. May she bring you the same luck she has brought me.' His words hit me like a punch in the stomach. My daddy was leavin' me with this woman. He had sold me for one hundred dollars. So I threw up all over Miss LuAnn's pretty dress and passed out."

"Short of shooting them both, that's the best thing you could have done." Beth smiled. Jenny's tears slowly changed to a small laugh, and Beth joined her. "Go ahead and sleep, little Jenny. I'll take pleasure in watching over you." Jenny wiped away a tear, smiled, and closed her eyes, sleeping well for the first time in four years.

✦

Looking at her in the glow of dawn, Beth knew she must help her. Beth knew just how she would do it too.

Sam rode into Smith just as the town was starting to stir. He was ready for some more hot coffee. The marshal drew some attention as he rode into town. Men nodded, and women smiled. He was a little better known than he liked. Sam was no Hickok, but he had lived a life of adventure and honor. Hard cases had died; women and children had been saved. The events of his life had been widely reported and exaggerated. That night at the Webster's farm had not helped. He saw the first "penny dreadful" about that night the day before he had left for Smith.

Sam had run into his first young gun slick trying to make a reputation on Sam's name just after the war. He did not like it, but short of disappearing, he did not see how he could stop the young fools from marching to their graves.

He scanned the town now for just such an unwelcome greeting. Smith was growing, and everyone seemed to be in town that day. The undertaker's plate-glass window caught Sam's eye. He had three fresh boys displayed in the window. Their hands were crossed on their chests, but the bullet holes were still visible.

It has begun. I had better check it out, he thought.

The town was buzzing about something. Folks were running around like it was the day before Thanksgiving. Sam stepped off of Buck and tied him off in front of the undertaker's window.

◆◆◆ —— ◆ —— ◆◆◆

Eli bought Jenny some breakfast. The other hotel guests and townsfolk who were enjoying Maggie's cooking watched them enter the dining room and smiled, thinking the worst. Beth saw their looks and knew what they were thinking. *Good,* she thought.

As Maggie poured them coffee, Beth began. "Jenny, what is your last name?"

"Richards."

"Well, Miss Richards, I've got a proposal for you."

"It's about time," Jenny cooed. She leaned in and waited for Eli to be like every other man she had known.

"Just hear me out, Jenny. How much schooling did you have?"

A questioning look came to Jenny's face. "My mama was a teacher in Georgia. She made sure I mastered my figures and read what she called the classics, but darlin', you don't need much education to do what I do. "

"Are you any good at it? The figures, I mean."

Jenny's face broke into a broad smile. "You will just have to try me."

Eli became serious. "Are you any good at figures?"

"My mama said I was very good. She tried to stump me with problems, but I would not quit until I got it."

"Do you think you could keep books?"

"I do it now for the saloon," she said with some pride. "Why are you askin' all of these questions, Eli?"

"After you fell asleep last night, I got to thinking about the Running J. I need some help out there."

Jenny listened with cautious interest. "Are you askin' me to cook and clean and...?" Her eyebrows went up.

Eli laughed. "No, no. I'm asking you to do something far more important. I like you. You're a bright girl. I can see the mark your mother left on you before she died. My place is growing fast. I can't keep up with my correspondence, and I'm no good at managing the big house." This was a lie of course. Beth was very good at managing her affairs, but being freed from the house and the books would give her time to focus on the ranch.

"Jenny, I need a personal secretary. I'll pay you thirty dollars a month." Thirty dollars was more than Jenny could make in two months, and Beth knew it. Jenny took a drink of coffee to cover her emotion.

Beth leaned toward her. "I have some conditions you will need to agree to."

"Go ahead," Jenny said, gulping back tears.

"One: you will need to quit whoring and move to the Running J. Two: you will present yourself as a proper, young lady." Eli threw a one-hundred-dollar gold piece on the table. "If you agree, take this coin as a signing bonus and buy some appropriate, modest clothes. Finally, you need to stay away from my crew. No men period, unless they are going to court you proper, and they will have to ask me first. Well, what do you say, girl?"

Through moist eyes, Jenny reached out and picked up the coin. "I say yes. May God bless you, Eli Kennedy." The tears began to fall. "I can be ready by lunch."

Beth struggled to keep Eli from joining Jenny in tears. "Meet me at the livery, and we will pick you out a horse and a saddle."

Jenny stood. "Well, I've got a few things to pack and some new clothes to buy." She leaned over and kissed Eli on the check. Then she turned and walked out with hope in her heart for the first time in four years.

A warmth filled Beth as she finished her coffee.

+++——◆——+++

Sam knocked the dust off his clothes with his hat and stepped into the undertaker's shop. The room was paneled in dark pine, and green curtains hung in the windows. "Morning."

A thin, long-faced man looked up from his carpentry. "Morning." He looked Sam up and down, measuring him for future business. "How can I help you, Marshal?"

"You can start by telling me what happened to these old boys," Sam said, pointing to the window display.

"Well," Long Face started and then paused. Sam thought he might have nodded off. Then he started again. "These three ruffians insulted Mr. Kennedy's mother. Moments later, they had gone to the Great Accounting."

"Was Kennedy hit?"

"Not in the slightest. The fight was honorable, but two of the ruffians did not manage to get their pistols out of their holsters. The young gentleman is technically flawless. He walked out of the saloon with a...soiled dove on his arm. Unfortunately, Carl Larson's sons will be quite angry about the untimely deaths of their friends."

"Of course, all of this is good for business," said Sam.

"Of course." Long face smiled, revealing large, yellow teeth.

"Thank you for your time, Mr....?"

"Black is the name. Marvelous, isn't it?"

Sam smiled. "It's always refreshing to meet someone who loves their work, Mr. Black." Sam tipped his hat and stepped back out into the street.

He walked Buck to the livery. A young man already missing his front teeth smiled at Buck and took his horse from him. "Rub him down good and give him whatever he wants," Sam said.

"Yessir, Marshal," Toothless said.

Sam gave Buck a good scratching around his ears. Buck usually loved that, but today he was paying no attention to Sam. His ears were up, and he was sniffing the air. He began to stomp, and Sam had to hold him steady. "What is it, boy?" Then Sam spotted the black mare. She was stabled at the far end of the barn and doing a fair amount of stomping herself. "You old rascal, you. Now, be a gentleman." Sam grabbed his gear and headed for the hotel.

He pushed through the front door and walked to the desk. There was no one in sight, but on the desk sat a pot of hot coffee on a pot holder with a clean cup right next to it. *What a blessing*, he thought and poured himself a cup.

Sam rang the bell. Suddenly there was a commotion in the back office. A moment later, George emerged, a little red-faced, followed by his wife, very red-faced. Maggie was a shapely gal who filled out her now slightly askew apron nicely.

Sam smiled at them both. "So what's going on?" he asked.

Both George and Maggie looked flustered. "We ah..." George began.

"I was just bringing George some coffee," Maggie finished.

"I mean in town?" Sam said with a wink.

"Oh, in town. Well, Miss Dunhill and her brother Quentin are arriving in town on the morning stage. The colonel has planned quite a celebration," George said.

"There is going to be a huge dance on Friday with a big spread of food. Everyone but the Double L folk is invited. You should come, Marshal. I'm doing the cooking," Maggie said.

"In that case, pretty lady, I'll be there." She blushed even redder. It was then she noticed she had not put herself back together quite right.

She made a few quick adjustments and said, "More coffee, Marshal?"

"Yes please, ma'am." He watched her go. "George, you have a fine wife."

"Thank you, Marshal."

"I told you last time to call me Sam. Now, I would like my usual room."

"I'm sorry, Mar—I mean, Sam. That room has already been taken by Mr. Kennedy."

"Where is this young Kennedy now?"

"I believe he just stepped down the street to the general store to order supplies for the Running J."

"George, give me the other corner room and make sure I have clean sheets, and would you pour me a bath?"

"Yes sir, Sam."

◆┼┼┼━━━━◆━━━━┼┼┼◆

"Thank you, Ed," Eli said to the two-hundred-pound storeowner. Ed was short, and his belly filled his overalls, but moving forty-pound bags of flour and beans all day had made him as strong as an ox. He was a kind and generous man with a keen sense of humor. When the time called for it, he could be as tough as nails. Ed had been Beth's father's dearest friend. She loved the old man and depended on him for a broad, mustached smile and advice. For his part, Ed thought of Eli as his own child.

"I'll have some of my men come in and pick up the supplies tomorrow."

"It'll be ready, boy."

Eli turned and began to go, but Ed's voice stopped him. "Why did you come back early, boy?"

Eli slowly looked back at his old friend. What could he tell him? He did not want to burden him with his troubles. "I like Salt Lake less and less, and I had pressing business here. That's all."

Ed eyed him, knowing there was more. He decided to dig a little deeper. "Are those three cusses in Mr. Black's parlor part of the business?"

"Could be."

"You be careful, boy. Last night you took this thing to a new level."

"Don't worry, old man. I'll be careful." The affection the two felt for each other hung in the air for an uncomfortable moment. Then Ed tried to lighten the mood.

"Are you coming to the dance?" Ed asked.

"Now, you know I hate those things, old man." She did not like dancing with women, and all of those other gals wearing dresses just made her mad.

· 62 ·

"You oughtta go, boy. How are we ever going to get little Elis if you don't start going to dances? Besides, I don't want to miss the show." He turned his back on Eli and began dusting the shelf.

"And what show would that be, old man?"

"Why, the Laurie Dunhill and Eli Kennedy show, or *When will she lasso him?* written by Colonel Dunhill." Ed began to laugh. "It has been a year since Laurie was home. She was always a fine-looking, little filly. We would all have to agree she has some of the most beautiful, big, round...blue eyes we have seen." Again he broke himself up, and this time Eli joined him. "I imagine all of that eastern schoolin' has made her quite an elegant, young lady."

"Ed, she has been a spoiled brat all of her life, and no school can change that. Even when we were little and times were hard, she thought she was the crown princess of the Bear River Range."

The truth was, Beth liked Laurie Dunhill. After Beth's mother, sister, and twin were killed, the only playmates for fifty miles were Laurie Dunhill and Vickie Larson. Laurie always bossed everyone else around, and if she did not get her way, she threw a fit, but Beth had felt sorry for her. Laurie's mother was sick and rarely left her room. Her bossiness covered up how much she worried about her mother.

Vickie, on the other hand, was just flat wild. Her parents did not know where she was half the time and did not seem to care. She was always climbing trees, falling in the river, tearing her dress, and finding new ways to scrape her knees. Beth envied her wild freedom.

By the time Beth, Vickie, and Laurie were twelve, the feud between Larson and Dunhill had grown so deep that Vickie and Laurie were forbidden to see each other. Still, the girls and Eli managed to secretly get together. They would ride off on their horses and meet, spending the afternoon talking and exploring the county.

This was a treasured time in Beth's memory, but as they all began to become adults and their bodies matured, things changed. Beth was lost and alone as her body began to change. She couldn't go to her father. By this time, Beth was gone in his grieving mind, and only Eli remained. She needed help, and Vickie was the answer. Laurie would never talk about such things, but Vickie would talk about anything. Beth managed to get all the information she needed, but it was still hard, and there were some quiet nights of just hiding and crying.

Finally, it all came to an end on Laurie's fourteenth birthday. Laurie decided that Eli belonged to her. He was the most eligible, young boy in the county, so naturally, her daddy would get Eli for her.

Vickie had always flirted with Eli in a tree-climbing sort of way. She naturally assumed she and Eli would be climbing trees and making babies the rest of their lives. The conflict was too great for the relationships to bear. The two girls became enemies overnight.

Beth's heart was broken. For all of their faults, Beth loved them both. For a while, she continued to see them separately. Laurie always wanted to play Queen and Consort of the Western empire, and Vickie wanted to play man and wife. By the time they had all turned fifteen, Eli was avoiding them both.

Ed came from behind the counter and put his arm around Eli's shoulders. "Someday you are going to have to stop being responsible for your father's promise and live for yourself. You need some joy in your life. I want to see you happy, Little K." That was the name Ed had called her on the first day he had met her. She was eight and had been Eli for almost two years. She loved the name. Ed had not used it in some time. "I know things are comin' to a head. I'm with you, Little K. You call, and I'll come a runnin'." Ed smiled warmly and offered his hand. Beth took it and looked into his eyes.

There was something there in his face that unnerved her. *Does he know?* she wondered. She gave him a hard slap on the back. "If I ever need anyone, yours will be the first name I call." Eli turned to push through the door, but before he could, Miss Vickie Larson came in.

She was wearing a rich, dark-brown riding skirt and matching vest over a cream blouse. She had picked the outfit to set off her fiery hair, and it was doing the job. Pulling off her riding gloves as she came, she didn't see Eli. When she did, she was so surprised she dropped one of her gloves and struggled to hang on to the other.

Eli and Vickie squatted down to at the same time to pick the glove up, almost bumping heads. Eli looked into her face and saw what she thought was confusion. The morning sun was shining through the glass in the door onto Vickie's hair. She wore it pulled back from her face and down around her shoulders.

Suddenly, Vickie kissed Eli, knocking them both over in the process. Eli scrambled out from under Vickie and back over to Ed's counter. Ed eyed them both and smiled. Vickie picked herself up and followed.

"Oh, Eli, I'm so glad to see you."

"We can all see that, Miss Vickie." Ed chuckled. Eli opened his mouth to speak, but Vickie covered it with her hand and began talking a mile a minute.

"I know I was too forward for you just now, but for some reason, I have been worried about you all week. I just couldn't get you out of my mind. I even went to that old Nez Perce witch to see if she could tell me something."

Beth's eyebrow went up. She did not like the old woman. There was heaviness around her. When Beth was with her, she felt the need to constantly be looking over her shoulder.

Vickie went on. "But she just kept tellin' me about 'the two in one' and 'the spear of the great spirit.' She was no help at all."

Beth's mind raced at those words. "It's all right, Vickie. You have been stealing kisses for as long as I can remember."

"That is only because you weren't givin' them away." She pouted. "Ed, don't you think Eli should be just a little more friendly?"

"As a matter of fact, I was just tellin' him that very same thing, Miss Vickie, but he seems to be getting a little bit deaf in his old age."

"Well, I am not goin' to wait forever, Mr. Kennedy."

"I hadn't noticed you had been waiting at all," Eli replied with a broad grin.

Vickie took a good swing at Eli, but he ducked away, laughing. "Damn you, Eli Kennedy. You haven't changed one bit since you was a boy.

"Oh, I've changed more than you know."

"Well, if I didn't know better, I'd think you didn't like girls." She turned and stomped out the door, slamming it on her way out. Both old friends turned and looked at each other then broke into loud laughter.

Like the rest of Smith, Sam was ready for a party even though it was still two days away. The ride from the lake had been long, but the beauty of the wild land and the mysterious young woman had made it most memorable. It had felt good to wash the trail off. Now he stepped out onto the boardwalk wearing a clean, white shirt, black tie, brocade vest, and pants. His colt .44 was in place, thong off, and he had folded his elk-skin riding gloves over his gun belt cavalry-style. He felt certain he was about to run into Beth, and he wanted her to be properly impressed. Granddaddy had always said, "Women love a clean, well-dressed man." Over time, Sam had found this piece of advice to be correct. He thought he might step over to the new tack and leather shop and see if anything caught his eye, but as he stepped off the boardwalk the sound of spurs stopped him.

Sam turned and saw him coming—new, high boots covered with large, Mexican-style spurs. Sam's eyes moved to Spur's guns: Remington .44s—one tied down and one set in a cross-draw holster. The guns were pretty enough for a woman. His hair was long, and he was just old enough to have grown a thin mustache and goatee. Sam recognized the look. Spurs thought if he looked as good as William Cody, he might be as good.

As a young woman passed, Spurs struck a pose so she could see the whole effect.

Lord save us, Sam thought in disgust. He turned away and began crossing the street to the tack shop.

"Where are you going, Marshal? We have some business together," Spurs said with a broad smile.

"I doubt it, boy. I already had my boots shined in the hotel."

"Oh, I understand Marshal. You're getting old and don't have the reflexes to fight a stallion like myself."

Sam stopped. *This pup is too pretty for his own good. Well, I'll fix that.* Sam turned and marched toward Spurs, pulling on his gloves as he walked. Spurs took a step back, puzzled. This was not how he had envisioned events unfolding. Before he could figure out what to do, Sam was toe-to-toe with him. Spurs's eyes were wide and confused.

"Could ya speak into this ear, sonny? I'm a little deaf in my right," Sam said.

Spurs, out of confusion, went for his guns, but Sam got there first. With one lightning-swift move, he pulled both of Spurs's guns from their holsters and held them in front of his face. Point made, Sam threw them into the horse trough in front of the hotel.

Spurs's eyes flashed with anger. Not knowing what to do next, he reached back with his right fist to hit Sam. Sam blocked the punch with his left and smashed a wicked right into the pup's jaw. Spurs staggered backward, spitting out teeth. Sam followed, stepped in, and buried his left in Spurs's middle. As the young gunman began to double over, Sam hit him with a sledgehammer left uppercut, straightening Spurs to his full height. Spurs weakly tried to raise his left as the full force of Sam's right landed on his nose, flattening it permanently. The blow took Spurs off his feet, and he landed flat on his back, out cold.

Sam pulled off his gloves. Spurs's face was ruined, but he was still alive. If Spurs had a lick of sense, he would thank him someday, but knowing human nature, Sam figured he'd have to kill the fool sooner or later. Sam wiped his bloody gloves on Spurs's already soiled shirt.

◆

The brightness of the summer sun caused Beth to squint as she looked east, watching for the stage. A crowd was gathering in the middle of the street. Beth guessed it was a fight, but through the glare and people, she could not make out who or what might be fighting. It could be dogs for all she could see.

———————◆———————

Sam heard it before he could see it. The stage was coming and Spurs was lying right in its path. The crowd began to scatter. Sam grabbed the young hard case by the shirt collar and dragged him to the north side of the street just as the stage rounded the bend. Sam propped him up on a hitching post and put Spurs's hat over his flattened face. For good measure, Sam crossed Spurs's legs to give him that casual look. Sam walked to the stage. He had heard a lot about this Dunhill girl, and he wanted a good look at her.

———————◆———————

The driver yelled, "Whoa!" and the team came to a halt. The stage almost disappeared as a cloud of dust swallowed it. Beth saw a man appear through the cloud at the rear of the stage, dressed in black and white. She gasped. He moved like a great, male wolf—total, deadly confidence mixed with a joy for living. She knew this shape, this walk. She had been thinking about little else for the past five days. Her heart began to pound. The ache in her center made her want to run to him, to press her whole body against him. The memory of his kiss lingered on her mouth.

As she leaned toward him, the reality of her situation hit like a slap on the face. She was Eli. He must not see her like this. She was false. He would hate her. She wanted to run, but she was trapped. People were gathering around her, greeting Eli. *I must run, I must run, but where, and to whom?*

———————◆———————

Sam walked to the stagecoach and opened the door. He put out his hand and took off his hat. "Miss Dunhill, I presume?" One of the most beautiful brunettes Sam had ever seen hesitantly took his hand. She wore a cream-colored dress accented with lace. It was expensive and had been tailored to show off all of her considerable assets. Tightly corseted, it added to her feminine curves.

Sam was once again impressed by God's blessing. Granddaddy always said the first look was a gift from God, "It's the second, third, and fourth look that'll git ya in trouble." Sam was in trouble.

She followed his eyes and took his hand more firmly. Miss Laurie Dunhill looked him up and down in a way a proper, young woman would blush at. She smiled. "Why, thank you," she said. She reached out and touched his badge. Her fingers caressed the star. Sam could feel the light touch all the way to the back of his spine. "And you must be the famous Marshal McKnight. I heard you visited our little town from time to time, but I have always missed you. We must remedy that. My father is throwing a dance Friday night. Will you come as my guest?" She batted her long, dark lashes.

"Call me Sam, Miss Laurie, and I wouldn't miss it."

Miss Laurie was followed by a dandy who looked as if he thought he was getting off the stage in Boston. Sam watched him looking down his long nose at everyone who had come out to meet Miss Laurie and judge them unworthy of his time. He moved with grace and wore a pearl-handled colt .45 set up in a cross-draw holster. The gun hung with ease as if he had used it often, but Sam guessed it had mainly been pointed at people's backs.

"Sam, I'd like to introduce my brother, Quentin Dunhill. Quentin, this is Marshal McKnight."

The handshake was firm as both men looked directly at the other. Quentin flashed the well-polished smile of a Mardi Gras mask at Sam.

"Oh, yes. I read about you saving some family of darkies last spring, from New Mexico outlaws, wasn't it?" Quentin watched and waited for Sam's reaction.

Sam smiled. "Yes, they were some hateful, old boys, and it was my pleasure to end their useless lives."

Beth saw the way Laurie looked at Sam and felt something she had never felt before: jealousy. She wanted to step right up and claim her man, but how? Eli couldn't take Sam in his arms, and what would Sam do when he saw her? Eli couldn't shoot Laurie, but he could draw Laurie away from Sam.

"Laurie!" Eli called.

Laurie's face turned quickly to the familiar voice. "Eli, you came to meet me. How sweet." She crossed to Eli, holding out her hand for him to take.

Miss Dunhill moved toward Eli, trying hard not to show her excitement at his presence. He stepped off the boardwalk and walked to her with purpose. Eli gave her a courteous kiss on the cheek. Laurie put her arm through Eli's elbow and turned to Sam.

"Eli, darling, I would like you to meet my new friend, the famous Marshal McKnight."

The first thing Sam saw was a beautifully made gun belt and holster holding a .36 Colt. The young man wore a strangely familiar blue cavalry shirt under a brown, leather vest. It was tucked into dark breeches. Kennedy's head was tipped forward so his Stetson covered his face.

Beth slowly looked up and met his never ceasing gaze. She watched his eyes widen and search her face then move to her clothes and colt, finally back to her face. With an ever-so-slight shake of his head he smiled at her—he *knew*.

Beth was terrified. What would the next moments bring? *Oh God, save me!* She had not prayed since the night of the burlap monsters, and she was surprised she was now. She had no use for a God who would let her mama, twin, and sister die so horribly, but there was nowhere else to turn, so the desperate prayer went up.

Laurie looked at the two of them. "You two seem to already know each other."

"As a matter of fact," Sam began, "uh...Mr. Kennedy and I had a brief but intense discussion not more than a week ago." Quentin shifted slightly and began to pay closer attention to the conversation.

"Seems you folks have been having a little trouble with cut fences and misbranded cattle. Not to mention the murder of the Amos boy," Sam said, watching for reactions. There were none.

Beth's heart began to slow. *He is not going to give me away. Thank you God,* she thought with relief. *What is he thinking?*

Quentin spoke first. "Our father wrote us as much. I am sure he will want to help you however he can. We all know Carl Larson is behind this. The sooner you clean out that riffraff, the better, Marshal."

"Is that right?" A deep voice came from behind the crowd of townsfolk who had gathered to see the local royalty arrive. The crowd parted, and there stood one of the roughest-looking men Sam had ever seen backed up by a slightly younger brother, judging by the resemblance. Three ranch hands completed the group. The big-voiced man was well over six feet.

✦━━━━━◆━━━━━✦

Sam guessed he was about twenty-five. He had a thick mustache, but the rest of his face was freshly shaved. His hat and boots were worn, but you could tell he thought they were perfect. The red shirt he wore could barely cover his massive muscles. This man's wrists were as thick as most men's forearms. Two Remington .44s hung in a double rig that could use some care. They were tied low, thongs off.

This has to be Rowdy Larson. The brother was a smaller version of Rowdy. Not quite as clean. Sam could tell just by looking that Little Brother was the follower and Rowdy was the leader.

These boys are ready to fight, Sam thought. He made a mental check of his .44, and wished he had added his second .44 in his cross-draw. Rowdy had Sam's full attention.

"Know yer enemies when ya see 'em, boy, and be ready to drop 'em where they stand. You'll live longer that way," Granddaddy would say. There were new enemies all around. Quentin was a snake waiting to strike, and Rowdy and his brother were the kind of wild dogs that killed for fun.

"Well, if it isn't my old playmate, Rowdy. Have you learned to read yet?" Quentin hitched his thumb in his gun belt, inches from the grip.

"You learn to like girls yet, Queeny?" Rowdy's whole crew broke into laughter.

Quentin's eyes flashed as the childhood taunt struck home. Sam thought lead was about to fly. Quentin's hand moved slightly—more of a twitch than an aggressive move. Then to Sam's surprise, Quentin dropped his hand to his side and stepped back. *He is outnumbered,* Sam thought. Quentin did not strike him as a coward, but he had expected more from him.

"Laurie, you look good enough to eat. When are ya going to start seein' a real man?" Rowdy said as he placed a finger on the center of Eli's chest and pushed.

Oh, no you don't, Sam thought. He was about to pull iron to protect the most surprising woman he knew, but before he could, Beth's .36 leapt into her hand.

"If you want to keep picking your nose with that finger, pull it back." It was quite a sight. Rowdy towered over Eli. Rowdy's finger was planted right in the center of Eli's chest, and Eli's .36 was planted at the base of Rowdy's rib cage. Unlike Quentin, there was no back down in Eli. Rowdy decided picking his nose was a habit he wanted to keep and slowly pulled his finger back.

"This ain't over, Kennedy. You killed three of my boys last night, and you're going to pay," Rowdy growled.

"You tell him, Rowdy, he cain't do the Double L like that and get away with it," Little Brother added.

Crack came the sound of a buggy whip. All eyes turned to a glossy, ebony buggy pulled by a magnificent, black trotter. The man at the reins was just as elegant as the rig he was driving. He wore a finely tailored, blue, frock coat with a matching vest and tie. The suit had a military look to it. Sam guessed that was the point. The buggy was escorted by four riders from the 7C. They were riding in perfect formation, all carrying scatterguns.

Sam had known many men like the colonel—men who saw their time in command as the highlight of their lives and could not let it go. Command marks a man for life. The officers who led men to hold this young land together saw more bloodshed and sorrow than anyone should have to bear. They could not help but be marred by it. Sam knew he was.

For his part, Sam did not miss command one bit. It is one thing to put oneself in harm's way for what is right, but putting other men's lives in danger was another thing altogether. Seeing his brave, young men riding into the teeth of .50 caliber musket fire under his command still caused him nightmares. He did not regret his time as an officer. It was something that had to be done, but if he never wrote another letter of regret to a grieving wife or mother, if he never held the hand of a young soldier until his life passed on, it would be too soon.

"Daddy!" Laurie shouted as the buggy pulled up.

"Baby girl!" the colonel called back as he leapt from the wagon to greet her. The colonel was in his midfifties, but he was still in fighting shape. They fell into a tight embrace. Their bond was deep. Laurie was a true daddy's girl. The colonel kissed her on the forehead. She took off his hat and ran her hand through his gray hair.

"I've missed you, Daddy."

"And I you, baby girl."

Quentin stuck out his hand. "Colonel."

"Quentin." The colonel eyed his son.

"Ain't that sweet, the Dunhill family back together again. I think I might cry, boys," Rowdy said and spat on the ground as his crew once again broke into laughter.

The colonel nodded to his men, and in one clean, military move, the 7C crew leveled four sawed-off shotguns at Rowdy and his boys.

Sam guessed the guns were probably loaded with buckshot and glass. At that range, that kind of load would cut a man in half. The Double L crew shifted uneasily. The blood drained out of one of Rowdy's boys all together.

With the scatterguns backing him up, the colonel said, "Open your filthy mouth again, and I will close it permanently."

The colonel knew he might run into trouble in Smith, so he had come prepared. The situation was far worse than Sam had thought. The feud had grown so deep that all sides were ready to kill each other on the street. In fact just coming to town required a battle plan.

Rowdy began to open his mouth but then thought better of it. He had had to back down twice in five minutes, and this made him furious.

Eli stepped between the two battle lines. "This is a happy day, Colonel. Your children have come home. No need to spill blood."

Reluctantly the colonel again nodded, and his men slowly lowered their side-by-side scatterguns. "Eli, my boy, it is good to see you. You are going to come to the party?"

"Oh, yes, sir. I would not miss it."

Sam stepped forward. "Mr. Dunhill, my name's Sam McKnight." He offered his hand to the colonel.

"Oh yes, I heard the US marshal's office was sending someone from Salt Lake. Personally, I think you are wasting your time. We in northern Utah can handle our own problems without the federal government getting involved."

Sam smiled slightly as he looked directly at the colonel. "Well, that may be, Mr. Dunhill, but I would still like to meet with you and talk over the details of what's been going on. How would tomorrow morning be?"

"I'll be expecting you, sir. Come, Laurie. We have much to do before the dance." The colonel turned to the buggy, but Laurie went to Sam.

She put her hand on his. "I look forward to seeing you tomorrow morning and at the dance," she said and then looked to Eli and purred, "See you Friday night, Eli." She swung around, and her father helped her into the buggy.

"See ya Friday night, Laurie," Rowdy taunted.

The colonel pointed his whip at Rowdy. "If you set foot on the Seven-C, I'll have it shot off, Rowdy Larson. Mark my words."

"I have had jest about enough of your high-and-mighty talk, Dunhill. You ain't no better than me and my people. You and my pa came from the same small town in Maryland, so just get off your high horse."

The colonel clenched his jaw and snapped his whip. The trotter leapt forward, and in moments, the 7C detachment was gone.

As the Dunhills drove away, Sam turned to Rowdy. "Tell your father I'll be out by your place this afternoon."

"I'll tell him, but I ain't sayin' he'll be waitin'. We don't give a damn about your badge or all the lies they tell about you." Rowdy hitched his thumb in his gun belt, watching for Sam's reaction. Rowdy's brother and crew all shifted slightly. Time stood still. For a moment, there was no sound except the hooves of the horses hitched to the stage.

Sam glanced at Beth, wanting to know where she was if lead began to fly. Her beautiful eyes were not on Rowdy. They were looking behind Sam. Suddenly her eyes widened, and her irises focused. At the same instant, she reached for her gun. All of this seemed to happen between heartbeats. There was no time to think, only react to the danger Beth saw behind him. The young gunman Sam had just knocked unconscious was back on his boots. He had pulled a .45 from a bystander's holster, and it was pointed right at Sam, hammer pulled back.

Sam turned, pulled, and shot as Beth's .36 cleared leather. The slug blew through the gunman's heart. Surprise and horror covered the back-shooting gunman's face as he fell backward and let out his last breath.

Sam was so fast, Beth had not even been able to get a shot off, but the hammer was back, and she swung it on Rowdy. Rowdy and his crew had begun to pull iron the moment they saw Sam go for his Colt, but as the reality of Sam's speed and accuracy hit them, their guns sunk back into their holsters. The crowd stood in stunned silence. Sam seeing Beth had things well in hand walked to Spurs, punching out the empty brass, and reloading as he went.

Kneeling down beside the body, he looked into its dead eyes. "I didn't want to kill you, boy."

Rowdy spat on the ground. His gray eyes went dark as he turned and walked away, the Double L crew following. Little Brother was the last to leave. He took a few steps backward, shaken by what he had seen and his brother's reaction to it.

Beth watched her knight. All she saw in Sam was deep regret. Each time she saw him, there was more to him. The depth of him made her want him all the more, but instead of making her happy, it made her mad.

Mr. Black walked to his prize and began going through the dead man's pockets.

"Show is over, folks. Go on about your business," Sam called out then turned to face Beth or Eli or—he didn't know what was going on. Out of frustration he said, "Mr. Kennedy, it is time for you and me to finish that conversation we started five days ago."

Beth's heart began to race again, and she didn't like it. She had told Sam to stay away, and he hadn't. She had enough to deal with without him showing up. "That conversation is finished." She turned and began to walk away.

Sam reached her in two quick strides. He grabbed her by the elbow and swung her around. "Now wait just a minute, Be—Eli. What is going on here?"

"I told you to stay away."

Sam pulled her close to his face and whispered, "My investigation brought me to Smith. It is just an added bonus that you are here."

Their eyes locked for just a moment. In that moment, they saw each other anew. Sam saw her soft mouth and those blue eyes. Beth saw the concern for her in his strong, tan face—a fine, handsome face. She wanted to touch it. At the same time, they both became aware of the crowd that was still watching them. Sam straightened, and Beth pulled away and began walking to the livery.

"Kennedy, you are not going to get away from me that easy," he said as he followed her into the stable. "You are in the middle of this range war. I need to know how you are involved. To start with, why did those two outlaws try to kill you back at the lake, and why are you pretending to be Eli Kennedy?"

"Leave me alone. This is none of your business." Her anger was back in full force.

"Everything that has to do with the murder of young Amos and your father is my business."

The mention of her father stopped her cold. "How do you know about my father?"

Sam looked around the livery; except for Buck and a few other horses they were alone. Sam crossed into an empty stall and leaned against a post, smiling slightly because now he had her complete interest again. "Let me see if I got this right. For years, your father, William Kennedy, kept the peace between Colonel Dunhill and Carl Larson by allowing both ranchers to water at the Juniper River."

"Yes."

"Both Larson and Dunhill tried to buy your father out, but he would not budge."

"Right."

"One day, four years ago, your father was found dead, thrown from a horse and badly beaten up."

"My father would never have fallen from his horse. Nothing would spook Old Blue. The two of them were old friends." She turned away. She could feel tears coming, and she would not cry in front of him again. He was the first to see what she knew was true: Her father was murdered.

He reached out and put his hands on her shoulders. She shrugged him off. She was desperately trying to stay hot at him for following her, but his mere presence and concern for her welfare were building another kind of heat in her.

"Now, I have had just about enough of you pulling away from me." He reached forward, grabbed her by the arm, and spun her around. "I did not ask for this assignment. I was sent. I did not ask to save your life, but I thank God He put me there when He did. You are in this up to your pretty, little neck. You need me, and I want to help."

"I don't need you or anybody else." The tears began to come now as she tried again to shake him loose.

Sam whispered angrily, "You may not need me, but I need you." He pulled her into him, and their mouths met. Her tears never stopped. Their bodies pressed tightly together—a perfect fit, as if they were made for each other. He released her arms. Her hands moved up his strong shoulders and around the back of his neck. She held him as close as he held her.

A board creaked behind them, and they broke apart, heading for opposite sides of the stall. Jenny stepped into view, wearing a brand new riding skirt, blouse, and matching, burgundy vest. She had a glow to her. The new clothes and new dream had almost been like a baptism to her, washing away the four years of a dark life.

"What is goin' on here? Have the two of you been fightin'?" she asked.

They eyed each other, and then they both began to laugh nervously. Eli spoke, "Of course not. The marshal and I are…old friends. Jenny Richards, this is Marshal Sam McKnight."

He reached out and took her hand. "Pleased to meet you, Miss Richards."

Jenny eyed them both, but before she could ask another question, Eli jumped in, pointing to the far stall. "Jenny, I bought that Palomino mare for you. She's six, real gentle, and quick. Her name is Freedom, but they call her Free."

"Oh! She's…she's beautiful!" Up to this moment, the clothes she was wearing were the greatest gift anyone had given her. "You are too good to me!"

Eli smiled. "I'm glad Free pleases you, gal. You be good to her, and she'll be good to you. She's all saddled up. Take her out in the corral and get to know her. I'll be along shortly." Eli glanced at Sam. "The marshal and I have some unfinished business."

Jenny walked to the blonde horse and reached out a hand for her to smell then gently touched the horse's soft nose, then face, and then finally jaw. Jenny's other hand began to stroke the Palomino's long neck. The horse and woman seemed to form an immediate bond. Jenny reached for the reins to lead Free out, but as soon as she stopped stroking the horse, Free complained. Like a big Labrador, she pushed Jenny from behind, wanting more attention. Jenny laughed, and the two of them moved on out into the corral.

When the girl and her new horse were out of sight, Sam gently took Beth's hand. "Tell me, Beth. Let me help."

They sat on a low bench, and she looked at him. Just like the night in the cabin, she felt she could trust him in a way she had never trusted anyone else. She sighed. "It started on that terrible day I told you about when those outlaws took most of my family. My daddy sent his men after the outlaws while he stayed behind to find us and buried my mama and Mary. He began to drink as he dug brave, little Eli's grave. He kept looking at me and shaking his head. That night he just sat in front of the fire, drinking and staring into the flames. I wanted him to hold me, but something had changed in him, so I waited. The fire slowly burned down. The room grew dim. Finally, he called me over. I ran to him, and he pulled me up on his lap."

"'Little sis,' he said, 'I never want you to be hurt like your mama and Mary. So we are going to play a game to keep you safe. This game will also help us keep little brother alive.' He went on to explain that we would pretend I was Eli. Then all the bad men would leave me alone.

"He sat me on the table and walked over to his desk. Opening the center drawer, he pulled out my mama's scissors. In just a few minutes, my long curls were on the floor.

"I didn't mind being Eli. I loved my twin, and it made my daddy happy. It was easy when I was little. Of course, as I grew older, it became more difficult. I was missing most of the equipment required to be a man, and my spare parts were growing." She blushed. Sam watched and listened, giving her his full attention.

She went on. "By the time I was fourteen, it became apparent I would be blessed—or perhaps cursed—with a boyish figure, and that was just fine with my daddy. So the game went on. By the time I wanted it to stop, it was too late. It was no longer a game to my poor, tortured daddy. He stopped mentioning my real name, always calling me only Eli." Sam could hear a little catch in her throat. "I loved that old man, and if that made him happy, so be it.

"The game was such a comfort to my father. His little girl was safe."

"After he was killed, I could have given Eli up, but as a woman, I didn't think I could find his killer or save the Running J. We both know it is a man's world. Men hold all of the cards. Women are property to be used and played with."

"My granddaddy always said, 'Women are to be loved and cherished...'"

"Oh yes, like a well-loved dog, or a favorite child," Beth chided.

"No. You are the most beloved of creation, a holy thing made by His hand, the heart of a masterpiece. You are the completion, made so wondrous that man cannot help dwelling on your form." The words he spoke brushed her face like delicate kisses. She longed for the world he spoke of.

"The plan is for a man to give to a woman with sacrifice and a servant's heart. When he does, he gets back from her ten times what he gave. I know all you have to do is look around to see that men have twisted the plan to serve themselves." He reached to touch her face. "But the plan is still there, and it still works. I have seen it."

Resting her freckled cheek in his hand, she listened to him. She had never heard a man speak of women in such a way. She knew that some men loved their women. Her father loved her mother, but he had never spoken of her. The time Beth had spent on cattle drives, in saloons, and in bunkhouses had convinced her that men viewed women as ignorant playthings. This man, whose green eyes searched her, spoke a language she could barely understand. The sound of it made her heart sore. It was so high and full now she could no longer hold it back. She leaned forward and covered the five inches between them. Once again, their lips met, ever so softly this time, searching. Slowly, she pulled away from him, blinking her eyes to clear the tears of joy. She wanted to look him in the face and speak plainly.

"You are a rare man, Sam McKnight. I need some time to think, but I want to hear more about this plan." She stood up, and—being a gentleman—so did Sam. "Maybe together we can find out who killed my father and who is trying to kill Eli. Will you come to dinner tonight at the Running J?"

"I'd be delighted to, Beth." She loved the sound of her name coming from him. Once again, she leaned in and kissed him. He wrapped his arms around her and pulled her close. Her heart began to pound as her body reacted to his touch, but suddenly he released her. She searched his face, and all she found there was warm acceptance. She walked backward to Belle saddled in her stall. She stepped to the horse and mounted. "We eat at five."

"I'll be there. Count on it."

She rode Belle out into the sun and called to Jenny, who loped over astride Free. Jenny began to talk with childlike enthusiasm, but Sam couldn't make out what she was saying, only that Eli's gift had made her joyful. He watched them ride out.

"You've got quite a heart, Beth Kennedy."

The summer sun was high and hot, but today Beth was not hiding from it. Her hat was hanging between her shoulders. The feeling of the sun on her face seemed to amplify the pure energy she felt at her core. She didn't know what the feeling was, but it made her want to play.

Jenny and Beth rode up to the crest of a hill and pulled up. From there they could see most of the Juniper River valley. This was Running J country. It was part of her. She had spent her childhood playing in and exploring every part of it. For the past four years, she had risked her life trying to hold on to it.

The Running J had two personalities. On the east side of the Juniper River stood tall, ponderosa forest. On the west side, it was all sagebrush, juniper, and high desert.

For some reason, the ranch seemed a brighter place this morning. All around her, the dark-green foliage of the junipers leaped out from the dusty, gray background of the sagebrush. The sky was as blue as a deep, high mountain lake. She took a deep breath. The sharp smell of sagebrush hung in the air. She gazed up at the blazing sun. It was hot and getting hotter, but instead of draining her, it took her back to childhood and long summer days. She felt like a twelve-year-old with a day of riding, swimming, and climbing in front of her. It struck her that she had not been this happy in years. She had almost forgotten the feeling. At the center of this feeling Sam was still standing there, hat off, green eyes shining. She smiled then laughed.

Jenny's voice brought her back from her daydream. The girl had not stopped talking about the virtues of Free since they left Smith.

"What a sweet horse, and yet she can fly like the wind."

"Is that right, Miss Jenny? Are you sayin' Free can beat my Belle?"

"I think she can, Mr. Kennedy. Yah!" Jenny and Free bolted down the road. Beth leaned forward and laid the spur to Belle. "Yah!"

Free stayed to the road, but Belle was a cow pony. Beth headed her straight across the sagebrush, cutting the corner. She had grown up in the saddle, and there was no place she would have rather been. Belle leaped through the brush like a mule deer. The young mare's body surged under her, and she anticipated every move. In moments, Belle had closed the gap. Now Beth moved Belle to the road. The two horses were side by side. Beth looked at her young friend, and they both laughed. As the bridge that crossed the Juniper came into view, they both leaned forward in their saddles and pressed their horses for more.

Again, they looked at each other. In that look, they shared this moment of joy. Both horses galloped side by side, hooves pounding together. Beth could have moved Belle ahead, but the moment was a greater victory.

Suddenly, they were on the bridge. The percussive sound of the hooves on the wooden decking signaled the race's end. They reigned up, laughing. Belle and Free stomped and snorted, ready to play some more.

"Oh Lord! That was wonderful. I have never felt so alive," Jenny exclaimed. "Thank you, thank you, Eli," The way she looked at Eli told Beth she expected something more. Beth understood Jenny's feelings. If Sam had been the other rider, Beth would be falling into his arms right now.

◆━━━◆━━━◆

Sam rode Buck up to the crest of the hill. He knew the Double L ranch house was just over the rise. He had been careful to stay off the road on his way in. Instead, he had kept to the ravines as he approached the place. After his encounter with Rowdy and Little Brother, he figured he had better play it safe. Rowdy was a back shooter if he had ever seen one. So Sam stayed in the draws, only topping the hills when he had no choice.

Sam eased out of the saddle, pulling the field glasses at the same time. Grabbing Buck's bridle, he pulled Buck's head around and said, "Now you stay right here, boy. I'll just be a minute." The big horse watched him go. Buck was uneasy, and Sam knew it.

As softly as a predator, he moved to a big juniper at the top of the rise. The central feature on the place was a large, squat ranch house. The square house was built out of gray rock. The tilting porch was held up with mismatched juniper logs. This place was just one step up from a soddy. It was in bad shape. At any minute, the porch might have fallen off, but the house itself was as solid as a fort. Sam figured that was the idea.

There were six men sitting on the porch steps or on crates in the shade. Rowdy and Little Brother were there. These men were not cowhands. There was an economy to what a cowboy wore. Everything on him had a purpose and was in good working order. The bone handle knife on his belt might have been worn smooth from use, but the blade was sharp enough to shave with.

These men on the porch wore too much iron. No one was working, and from the looks of the place, it could sure have used some. No, these men were hired for their guns, not their ropes.

The front door opened, and out walked a mountain of a man. His body was built like an oak barrel and looked just as hard. As one the lazy gunmen snapped to alert. His jaw looked to be carved from granite. His eyes fell on each man, looking for weakness. They all looked away like schoolboys, hoping not to be picked as an example. His sleeves were rolled up to the elbow, revealing massive forearms. A man of his size and age would have been slow, but there was no doubt in Sam's mind about Carl Larson's strength. His mere presence on the porch commanded attention. Larson began to speak, but Sam could just see the reaction to what he said through his field glasses. There was no way to get closer without being seen.

———————◆———————

"Boy," Larson bellowed in a deep bass.

"Yes, Pa," Rowdy weakly replied.

"Did you find out what happen ta Bass, Leach, and Collin?"

"Yes, Pa. Kennedy killed 'em."

"All three. Where?"

"At the saloon, Pa."

"How is Eli?"

Little Brother piped up. "We went to settle the score this afternoon, and he looked just fine, Pa. We would have taught him a lesson, but that Marshal McKnight got in the way."

"Marshal Sam McKnight is in town? I hear he's good, one of the best."

"Rowdy coulda took 'em," boasted Little Brother. The other gun hands glanced around at each other. None of them seemed quite as sure about Rowdy's luck against McKnight. "He said he comin' out to speak to you this afternoon."

"You are jest lucky Eli Kennedy or McKnight didn't teach you a lesson you couldn't get up from. Tex was a good hand. In a fair fight, there ain't many who could take him."

"That's the point. It probably weren't fair," Rowdy said.

"Eli Kennedy is his daddy's boy. If he killed 'em, it was fair," Larson said. "Did you see that Dunhill gal?"

"Yes, Pa."

"Well, did you talk sweet to her like I told you?"

"Yes, Pa, I sure did, and Pa she sure is pretty," Rowdy said.

"She liked him, Pa," Little Bother lied.

"How'd it go, boy? Tell me everything. Did you treat her good, like a lady?"

He rubbed his hands together. "If it don't work out with your sis and Kennedy, maybe you and the colonel's gal can be a match. You bedding Laurie Dunhill would be like rammin' a hot poker in the colonel's gut."

"Oh yes, Pa, Rowdy did just like you said." The two son's eyes darted to each other and then back to their Pa. "You'd have been proud, real proud, Pa. You taught us how to handle women," Roland said as he sat down on a crate by the door.

Larson eyed Roland then Rowdy. His eyes narrowed. Just as he was about to push the point, Rowdy said, "Pa, Dunhill said we were to stay away from the dance on Friday. He said if'n we stepped foot on the place, he'd see it was shot off."

"Damn that Dunhill, always thinkin' he and his are better than the rest of us. Well, we will just see who gets their foot shot off at that party."

Sam had seen enough; he walked back to Buck. "This looks like as good a time as any. Let's go do some digging, boy." He stepped onto Buck, and they started down the hill.

Eli and Jenny rode up on the Running J's outer corrals in the early afternoon. The place was busy. Men were working on the hay barn roof, and horses were being broke for the fall drive. Three cowhands were breaking some new mustangs in the first corral. They had a rope on a strong, young mare. Eli and Jenny stopped to watch.

Jake, Eli's foreman, had a hold of the rope. He was working the mare to a post in the center of the corral. The mare did not know what he was doing, but she didn't like it. Pulling as hard as he could, Jake finally worked his way to the post. The strain of the struggle had caused him to completely sweat through his shirt in the early-afternoon sun.

Jake swung the rope around the post, getting one wrap on it. The mare, feeling more and more trapped, pulled back hard. Jake let the rope slip through his buckskin gloves. Smoke rose from the friction of the rope around the post. The rope fell into a slot worn in the post by many past struggles of horse against man.

During all of the mare's thrashing, Jake kept speaking softly to her. "Good girl, pretty girl, it's all right. I ain't goin' to hurt you. That's a good, little gal." She calmed some.

Beth looked at Jenny and saw just what she had hoped. Jenny's eyes were locked on Jake. She was totally smitten. Her face reflected every new step Jake took with the mare.

"He's good, isn't he?" Eli said.

"Wonderful."

Every time the mare gave ground, Jake took up the slack. Whenever he got enough rope, he put another wrap on the post. His grip on her was now strong. She pulled against the rope but only managed to wear herself out. Breathing hard, the mare gave in.

"How come I have never seen him at the saloon?" Jenny asked.

"Jake spends time where his heart is. I'd have to order him off the ranch to make him leave. He's got a mission."

"Is he religious?"

"You might say that. He is saving for his own place. He says one more year and he'll have it. He wants to raise horses, and he should. I've never seen a man so good with the animals."

Jake passed the rope to a round Mexican who was helping him. A third man, about six foot and no wider than a six-by-six, handed him a blanket. The two assistants were smiling, enjoying the work of a true master.

Jake never stopped talking to the mare, and his hands were always on her. After the blanket, Slim handed him the saddle. He placed it on her for the first time. She shied but did not bolt. She was beginning to like this man, until he cinched it down. That, she did not like. She liked it even less when he stepped into the stirrup and eased his long, strong frame onto her.

"What a good girl. Now let's play. Let her go, Jesus," and Jesus gently pulled the rope from her head. Away she went. She may have liked this man, but he was not supposed to be on her back. So she tried to remove him.

"Oh Lord! He's goin' to get killed." Jenny gasped and looked away.

"Not Jake. Just watch."

"I can't."

"Watch." Eli said with more force, and Jenny looked up again, just as the mare gave in. Jenny could almost see her listening to Jake's calming voice. Now he began to teach her as he moved her around the corral.

Eli waved the men over. Jake walked the green broke mare slowly to the fence. "Miss Jenny Richards, I'd like you to meet my top hand and the foreman of the Running J, Jake Brown. These other two are Jesus Domingo and Slim Parsons. Miss Richards is my new secretary and business assistant."

With their hats in their hands, each man greeted her, Jesus first. "I am very pleased to meet you, senorita."

"Howdy, miss, I believe we have met," Slim said.

"You know we have, Mr. Parsons." Jenny smiled. She knew most of the men for one hundred miles around, but she did not know Jake.

In the same voice he used with the mare, Jake greeted her. "Miss Richards, you have come to work on the best ranch in northern Utah, for one of the finest, most honorable men I've ever known. He knows how to pick people, so it is a pleasure to meet you."

His greeting took Jenny's breath away. The others just stared at him.

"Damn, Jake," Slim said. "That is the most I have ever heard you say to a human." They all broke into laughter.

"Miss Richards is going to work closely with you, Jake. Tomorrow I would like you to take her around the place. She needs to know how we do things and what it costs."

"No problem, Eli. No problem at all," Jake said. Jesus and Slim were just staring at Jake.

Beth noticed Jenny was blushing ever so slightly. "Jake, come to dinner at the house tonight. I want to get caught up."

"I'll be there." Jake jumped down from the green-broke mare and walked into the barn as Eli and Jenny turned their horses toward the main house.

They rode past a large log cabin on their right. Men were coming and going, but when they saw Jenny, most stopped and took note. Some called out, "Howdy, Jenny. What brings you up here?"

Eli turned Belle hard to the right. "From here on out, you will call Jenny 'Miss Richards.' She has a new job. Miss Richards is my new secretary and business manager." Jenny seemed to sit up a little taller on Free as she looked at her old customers.

"Howdy, Miss Richards. Does this mean you won't be at the saloon no more?" Hank asked. He was a young cowhand, blond with just the start of a mustache.

"That's right. I have a proper job with Mr. Kennedy now. I won't be back to the saloon again."

"Damn—I mean, darn," said the disappointed cowhand.

Jenny smiled.

"That's where I grew up," Eli said, pointing to the simple, one-story, log ranch house. A covered porch dominated the front of the house. "Now it's Jake's house and the center of ranch operations. The men eat there, and all short- and long-term projects are directed from there."

"I see," Jenny said.

"You will be spending quite a bit of time there with Jake." They both stopped at these words and smiled. Eli added, "During the day, working on reports and financial statements."

As they passed the northwest corner of the old log homestead, the three-story, log main house came into view. Jenny had heard about the place from Eli's cowhands, but their description had not come close the reality of it.

The main floor was dominated by a huge, covered entry that served as a spacious deck for the second floor. The deck looked large enough for a town dance. Jenny thought this was odd, since Eli never entertained. There was also a large balcony on the third floor. Jenny guessed that was Eli's room. From there, she could see the whole valley.

A young, Mexican boy ran out to meet them. "Senor Eli, Senor Eli!" he called. The boy was smiling from ear to ear. Eli jumped off Belle, lifted the boy off the ground, and spun him completely around before putting him down. Jenny was a little surprised at the obvious affection Eli had for the boy.

"Jo, you have grown a foot while I have been gone." The boy glowed as he tried to stand even taller. "Jo, this is Miss Richards. She is my new secretary."

Jo looked her up and down as she climbed off Free. "Senorita Richards is very pretty. Is Senor Eli going to marry her?"

Jenny blushed, and Eli spoke carefully. He wanted Jenny to know that he thought she was good enough for anyone, but he did not want to lead her on. "A pretty senorita like Miss Richards will have a line of men asking her to marry soon enough. Besides, I don't want to make your mama jealous."

"Oh, you won't. She says, 'The sooner Senor Eli gets married the better.'"

"Well, you go tell that old matchmaker that we will have company for dinner. Miss Richards will join us at the table from now on, Jake will be there, and Marshal McKnight will be coming to dinner."

"Marshal McKnight, the gun fighter?" The saucer-eyed boy asked.

"That would be him."

The boy spun around and ran back to the house. "Mama, Mama! We are having company."

"Does he run everywhere?" Jenny asked.

"Everywhere."

"Rider's coming!" All eyes turned to the bluff. The sounds of bullets being levered into rifle actions and gun-leather being adjusted filled the air as Buck and Sam rode in. Larson stepped to the edge of the porch. Rowdy was right beside him, leaning on a juniper post. Sam slowed Buck to a walk and then came to a stop. He stayed in the saddle so he could speak to Larson eye to eye. He leaned against his saddle horn with his right hand just inches from the .44 in his cross-draw holster. The men on the porch were all ready to fight, but standing easy. No man would stand against eight, not even McKnight.

Sam smiled. "Afternoon Mr. Larson. My name is Sam McKnight." No move was made to shake hands.

"Afternoon, Marshal. My boys said you'd be comin' out. What can I do for you?" There was no worry or concern in Larson's tone. If anything he seemed interested to meet McKnight.

"I thought you and I might have a little word about all the trouble that has been going on around here. I'm told you were one of the first men to tame this country and that you know more about the land and the people than just about anyone. I thought you might be able to shed some light on the trouble."

Larson smiled. "Well, it is about time someone with a little sense came to the right place. I can tell ya how to solve your problem. You just ride on over to the Seven-C and tell the colonel to stop cuttin' the fences and rustlin' cattle, and I'm sure it will stop." All of his crew mumbled in agreement.

"That is just about what Mr. Dunhill told me to tell you."

"Well, the colonel is a damn liar." All heads on the porch nodded.

"Mr. Larson, if you have any proof that Mr. Dunhill is behind the rustling, I'd be happy to hear it."

"Everyone knows Dunhill is without honor. I'm missin' more than a hundred head of cattle since spring. There is only one man in these parts who would want to harm me like that." Larson was sincere, and Sam believed him.

"That's right, Pa. You tell 'im," Roland said.

"Shut up, boy. When I need a half-wit to help me talk to the marshal, I'll let you know." A low snicker ran through the gun hands. Roland's face turned red as he backed away from his father. Hand on his gun, he turned on the men. They all just stared back at him with looks of contempt. "You'll have to excuse my boy. His worthless ma ran out on us when Roland was born. Guess the sight of him was too much. Being raised out here, my boys haven't learned to be real gentlemen. You can see how spineless the youngest boy is, but I have hopes for Rowdy."

Roland spun on his heels, ran to a horse, mounted, and rode out. Larson shook his head in disgust. *He wanted that boy to strike him,* Sam thought.

"Rowdy is the only one of my three offspring who seems to have any of me in him." Rowdy smiled at his father's praise. The only thing Sam saw in Rowdy Larson was flat evil. The sooner he was in prison or dead, the sooner people in Smith would be safe.

"Why would Mr. Dunhill want to harm you, sir?"

"The water. Dunhill wants the water to himself. It's the lifeblood of this land, and he wants it all. The only reason this did start years ago is Bill Kennedy. He was a man of honor. As long as he was in control of the Running J, I had no reason to worry. If something happens to his boy, or if Eli forms partners with Dunhill, I'll fight for my land. I'm not goin' to watch my cattle die of thirst."

This man was speaking from his heart, and Sam believed him. If pushed, Larson would do anything, but so far he was not involved in the rustling. Of course that did not mean Rowdy was not behind it. He would not put anything past Rowdy.

"What can you tell me about the Amos boy?"

"Not much. Haney is the one who found him. Come over here, Haney." Larson motioned for the thin, weathered gun slick to come over. "Ask him."

Sam asked, "Where did you find him, Mr. Haney?"

Haney looked up at the marshal squinting into the sun. "I found him on the rim." Haney spoke slowly as if he was out of practice.

Sam waited, but Haney seemed to be through. "And where would that be?"

"It's at the northern most reach of the Running J"—he paused— "where all three ranches meet."

"If I were to head up there for a look, how would I know that I was there?"

Haney's brow furrowed. He was going to have to use vocabulary. His eyes narrowed, deepening the lines in his face created by years in the saddle under the sun. Finally he found the words. "The rim is a small valley where all the fences meet, overlooked by a steep ridge to the east, on the 7C side. Is that 'nough fer ya, or do I have to describe the trees?" Snickers rippled through the porch.

"No, that will get me there." Haney turned away, smiling at his friends. "But I do have a few more questions. How long do you think he had been dead, Mr. Haney?"

Haney turned slowly around, throwing Sam a sideways look. "He was fresh. Found him around noon. The boy'd been shot that morning. Blood still wet."

"Rifle?"

"Ya."

"How can you be sure?"

Haney began to squint again as he pulled himself back to the scene. "His horse was still grazin'. He was wearin' an old Colt he never pulled. Grass was still young. You could see every print clear like. Hadn't been 'nother horse up there in days."

"Can you tell me anything about the caliber?"

"Big. Had to be more than three hundred yards. Sharps, maybe. It came from the ridge."

"That was very helpful. Thank you, Mr. Haney."

Haney puffed up a little as he walked back to the other men.

Rowdy said, "You must be plum tuckered out after all that talkin'. Do you want ta hit the bunk house for a nap, old man?" All the men laughed at Haney's expense.

"Where were you that morning, Rowdy?" The question caught Rowdy off guard. He looked up at McKnight and found Sam's eyes drilling right though him.

"Was still at the saloon in bed with that whore, Jenny. I wasn't through with her until mid-morning." All of the hands whooped at that.

Larson hit Rowdy with the back of his hand, and his son stumbled into the crates behind him. Rowdy sprung back to his feet ready to fight but then reconsidered. He put his hat back on.

He spoke low, full of rage. "Pa, I'm telling ya. Ya gotta stop doin' that."

Larson stared at his son, breathed out a sigh of disappointment, and turned to the Marshal. "I can see ya are true Texas gentlemen. Fought beside many of them in the war for Texas independence. You should meet my little girl, Victoria. I think the two of you would get along just fine." He looked back at the house.

"Victoria, Victoria!" No answer from the house. "Where is Victoria?"

"I don't know, Pa. She went out early this mornin' for a ride. Looked like she'd packed lunch for two." This news did not please Larson.

"Damn that girl," he said. "Why can't she just stay home, instead of running off with every...? Well, she will be at the dance, Mr. McKnight. I think you would like her."

"I would be happy to meet her, sir. I'm looking forward to it," Sam lied. If Vickie Larson was anything like her brothers, she would be dangerous.

Sam and Buck were thirsty. The sun had been on their backs for the past two hours. Sam had been pushing hard. The memory of his last embrace with Beth drove him on. The thought of her soft cheek resting on his shoulder was almost more than a poor Texas boy could handle.

He was now on the Running J, and he liked the country. It was Rocky mountain pine forest giving way to high desert juniper. If the Bear River range was the foothill of the Rockies, then these were its toes.

They were now cresting hills and dropping into draws. At the bottom of this draw, Sam saw a small creek. "I think we could both use a drink, boy." But Buck did not need encouragement. Down they went.

He stepped off his thirsty friend and let him drink. The water was cool and fresh. He took off Charlie's bandana and soaked it in the crystal water and retied it around his neck. The fresh water trickled down his back and chest. It felt good. In fact, everything about this moment seemed good—the cool, soft grass beneath his boots, Buck drinking, the sound of water over rocks, and being that much closer to Beth. He felt blessed. Looking up, he said, "Thank you."

Bright laughter rang out in the stillness. Sam stood and stepped to Buck. Buck's head was already up, and his nose was working. "Smell the perfume, boy? Hold, boy. I'll be back." Buck watched him go, never taking his eyes or ears off of him. Sam might call for him, and Buck wanted to be ready.

Sam carefully moved upstream around a bend in the creek. He stepped on rocks and soft grass to conceal his approach. Here, the creek was blocked by a beaver dam, creating a clear pool. The little draw opened up into a lush green meadow, and on the edge of it sat the source of the laugh.

Her red hair and cream-white shoulders stood out against the green background of tall grass. Sam was within twenty feet of her, but she had no idea he was there.

She laughed again. "No. Now you get home. You have had enough. See ya at the dance." Sam heard a muffled response then a horse breaking into a gallop and moving away.

He gave the horse a moment to move well away, and then he introduced himself. "Good afternoon, Miss Larson." She turn, startled and on guard. She held a .45-caliber derringer in her left hand. He made no move, just held his ground and let her sort things out. She did.

This female wildcat quickly observed everything about him, including his badge. "You must be Sam McKnight."

"My friends call me Marshal."

She considered the derringer and put it down. She had not quite had time to put herself back together after her picnic, but she was not the kind of girl that minded men taking a peek. Buttoning up her blouse, she said, "I heard you met my brothers this morning, and they ended up leavin' with their tails between their legs."

"They left, but I don't usually notice men's tails." She tightened the belt around her waist, grabbed her boots, and began to pull them on.

"Who was your friend?"

Now she turned her attention to the picnic basket. "It's not really any of your business, but if you must know, it was Eli Kennedy."

Sam had to smile. What a smooth liar she was, but there were a few things about Eli Miss Vickie obviously did not know. Sam decided to have some fun at this talented liar's expense. "Is that right? I just happen to be eating with Eli tonight. He and I are old friends. I will have to ask him how he liked the picnic and the swim."

The irises of Vickie's eyes widened, and a faint pink flashed in her checks. "He told me it was one of the best dips he ever had." She began to pull her red hair into a loose braid. "Tell him hey for me. How do you know Eli?"

"We have a young woman in common," Sam said. "She introduced me to Eli on a trip." The mention of a woman caused her to pick up the picnic basket and move to her horse. She began to tie the basket to the saddle the way he had seen his young wife slam cabinets when she was "not upset."

Sam changed the subject. "I met your father today. We had a good talk. He thought you and I should spend some time together." Sam was playing with her and enjoying every minute.

"How is my old fool of a daddy?"

"He was very helpful. I was able to get a clearer picture of the Amos boy's murder. It appears to be as cold-blooded as they come."

Suddenly her edge came off, and she spoke with a tone as sweet as a Sunday school teacher. "He was a nice boy. Only problem he ever had was that he was sweet on that little spic whore the colonel raised." These words were part of her everyday life. The foulness of them hung in the air like a dead animal. It did not matter how hard she pretended to be a lady; Sam could see the crudeness at the heart of her.

He could see his granddaddy rocking on the front porch of his house. "Some people look all fine on the outside, like a fresh, white-washed house, but jist under the paint, the wood is rottin'. Them's the folks you got to watch." Vickie Larson had his full attention.

"You are the first person I've talked to who seemed to know the boy. Why do you think someone would want to kill them?"

"I don't really know. He did have a habit of sticking his nose in where it didn't belong, but he was harmless. Never picked a fight, but I saw him end a few."

Sam watched her eyes and mouth. She was not out-and-out lying, but she was holding something back. "So you saw him end a few fights. Did he have any enemies?"

"Not that I know of. Of course we have the usual bunch of boys who will kick butt for any reason." She stepped up into the stirrup and pulled herself onto her horse. As she threw her leg over, her bare thigh was in clear view. She looked to see if Sam noticed. Of course he did. She smiled. "My daddy will be wantin' me home."

"I'll tell Eli you send your regards." Again the color rose in her cheeks as the clear sarcasm struck home. She wheeled her horse and was gone.

Sam walked back to Buck. The Amos boy was beginning to take shape in his mind. He thought about what he had just learned. "Someone took time to kill this boy, Buck. He was in someone's way, just like Beth's father. I'll bet my hat they are the same person."

The summer sun was still high when Sam rode up to the main house on the Running J. The artistry of the little cabin on that shining mountain lake was all over this place. Gazing at the main house, Sam knew he had to meet this architect. The house sang out joy carved in logs. It had a life to it. But it was missing something. "People. This place should have people all over it," Sam said to Buck.

As Sam stepped off Buck, a little boy burst through the main door. He was decked out in the glory of old Spain: white shirt; beautiful, brown, short coat; matching pants; and boots. "Senor Marshal! Senor Marshal!" the boy shouted as he ran up to him. As the little Don reached Sam, he slid to a stop and came to attention. Before saying a word, the little Don gave Sam and Buck a thorough inspection. Sam watched his big, brown eyes as they moved over every detail of Sam's rig. His eyes blinked twice, and he gulped as he looked at the famous Colt and new Winchester in the saddle scabbard. Finally, the big eyes came to rest on Sam's face and broad smile.

"My name is Jo."

"Pleased to meet you, Senor Jo. I'm Marshal McKnight."

Jo smiled at the senor. "Senor Marshal, you are to please come with me."

With that, Jo grabbed Sam and began to pull him toward the house. "Whoa, Jo. Just a minute. What about my horse?" Sam pulled loose long enough to grab his saddle bags and pull the Winchester loose.

"Do not worry, Senor Marshal. Senor Hank will take your fine horse for a good cool down." At that moment, a young cowhand appeared from the bunkhouse. He walked up to Buck, and the two were immediately friends. He tipped his hat and extended his hand. "Hank Redford, Marshal." They shook hands.

"His name is Buck," Sam said.

"I'll take good care of him." Hank led Buck away.

Sam put his hand back out, and Jo grabbed onto it with glee, towing him into the house. Jo pulled him though the front door into an amazing space. The center of the house was open from floor to ceiling, three stories' worth of open space. The house wrapped around this space. The second floor hallway was a balcony that circled the entire room. The railings and post were all made out of the burled pine Sam had seen at Beth's cabin. There was a massive stone fireplace on the far wall. The hearth was big enough to walk into.

Sam looked up. Light was streaming in everywhere. The builder had placed a thin row of windows along the tops of the third floor walls as they met the vaulted ceiling. The sun was setting, and its golden light poured through the narrow window pains, illuminating the rich tones of the wooden rails. Off of the third floor, a burl-railed staircase led up to a single door.

A large table was set for twelve on the ground floor of the great room. A plump Mexican woman was bustling about with what appeared to be her teenage daughters.

Jo pulled on Sam's arm. "Senor Marshal, Mama has poured you a bath. It is waiting for you in your room."

"Do I smell that bad, Jo?"

Jo only smiled back at Sam. Sam tousled the boy's hair and said, "Lead on, Aladdin." This little boy's energy and spirit reminded Sam of the young hero. Jo only looked back at him like he was surely *loco*.

<hr />

Laughter and good talk was the icing to a meal of grilled steak smothered in onions and vegetables, all wrapped in flour tortillas. Tex-Mex, Sam felt like he was at Granddaddy's for Sunday supper. He could hear him now. "Boy, no one can cook like them Mexican gals," he would say as he slapped his young wife's behind in appreciation.

Eli sat at the head of the table dressed in him a frock coat, brown vest, and slacks. The suit was linen and well made. It hung well on him, just loose enough to lose Beth. Sam looked at her, wondering when and how they could be alone. *For now, business,* Sam thought.

What made a meal great were the people at the table, and these were fine people. Sam watched them as they talked of the day's work and what was ahead of them the next day. They made friendly jokes at Jake's expense, while the Running J's cook, Maria, hovered around the table, making sure everything was perfect for the boss.

Maria was full of efficient energy. Sam had no idea how old she was. She could have been anywhere from forty to sixty. Her skin was perfect, and Sam could see the beauty she must have been still shining through. She and her daughters were dressed in colorful, traditional Mexican dress.

As Maria and her daughters moved around the table, Sam watched Jenny and Jake stealing short glances at each other. Then he turned and looked at Beth as Eli. She was smiling, laughing, and enjoying her family. He admired all she had done for the ranch and its families since her father had been killed. She looked to him, and truth passed between them. He knew her, not all of her, but the beginnings of her truth.

Finally Sam said, "Maria, I cannot eat another bite. Thank you so much for that magnificent meal."

Maria beamed.

"Oh, Marshal," Eli said, "Maria is without a doubt the finest cook in Utah, but she is not done yet. You and Miss Jenny are about to experience the most amazing dessert this side of the Great Salt Lake." Jake and all the other ranch hands nodded in agreement as Maria's daughter cleared away the dishes and disappeared into the kitchen.

Sam could smell it before he saw it. Maria came out of the kitchen carrying a great Dutch oven hanging from an iron hook. Her daughters rushed ahead of her to place a large trivet on the table to protect it from the heat. She put down the Dutch oven in the center of the table and pulled off the lid. Steam and an explosion of heaven-sent aroma came from the golden blackberry cobbler inside the oven. The oldest daughter served Sam the first bowl, and everyone waited for him to try it. Sam guessed Maria must have used a pound of butter in the cake topping and then sprinkled brown sugar over it. The first bite of warm wild berries and topping melted in his mouth. He smiled and said, "Eli, my friend, you are wrong about Maria." Everyone seemed to hold their breath. "She is not only the best cook in Utah, she may be the best cook this side of the Big Muddy." All laughed as the daughters dished up cobbler for everyone.

Finally they could eat no more, and several of the key ranch hands said good night and headed for the bunkhouse. Eli's remaining guests moved to the massive hearth. A small fire was going more for effect than heat. Looking at Beth, Sam felt the heat all the same. The fireplace was surrounded by leather armchairs and a large, leather couch. Cigars were passed out, and brandy was poured.

Sam looked around at these good people. He felt blessed to spend this time with them. Jenny was at the couch with Jake next to her, sitting on the arm. The two of them were acting like school kids.

"Jake, did you know the Amos boy?" Sam asked.

"Yes. Jeff was a good kid. We would sign him on for the spring round up. His folks work a little spread just south of Smith."

Sam sipped on his brandy. "Why do you think someone would want him dead?"

"I don't rightly know. Everyone seemed to like the boy." Jake paused then went on. "There was somethin', but I don't even like bringin' it up. I hear it in the bunkhouse, and most everything said in there is tall tales or just plain bull. Well, I heard the boy was sweet on this little Mexican gal that works in the big house on the Seven-C.

Jeff Amos had gone by to see her that morning and some big row happened. I'm not sure what it was, but supposedly, the colonel ran him off the place."

"Do you remember the gal's name?"

"Desiree, I think, but I'm not sure."

Sam thought for a moment then asked, "Were Laurie and Quentin back from the east at the time of the murder?"

Jenny piped up, "Yes, sir. I know Quentin was." A little half-smile crossed her face.

Sam felt no need to ask her how she knew.

Jake stood up. "If there are no more questions, I need to get some shut eye. Sun is goin' to be up mighty early. Thank ya for the fine evening, Eli. It has been a pleasure to meet ya, Sam." Then he turned to Jenny, "Good night, Miss Richards. I'll see ya in the morning."

"Please call me Jenny, Jake"

"Well, good night…Jenny."

"Good night, Jake."

Jake backed out of the room, bumping into a chair as he went. Finally, he found the knob for the front door and was gone.

Beth began to laugh first, and Sam joined in. Soon Jenny was giggling.

"That boy has got it bad," Sam said.

Eli added, "For a man who never met a bronc' he couldn't ride, he seems to be plum thrown by our Miss Jenny."

"Now you two stop it," Jenny said. "He seems like a very nice man. I wish I had met a few more like him at the saloon."

"Not likely," Sam said.

With a dreamy look, Jenny stood and said, "Well, I will head to bed too."

Eli gave her a stern look. "To your own bed?"

"Yes, to my own bed, by myself."

They watched Jenny go. She took her time trying to take it all in—firelight dancing on the dark, log walls, and stars just peeking through the third story windows. She walked up to the top of the stairs and stopped. Yesterday she had been a tramp with nothing but nights full of smelly cowboys ahead of her. Tonight she would sleep in a castle.

She leaned on the second-floor railing and said, "It's too much, Eli. Just this one night is too much. I…I will never be able to repay ya, but I will. I will if it takes me my whole life."

"Jenny, you owe me nothing. You are doing me the great favor. I'm the one who needs you. Now get to bed. You have a big day in front of you."

"Yes, sir, Mr. Kennedy." Jenny turned and almost skipped to her bedroom door.

As the sound of Jenny's door closing began to fade, Sam and Beth looked away from the reborn girl to each other. The fire popped.

Beth was standing at the great, stone hearth. She turned to the fire.

Sam watched her as she stared into her brandy. The warm glow of the flames reflected in the irises of her aqua eyes and the honey tones of her short hair. The fire seemed to be alive in the amber liquid. She took a drink to steady herself.

Sam thought back to what Beth had done for Jenny. Sam wanted Beth, all of her. Not just her mouth and body, he wanted her story, her heart, her soul, and her brokenness. He moved to her slowly, carefully, like she was a wild mare that might spook.

He took a drink from his brandy and set it down. As he reached her, Sam ever so lightly placed one hand on her waist and one hand on the back of her elbow. He felt a slight tremor move through her body.

Sam breathed her hair in. It was the same sweet fragrance he had smelled out on the trail the day he watched her cut it. She leaned back into him. Softly he kissed the back of her neck, moving down to her white, starched collar. She turned to him, and he held her close.

He leaned in to kiss her, and she welcomed him. Time and pleasure melted together.

◆◆◆ ——— ◆ ——— ◆◆◆

The sound of a dish breaking in the kitchen followed by a flood of Spanish brought them back to reality. They were not alone. Beth broke from the embrace, grabbing her brandy and gulping it. She looked down at her clothes, straightened her vest and smoothed her jacket, then emptied the rest of her brandy.

Sam smiled as he retrieved his snifter and sat on the arm of the leather couch. He gave her time to think. Granddaddy had always said, "Smart gals gotta think things through. Ya'll never regret given them the time they need."

Out of frustration building to anger, Beth said, "How can this ever work? You see the men, women, and families that work this ranch. They are my family now. They need Eli, not Beth. Eli can hold this land. He is respected. Friends trust him. If they knew who I really was, they'd know I was a liar. That everything about me is a lie. They'd hate me. Beth can't hold the Running J, but Eli can. How can I choose between my family and you?

"Then there's Larson and Dunhill." Beth threw the snifter into the fire as her anger boiled over. "For some damned reason, it is up to me to stop them. Stop them from starting a range war. Stop them from killing each other's families and any innocent folks who get in the way."

Maria came in from the kitchen at the sound of breaking glass. "Mr. Eli, are you all right?"

Sam stopped her. "He's fine, just blowin' off a little steam. I'll clean up the glass."

Maria eyed Eli then Sam and headed back to the kitchen. She stopped at the door and took one last look. "You jist call if you need me, Mr. Eli." And then she was gone.

"Miss Elizabeth Kennedy, are you through?"

"I guess so."

"Do you want to know what I think?"

"I'm not sure."

"You are one of the strongest, most self-sacrificing people I have ever met, man or woman."

Beth started to protest, but Sam pushed on. "You have given your life for the ones you love. Now someone is trying to kill you, and what do you do? Do you run, or look for help? No, you turn and head right at the danger. In fact"—he stood and walked to her—"I don't think there is any back down in you. Not to mention the fact that you are only twenty-one. Most men your age are so wet behind the ears they aren't even worth being around. Lord have mercy, Miss Elizabeth, if you were a man, I'd say you must have…" He paused and smiled at her. "Well you've got nerves of solid granite."

Her set jaw gave way to a smile, and then they both laughed.

Sam took her hand and said, "Besides, as a man, you're not much to look at"—he swept her off her feet and into his arms—"but as a woman, you are an iron-willed beauty, the likes of which I have never seen before." With that, he kissed her.

She reluctantly pulled back from his lips. "Sam, put me down." He did. "We are still in the same spot. I will not give up my family or the ranch, and I don't want to give you up. What will the two of us do? Meet in dark corners the rest of our lives?"

"No, no, gal. You do not have to give up your family, and we are not going to be a secret."

She looked at him like he was crazy.

"I know it seems impossible, but all things are possible for those who believe in truth. First, you are wrong about you. I believe Beth Kennedy can hold the land. Lord knows you are smart enough and can shoot fast and straight enough. Those Double L boys found that out the hard way."

She turned away, shaking her head. Sam took her by the shoulders and gently turned her back. "Now hear me out. The only help you need is how to lay your brother to rest while we bring that brave, little, dead girl back to life."

"That can never happen."

"It has to. Truth is the only thing that can win here. The truth of who killed your father and the Amos boy. The truth of who killed your mama, sister, and brother. They are the same truth, I swear. I feel it in my gut." Her eyes began to shine as his words worked deep into her, and she started to believe.

"Truth is a bright light that pushes back the darkness. Lies cannot stand in it. If we are going to use that light, we must shine it on you first."

His words washed over her like a spring rain. That seedling of hope that she had been nurturing down at the cabin began to grow. "I want the truth, but, Sam, I don't know where to start." She took his hand and asked him for something she had not asked of anyone in years. "Help me."

"How did that taste?"

"Dusty."

He pulled her into him. "Of course I will, but we're going to need more help than even a marshal can give. We need a mother's help, and I know there is one we can trust on the other side of that kitchen door."

"Now?" she asked with the look of a child who was about to have to take a spoon full of castor oil.

He could not help but kiss that face. "Yes. Now. Maria!"

The kitchen door opened and out came Maria wiping her hands on her dishtowel. All the other help had gone to bed. "Si, Mr. Eli. I was jist finishing up. Do you need something?"

Her gift of hospitality in combination with her mother-bear love for the young man she served made her the perfect ally.

Beth and Sam both hesitated, not knowing just where to start.

"What is wrong?" she asked. "Is the marshal trying to hurt you?"

"No," they said together, chuckling.

Sam started, "Eli needs some help and wisdom only you can give him."

Beth stepped to Maria and took her hand. "Please come and sit with us, old friend. I have something I need to tell you." The two women sat on the couch, and Sam stood behind Beth.

Maria looked from her boss to Sam and then back to Eli. "You are scaring me a little."

"I am scaring me a lot." Beth looked back at Sam. He put his hand on her shoulder. She went on. "Maria, I have been lying to you. I have been lying to you for years, and I am so sorry." Her eyes began to well up.

"Is dis marshal trying to hurt you, arrest you?" She stood and pointed at Sam. "You try anything, and I will kill you."

Beth jumped between them, chuckling as a tear rolled down her cheek. "No, Maria, Marshal McKnight is here to help. I trust him." She looked to Sam, not wanting to start.

"You can trust her with this. She loves you. Damn, she would kill an innocent man for you," he said.

Maria, still pointing at Sam, said, "I never met an innocent man."

"Point taken." Sam smiled, and the women sat again.

Beth took a deep breath. "Here it goes. I know we've never talked about it, but what do you know about the day my mother and sisters were murdered?" Beth saw Maria hesitate. "It's all right, go on."

"What everyone knows. Raiders came to the main house. Your brave mama tried to fight, but it was no good. She and your sister were…were tortured and killed. You and your sweet, little twin ran, but she was hit and died next to you in the scrub."

"You have it just about right." Beth paused. "You see, Maria, my father found us that night asleep, curled together."

"Your papa was such a good man. When I came to work here, your mama had been gone for three years, but he grieved her like hit jist 'appened. The whole time I work for 'im, he never stopped grieving and blaming 'imself."

Beth nodded and continued. "The lie begins that terrible night out of his love and guilt, out of a desire to never let it happen again. That day when the twins ran into the scrub, it was brave, little Eli who took the bullet for his sister Beth. He kept her in front of him. He was always the protector." Beth stopped and let the words hang in the air. Maria was quietly listening but not understanding. "I am not Eli. He died saving my life sixteen years ago. I am Elizabeth." She searched her friend's face for a reaction. Beth expected rejection but hoped for acceptance.

Sam held his breath.

Maria looked hard at her Eli's face. She stood slowly and backed away a step, shaking her head no and then nodding yes. "Si, si, I always knew there was something jist not right with you. I thought it was all dat 'appened to you, what you saw dat day. Little things. How shy you were about your body. You never swam with your friends."

Beth stood. "Please forgive me"

"Oh, little niña." Maria cupped her freckled face and said, "How could I not 'ave seen it?" She pulled Beth into her arms. Beth moved into this mother's hug she had wanted since she was five. "How alone you have been, becoming a woman by yourself. I am ashamed I did not see. It is you who needs to forgive me."

Maria looked to Sam. "You brought my niña back to life. But how did you know she was a woman? I have been with 'im—I mean 'er since she was eight. I am a woman, and I never knew."

Sam took Beth's hand. "It's a long story. Let's just say that when I first met Miss Beth, she hid very little from me."

Beth began to blush.

"You care for 'im?"

Not knowing quite what to say, Beth decided to go with this new truth. "Yes, yes I do."

"And you for her?" Maria eyed Sam, one eyebrow arched high.

Sam looked into Beth's aqua eyes. "Yes." He kissed her.

"You must stop doing dat until we put Miss Beth into some clothes for a girl. It jist does not look right. How can I help?"

They had moved to Maria's domain—the kitchen. Like the rest of the house, it was a masterpiece of beauty and function. The eastern wall held a large sink with a hand pump, large cabinets, and what many would consider too many windows. The way they were set, looking to the east, the sun would rise in those windows and fill the kitchen with its light in the morning. On the western wall stood a massive, wood stove that looked like it could feed a regiment. It was surrounded by serving and prep tables. In the middle of the room stood a sturdy, pine table that looked to be old but well cared for.

Maria poured Sam and Beth cups of strong coffee and joined them at the table.

Sam started, "We need to get the truth out as soon as possible. The top is about to blow off this town, and I don't see how we can stop it unless the truth comes out first. Maria, you are the first person in Smith to know the truth. We need you to help Beth tell the people who are most important to her, the folks here at the Running J. I've seen what Beth has created here. It is special. The men and families seem very loyal to the brand and to Eli, but how will they see Beth?"

"There will be a few who will not work for a woman. Maybe even a few who feel lied to, Marshal."

"Call me Sam. What about Jake?"

"It will knock 'im out of the saddle, and I don't know if he can climb back up. He 'as an open 'eart and mind, though. Look at the way he took to dat Jenny." She leaned in. "'e knows what she was.

The whole town does, but 'e treats 'er like a lady. I jist don't know. His sense of right and wrong is great."

Sam looked at Beth. It was late, but she still looked so fresh and young. She was worried, yet hope was growing in her. You could see the weight of Eli lifting off of her. "How are you doing?" Sam asked her.

"I'm not really sure. Thing are moving pretty fast. I'm glad you know the truth, Maria." Putting her hand on Maria's, she said, "How do we start, Sam?"

"Well, in Texas every beautiful, young lady has a coming out party, and Laura Dunhill's dance is going to be just the place."

"No, Sam. The whole town will be there. I can't."

"Beth, that is the point. The whole town will be there. The killer will be there. When he sees the truth about you, he will be thrown off balance. If you have been hiding the fact that Eli has been dead all these years, maybe you have more secrets you haven't revealed. He might tip his hand."

"But, Sam, I just—"

"Besides it is about time Miss Laurie Dunhill had some competition for 'Belle of the Ball.'"

Maria laughed. "I would not miss dat for the world."

Beth pushed her chair back. "I'm glad to see you two are enjoying yourselves, but I'm not going to do it." She stood and walked to the window over the sink and looked out over the sleeping ranch. "Ask me to ride into the Double L, guns blazing, looking at certain death. That I can do. But dress up as a woman and go to a dance? I'm not that brave."

Sam nodded to Maria.

Maria stood and stepped to her. "I will be with you. Sam will be with you."

"Oh, yes, you will be with me as I make a fool of myself." She turned to Sam. "You do realize that when I show up in a dress, most folks are just going to think Eli has started to dress as a woman. I don't know how the good, old boys in Texas take to a man dressing as a woman, but up here in northern Utah, we shoot them."

Sam smiled. "You could show up buck naked. That sure convinced me."

Maria did not know what to make of that comment. Beth, seeing her concern, tried to soften it. "Don't worry, Maria. I still had my skirt on." The lines of concern only deepened on Maria's face. "Well, I'm not going to show up with my shirt off. Have you got a better idea?"

Seeing her struggle, he said, "You asked for help."

Her shoulders started to relax. "I know, I know. I guess this truth…I don't even want to say it. It makes me frightened. I know you think this is the right thing to do, Sam, but I'm not so sure, and if you are wrong, I could lose everything." She paused and sat back at the table. "Lay the rest of it out so I can think on it."

Sam and Maria came back to the table. Sam said, "You will need your real friends and family behind you before we get to the 7C. So we will need to tell the ranch on Friday morning. It will give us a better chance of surprising the killer at the dance."

"All right, Marshal McKnight. If I do consent to making a fool of myself, where does Cinderella find a dress?"

"Well, from a fairy godmother, of course. We go out to meet her tomorrow, but we need to make an early start. It will take the whole day to get ready for the ball."

Beth stood. "I'm going to bed. I'll think on it, and if Cinderella is going to the ball, I'll be ready at four." With that, she turned and left the kitchen.

Sam and Beth were up early. They met each other in the great room. Sam liked what he saw. She was dressed as Eli in a red work shirt tucked into loose jeans held together by a fine, hand-tooled, leather belt. Over this, she wore a leather vest and an old, blue bandana. Her Colt and gun belt were slung over her shoulder. She was wearing her Stetson. Dressed like this, the beautiful tomboy was well hidden. Sam could understand how folks missed her, but if you knew the truth, she shone through.

For his part, Sam was dressed as a US marshal. He had on his best blue-bib Cavalry shirt tucked into brown jeans. His belt was made over the border, and the silver buckle was probably too flashy. When Sam looked in the mirror before coming down, he said to his Father, "Too much, I know. Vanity again, but I like it. I hope she does." Sam had already spent time in the Word and with his Maker, but he added, "Guide me as I try to help her."

Their meeting was a bit awkward. Sam was just glad to see her. It was a first step, and they had said they cared for each other the night before. There was a lot hanging over this early-morning meeting.

"Good morning, Sam." She stood on the steps just above him so they were eye to eye. "This doesn't mean I have made up my mind, but I'm willing to go down this path for a piece."

She passed him with the ramrod stiffness Sam had seen in his soldiers right before they charged into rifle fire. "Not so fast, Beth." He grabbed her by the elbow and pulled her in. "Where are you in there?" He pulled off her hat and smiled. "There you are." He kissed her softly. Slowly, her hands came up around his strong shoulders as the passion from the night before rekindled. He pulled back. "You should be kissed like that every morning. Stop worrying. This is going to be a good day. We will be riding together. I know Buck wants to spend more time with Belle, and the idea of riding in this glorious country with you takes my breath away." He kissed her forehead. "Now try that 'good morning' again."

"Good morning." She smiled, kissed him, and then gave him a good shove. Sam looked confused by her unorthodox combination. She pointed her finger at him and said, "You need to watch yourself, Marshal McKnight. I have run this ranch for the past four years, and I am not used to being bossed around. Oh, and it's easy for you to say, 'Don't worry.' You aren't going to have to try on dresses today."

With a sober look, Sam said, "Yes, sir—I mean, ma'am." And into the kitchen they went.

Maria was at the wood stove working magic with her cast-iron pans and Dutch ovens. Bacon and eggs were sizzling, and the smell of buttermilk biscuits filled the air. Two other young women were assisting her. One, Sam assumed, must have been one of the cowboy's wives. She was young. Sam guessed sixteen or seventeen, light-brown hair, and about six months pregnant. She had a fresh face with the glow of new life on it. There was flour on her cheek as she worked at more biscuits, which were needed for the all of the ranch hands who would soon be up.

Helping her, while spinning through the room like a flamenco dancer, was the spitting image of Maria at about fourteen. This little gal was talking a mile a minute in both Spanish and English when Sam and Beth pushed through the swinging door into the kitchen.

Beth introduced the two young women. "Marshal McKnight, this is Katherine Young. She is a hard worker and bright as a new penny. Kate is married to my blacksmith, Dobb."

"Pleased to meet you, Marshal."

"The pleasure is all mine. Pardon my saying so, but you are lovely. I don't think there is anything quite as beautiful as a woman in the family way." At these words, the sweet, innocent, young wife blushed. She had never heard such words from any man other than her husband.

Kate shyly said, "Thank you," and returned to her biscuits.

"And this Spanish princess is Angelica, Maria's youngest daughter."

Angelica gave Sam a little curtsy. "Pleased to meet you, Marshal McKnight."

"I am pleased to meet you, Princess Angelica." He took her hand and kissed the back of it.

Both girls looked at each other and giggled. The two of them behaved as if they were meeting Bill Cody.

"Kate, Angelica," Maria said sternly, and both girls rushed back to work. Sam and Beth sat at the table as plates appeared full of bacon, eggs, and a side of hot salsa. Next came a plate of hot biscuits with butter and preserves. Maria brought hot coffee strong enough to stand a spoon up in. She hovered around the two riders as they ate, making sure they had everything they needed. Beth finally said, "Maria, stop. I haven't changed overnight. I'm the same as I've always been."

"I know. You are right. I am sorry, but in my mind, you 'ave changed. I guess I am jist trying to make up for the years we 'ave missed." Both young women looked up, puzzled at this comment.

"Eli, Maria, this might not be the best place for this conversation," Sam said. "Could we continue it when we come back this evening?" Both women looked at the curious girls and nodded yes.

Grabbing his empty plate and coffee cup, he headed for the sink. "Eli, if you are done with that man-sized meal, let's get into the saddle. We have two stops to make before we reach Smith this afternoon."

Maria grabbed Beth's plate and cup before she could take them to the sink. Beth smiled and asked, "Where are we going?"

Kate and Angelica were hanging on Sam's every word. "First we are heading out to the Seven-C to talk with the colonel and, if we are lucky, the Amos boy's girl." He turned to the girls. "Then we are off to find your fairy godmother." Sam winked at the girls and headed for the door. The girls looked at each other in utter confusion. They looked to Eli for some sort of explanation. Beth just shrugged, grabbed her gun belt and Stetson, and headed for the door. As she reached Kate, she stopped and patted her baby-filled belly.

"He's right, you know," Eli said. "You are lovely." And then Eli was out the door. Kate stood there in the glow of the kind words that had been spoken to her this morning.

◆

They reached their horses under a dark sky so full of stars that they could find their way without a lantern. Buck and Belle were waiting at the rail in front of the house. They were saddled and ready to go. When they saw their masters, they both stomped and threw their heads in greeting. The riders returned the greeting as they reached the horses, stroking their faces and necks. Sam gave Buck a carrot as Beth slipped Belle a slice of apple. They both moved back to their saddles, checking the cinches, saddlebags, and gear. Jake had prepared the horses, and he had done his job well. Sam pulled his Winchester from its scabbard just a breath before Beth did the same. Sam had to chuckle.

"I don't think I've ever had so much in common with a gal. It's a little scary."

Now Beth laughed as she levered open the rifle's magazine. "Well, I have spent more than half of my life as a man." She pushed her Winchester back into its scabbard.

Sam saw that Buck was nuzzling the black beauty next to him. Moving up to Buck's face, he grabbed the horse's bridle and said good-naturedly, "Look at me. We have got a lot of ground to cover today. I know you like her, but I need you to stay focused. Understand?" Buck just threw his head a few times and turned right back to Belle. "Fine, have it your way."

Beth laughed. "He's got it bad."

"I know just how he feels." Sam wanted to do some nuzzling of his own, but the ranch was just starting to wake up, and they could not risk being seen quite yet.

For her part, Belle was pretending Buck was not there. She was the perfect lady.

Both riders stepped into their saddles as the sky began to hint at morning. *Doing the thing I love, riding with Beth right beside me. How blessed I am.* He wanted to kiss her again, but it would have to wait. There would be time. They headed for the Running J's main gate.

✦

Riding at dawn, they saw the land when it was most alive and lovely. When the sun started to push through the trees, they heard the sound of a bull elk bugling and another calling back. The farther they rode, the closer they got to the calls. Soon they could hear the sound of antlers crashing together. They rode to the edge of a great meadow and saw the herd. There were about twenty cows. Steam was rising off of them as the sun hit the dew on their coats.

The two bulls were fighting only fifty yards in front of them. One was at the end of his prime. He had a heavy set of six-point antlers, and he still had a powerful build. The cows were his. The challenger had a large set of five-point antlers. He was well muscled, was equal in size to the old king, and had youth on his side.

The two bulls had been fighting for some time when Sam and Beth rode up. The old king looked winded, his mouth open, and he was breathing hard. There was a gash behind his left shoulder. Their horns were locked together, and they appeared to be at a stalemate. Sam pulled his Winchester just in case an angry loser came their way.

"Looks like the old king is about to lose his harem," Beth said.

"I wouldn't be too sure of that. He didn't get to be that size without learnin' a few tricks." At that moment, the old king dug deep and started to push hard. The younger bull staggered back, his horns still locked with his opponent's. Steam rushed from the young bull's nostrils as he prepared to return the pressure. Just as he began his charge, the old bull let up and stepped back to the side, twisting his locked antlers hard as he moved. The young bull's momentum caused him to fall forward as his head was wrenched back by the old bull's trick. The young bull's shoulder hit the ground, and his right antler snapped. Now the old king had an open target. He gored at the young bull's unprotected side. The young bull leaped up and moved off a good thirty yards. They both just stood for a moment, heads up and proud. It was a kind of salute. The young bull dropped his head first and limped into the trees. The old king stepped to the cows, looked them over, and began grazing as if nothing had happened.

"You were right. How did you know?" Beth asked.

"I have seen many a young gunman come up against my granddaddy. They always think they have the upper hand because of their youth. Time after time, he shames them with one of the many tricks he has learned over the years. He is still wearing that ranger star."

Beth watched him as he turned Buck back to the road. "Wasn't that outlaw yesterday my age?" she teased.

"Miss Beth, don't go there." He smiled.

As the sun cleared the tops of the trees, they came upon large herds of cattle being guarded, more than watched, by 7C cowboys. Sam was struck by how neat and clean these cowhands were.

Pointing to a cowboy off to right, Sam said, "These boys are dandy dressers."

"The colonel won't have it any other way," she said.

The closer they got to the main house, the more guards they came across. All greeted them nice and friendly as soon as they saw it was Mr. Kennedy.

The 7C sat at the foot of the Bear River range. It was made up of big stands of ponderosa pine opening up into large, dry meadows perfect for grazing if there was enough water. Of course, Dunhill had enough because of Beth's generosity.

Now they approached the grand gate of what could only be describe as regimental headquarters for the 7C. They saw more men placed strategically throughout the compound. "If I didn't know better, I'd think the colonel was expecting a fight, not a dance."

"I haven't been up here in a year or more. These armed men weren't here then. He's worried," Beth said.

Everything was freshly painted white with red trim. Dunhill's mansion stood at the east end of the compound. It dominated the headquarters. It was two stories with six Greek columns holding up the roof. A large balcony stretched the length of the second floor and covered the expansive front porch. On the veranda eating breakfast were the colonel and his family. Mexican servants dressed in white were moving in and out of the house, serving them.

On the south side of the compound were two large bunkhouses. Sam guessed there must have been sixty cowboys just working the herd and another thirty guarding and working the headquarters. To the north were corrals and stables, and next to them stood a huge barn.

Men and women were busy in the barn, decorating it for the dance. In the barn, at least, folks seemed to be having a good time. There was laughter, men on ladders hanging lanterns, and women stringing colored paper from post to post.

Two horses were already tied to the rail as Sam and Beth reached it. The horses were still wet from a hard ride. Their riders, who were now standing behind the colonel, had no doubt announced Sam and Beth's approach. The colonel stood and came to the edge of the veranda as they neared the house. The two cowboys followed the colonel. They both carried double-barreled, sawed-off shotguns resting easy in the crooks of their arms. The younger of the two was a gun fighter. He was well kept, about five ten, a hundred sixty pounds with dark hair that had recently been cut. His rig was not new, but it did not show much wear. It had not seen the rough treatment leather gear gets while working as a ranch hand. The Remington that hung in his well-made holster was the new model 74. Sam had only seen a few. It must have cost twenty-five dollars. *He is no cowboy*, Sam thought. The second sentry was almost twice the young gunman's age. He had a patch over one eye. His rig was newer but worn. He was a cowboy, probably the foreman. Judging by his sidearm, he was being paid well. It was the new Smith & Wesson break-breach .45. Backed by these two the colonel looked formidable.

"Welcome to the Seven-C, gentlemen."

"Will you join us out here on the veranda for some breakfast?"

Beth put Eli back on like a comfortable hat. "No, thank you," Eli said, "but we won't turn down a cup of coffee, Colonel."

"Excellent. Gonzales, two more cups." A handsome, older Mexican nodded to the colonel and headed back into the house. Sam was struck by the nobility of the man's presence. Put him in a fine Spanish jacket, and he would pass for a Don. Sam and Beth stepped off their horses and tied them at the rail.

Sam whispered, "I miss your sister."

"Shut up," Beth said.

As they reached the colonel at the top of the stairs, he put his arm around Eli and led them both to the table. The colonel's two sentries followed in his shadow. "Son, it has been too long since you were here last. You know this is your second home. We"—he looked to Laurie who was seated to the right of his chair at the table—"have missed you. Quentin, get up and give Eli your seat." Quentin had been seated to the left of the colonel's chair. He cut his eyes to Eli, his resentment showing, and reluctantly got up. He moved to the end of the table.

Laurie stood and came to greet them. Her rich, brown hair was up, accented with a blue, velvet ribbon that matched her lush, velvet riding skirt. Her considerable assets were covered today with a white, satin blouse wrapped together at her waist with a red sash.

"Eli, how good it is to see you." She embraced him and gave him a kiss on the cheek. Eli gave her a little half-hug in return. Sam saw a small shift in the young gunman who was standing behind the colonel. The kiss made him angry, but he was trying to hide it.

"Tomorrow night, you must give me the first dance." Now Laurie turned her charms to Sam. "And, Marshal McKnight, I have been looking forward to seeing you this morning. I do love a man with a badge." As she had the day before, she caressed his badge. "You must have my second dance. You are coming to the dance?"

Sam met her overconfident flirtation with a look of pure, male power. Laurie Dunhill was used to men who turned into schoolboys in her presence. Sam met her direct gaze and smiled in a way that told Miss Dunhill there was nothing about her he had not seen before. He said, "Oh, I would not miss it. The night promises to be full of surprises." Laurie backed away, rattled and slightly flushed, and now Sam saw a slight shift in Beth, her ears turning a light shade of pink. She was uncomfortable with Laurie touching Sam. Eli and Sam sat as Gonzales appeared with two cups and poured coffee for them. The colonel turned to Laurie and asked, "Where is your mother, baby girl? She won't want to miss seeing Eli."

Laurie, not wanting to make eye contact with her father, said, "She is in bed with another one of her headaches. She told me to ask you to forgive her for not coming down again this morning, Daddy." She picked up her cup and took a quick sip of coffee.

"Of course," he said, trying to hide his frustration.

Sam decided it was time to get to the point. "Mr. Dunhill, I don't want to take too much of your time. I just have a few questions."

"As I told you yesterday, we don't need federal help up here in Bear River country. We can handle any problem that arises ourselves. Eli, of course I am glad to see you, but why, may I ask, are you with the marshal?"

With calm authority, Eli lied. "When I was in Salt Lake earlier this month, I paid a visit to the federal marshal's office. I am the one who asked the marshals for help."

"Well, I have always been impressed with your decisions, son, but I wish you would have asked me first." Sam could see Quentin tighten every time the colonel called Eli "son." "All right, since you were invited here by my good, young friend, I would be happy to answer your questions, but will you answer two for me first?" He motioned to Sam's Cavalry shirt. "Who did you serve with in the war and at what rank?"

Sam was reluctant to talk about the war, and he did not like the rank question. When men were dying on the battlefield, their rank meant nothing. But his granddaddy taught him to be polite, so he would go down this road for a little while. "I enlisted as a private in the Cavalry Corps of the Army of the Potomac. Most of the northeastern boys didn't know how to ride, so the Union was looking for horsemen. Being born in Texas, I had a horse under me almost before I could walk. The last two years of the war, I served under General Phil Sheridan's command. I was field promoted to Captain."

The mention of Phil Sheridan caused the colonel to lean forward with excitement and ask, "So were you there at the battle of Yellow Tavern when the little Irishman led the attack where Jeb Stewart was killed?"

Sam sighed and said, "I was with General Sheridan."

Turning to Eli, the colonel said, "What a great victory." Turning back to Sam, he continued, "It must have been glorious to have been part of it."

Sam sipped his coffee, considering whether to take the easy way out of this conversation and just tell the colonel what he wanted to hear or go with the truth. He decided to go with the truth. "The only glory taken from the field that day was by those brave, outnumbered Confederate boys who struggled to protect the general they had served and loved. General Stewart was a great and honorable man. None of us, including Phil Sheridan, took pleasure in Stewart's death." Sam could feel Beth's eyes on him, watching, listening, and learning about him.

Thrown off balance by Sam's answer, the colonel struggled to recover. "I am surprised that a Texan would serve the Union. What, may I ask, made you join?"

Sam did not like the implied accusation and, with quiet conviction, said, "I was taught at my granddaddy's knee that when we Americans say, 'all men are created equal' we mean *all* men: black, yellow, brown, and red."

Not liking the answer, the colonel said, "I see. That is all well and good, but we all know the war was not fought to free the darky. It was fought to put down a rebellion over states' rights."

Sam got very quiet. He was so sick of this tired argument. He put his coffee down and leaned toward the colonel. "Colonel, perhaps what you and your men fought, bled, and died for was the government's desire to exert its power over the South, but not Sheridan's boys. I would not ride with my men into battle for that cause. I would not shed the blood of those brave, Southern boys and old men so some politician could have his way. Only for God-given liberty would I pay that price."

The quiet power of his words silenced the table.

The colonel was waiting uncomfortably for Sam to return the courtesy and ask about his service. *Enough of this,* Sam thought. *I'll be damned if I'm going to ask him about his time in the war.* He had no desire to reminisce any further about all the American blood spilt by both sides on American soil. Sam moved right to his questions, "Colonel, who do you think is behind the fence cutting and rustling?

"Why, Carl Larson of course," answered the colonel, surprised the conversation about the war was apparently over.

"Funny; that is the same thing Larson said about you."

"The man is a liar, without honor," the colonel said as if he was stating a fact known far and wide.

"Weren't the two of you and William Kennedy once friends and comrades in arms?"

"You are surprisingly well informed, sir." The colonel leaned back in his chair. "Yes it's true, but my relationship with Carl Larson ended years ago, when Laurie, Eli, and his twin were still just crawling. William and Ellie Kennedy were my wife's and my dearest friends. Oh, Eli, your parents were such fine people, and your mother a true beauty. I still miss her." He emptied his coffee cup, and Gonzales refilled it.

"I can just remember her dancing with my father," Eli said.

"Yes, well, your father wasn't much for dancing, but your mother loved to dance. She would not miss an opportunity. In those days, she and my wife would put together some kind of event almost every month. I can remember dance after dance with her." He drifted off. Then he snapped back. "What does any of this have to do with the rustling?"

"Probably nothing," Sam said. The colonel's comments about Beth's mother interested Sam. He pushed a little further. "Terrible thing what happened to Eli's mother and sisters."

"Yes, terrible. I remember coming out to the Running J the day after. William was drunk, his Irish weakness. Eli, I will never forget the sight of you sitting in your mother's rocking chair, wrapped in her quilt, holding your sister's rag doll. I told William he should sell out and leave this memory behind. He literally threw me out of the house. Said he wouldn't leave his Ellie behind. We rarely spoke after that. He never got over her. The man loved her more than his own life, more than she could love him."

"Why do you say that?" demanded Eli.

"I don't mean to offend you, son. I know your mother loved your father, but your father worshiped her in an unhealthy way. He was extremely jealous of anyone's attentions toward her."

"Jealous of *your* attentions toward Mrs. Kennedy?" Again Sam locked eyes with the colonel. The colonel just stared back.

Laurie, not wanting to be ignored, broke the uncomfortable silence. "Daddy, I do not have time to sit here and talk about dances that happened twenty years ago. I have a dance to prepare for tomorrow night. So if you gentlemen will excuse me, I must ride into town." She stood, so Eli and Sam stood. She crossed behind Eli, placing one hand on his hip. "Eli, would you ride into Smith with me? It just isn't safe for a woman on the road with the Larsons out looking for trouble."

Eli subtly removed her hand. "As much as I enjoy your company, I will have to say no. The marshal and I have business north of here today."

"May I ask what could be so important?"

Beth could not say, "I'm looking for a fairy godmother," so she lied. "The marshal would like to see where the Amos boy was shot."

The colonel turned to his daughter. "Baby doll, take Johnson here. He is as good as the marshal with a gun—or so he says."

"Better," the young gunman amended as he straightened and adjusted his gun belt. From where the colonel sat, he could not see the look of pleasure on Laurie's face at his suggestion. *Who is going to protect Johnson?* Sam thought.

"Have you seen the marshal in action?" Eli asked.

"No," Johnson replied.

"I thought not." Eli smiled.

"Good-bye, gentlemen. I will see you both at the dance," Laurie said as she pulled on her riding gloves and headed for the corrals with Johnson in hot pursuit. Everyone on the veranda watched her go. Sam returned to his questions. "Colonel, you believe it was Larson who had Amos killed."

"It goes without saying," the colonel said firmly.

"Why would he want the boy dead?" Sam asked.

"The young man was riding for the Running J. Larson wants the water. Anyone on the J is a target," he said.

"Yesterday I spoke to the man who found Amos. He said the young man was killed by a big-bore rifle, like a Sharps." Sam watched for a reaction. The colonel made none, but Quentin picked up his cup and drank. Sam asked, "Do you have a Sharps on the place?"

"Of course. When we first came to this part of the territory the land was thick with buffalo. The Sharps was and is the best gun for downing a buffalo. Are you implying someone on the Seven-C shot the boy?"

Sam deflected the question. "Don't you want the water on the J?"

"No. I am perfectly happy with the current arrangement. Eli knows I would like to have the J. I have offered him a fair price in the past, and the offer still stands. I would also be open to a partnership. I am a man of honor. I would never take the water with guns. Eli is my best friend's son, and I am offended at your question." The colonel rose and said to Eli, "I am surprised you brought this man out here to insult me."

"You have always been a good friend to me, Colonel, but the marshal has got to get to the bottom of this," Eli said.

"Did you know Amos?" Sam asked.

"No."

Just then a young woman came out to the table and began to clear away the dishes. She was a dark beauty, the perfect mix of conquistador and Aztec blood. She was small, about five feet. Her long, dark hair fell over her proud shoulders. There was a clear bruise on her right cheek and bruises coming on her neck. Sam had seen this kind of bruising before. The girl had been choked.

Quentin, putting his coffee cup down, said, "Father, Amos was often here last spring hanging around this Mexican tramp." She flinched at Quentin's insult, but she just kept to her task.

This must be Desiree, and she was hit last night by someone who is left-handed. Sam watched Quentin pick up his coffee cup again with his left hand and asked, "Quentin, where were you the morning Amos was shot?"

"I was in the bed of that whore, Jessica. Or is it Jenny?" Quentin said, trying to shock with his words.

Both Rowdy Larson and Quentin in the same bed with Jenny. Must have been crowded, Sam thought. "Sounds like she had a busy night. What did you think of Amos, Quentin?"

"I thought he didn't know his place. He didn't understand the order of things." He smirked.

Sam waited for the colonel to slap Quentin down as usual, but he didn't. Either he was giving him enough rope or he approved of what his arrogant son was saying. Sam thought it was the latter, and so did Quentin. His father's apparent approval emboldened him. He sat up and leaned toward Sam.

"'The order of things?' I'm not sure I catch your meaning," Sam said.

"I thought a famous gunfighter like you would understand. Why, just yesterday I saw a schoolboy in Smith with a penny dreadful about Marshal McKnight in his grubby hands. Someone who is the subject of such great literature should have a deep understanding of the order of things. I guess I overestimated your depth, but I would be happy to enlighten you."

Sam's desire to enlighten Quentin was growing. The colonel now sat, hands folded, his eyes on Sam, with a small smile growing on his face.

Playing dumb, Sam said, "Being just a shallow, illiterate US marshal, I would appreciate your tutelage."

Quentin, encouraged by the colonel's silence, started to point his finger at Sam. "If you are a young, no-account, stupid saddle tramp from some nothing dirt farm south of Smith, you do not come to the Seven-C without an invitation." He looked directly at Desiree. "You certainly do not nose around property trying to get into its skirt without asking for permission, no matter how worthless or well used the property might be." He leaned back in his chair, looked directly at Desiree, and laughed.

Desiree's back stiffened, and tears began to well in her proud eyes.

She circled the table to Quentin, picked up his hot coffee, and threw it in his face before he could react. "Jeff was a good man, better than you will ever be. You are not worthy to shine his boots!"

Quentin screamed like a child, "You damned, little squaw! I guess the marshal isn't the only one who needs to learn a lesson." He moved to strike her. Sam was about to do some teaching of his own, but Beth beat him to it. Her ears were red, and she was in a rage. She stepped between Desiree and Quentin, smashing her knee into Quentin's crotch. Quentin doubled over, and Beth grabbed his shirt and straightened him back up. Quentin, still holding his badly bruised manhood, made no attempt to block Beth's next blow. Beth landed a left cross on Quentin's grimacing mouth. The blow sent him off the porch and into the dust at Buck's feet. Buck promptly stepped on his hat.

Quentin began to reach for his gun, but looked up in time to see the barrel of Sam's Colt pointed at him.

Eli pointed his finger at Quentin. "I'm so tired of your bullying. You tormented me as a small child because I was too small to do anything about it. Now you're doing the same thing and probably worse to this poor girl because she doesn't have the power to fight back. It's time you learned the *order of things* has changed. You don't own anybody on this place or in Smith. You are not worth any more than the folks around here. The truth is you are worth less than most. If you ever touch this girl again, I will kick your sorry butt around this town."

Quentin looked to his father for help, but the colonel looked disgusted. He did not move or speak, so neither did his foreman. Quentin growled, "This isn't over, Eli. You won't always have your new friend with you. I look forward to seeing you later."

"Quentin, shut up," said the colonel. Quentin got to his feet, picked up his crushed hat, and limped off toward the barn.

Eli turned to the girl. "Desiree, will you leave with us?"

Desiree nodded yes.

"Colonel, I'm sorry about this trouble," Eli said.

"So am I." The colonel turned to Desiree. "Girl, you are fired. I will send your pay and personal items to the Running J."

Sam just shook his head. "You are quite the gentleman. Your son makes fool of himself, and your response is to fire the girl he has been abusing."

Now with the same smirk that had been on Quentin's face, the colonel said, "A true gentleman knows the order of things. I think it is time for you to leave. I look forward to seeing you both at the dance," he said, smiling as if nothing had happened. He picked up Elma's weekly newspaper and began to read.

As they stood to go, Beth could see Gonzales standing on the other side of the glass French doors. He mouthed, "Thank you," to her. She nodded back to him, and they were on their way down the front stairs. Beth stepped up onto Belle first and offered Desiree a hand up. Sam helped her up behind Beth and said, "Not exactly Marquis of Queensbury rules."

Beth smiled and shook her head. "He outweighed me by forty pounds. Smaller men can't always afford to fight fair. Besides, that moron's idea of a fair fight is hitting a hundred-pound girl."

Sam swung up onto Buck. "I just need to remember to watch your knees the next time we get into a fight." He laughed, and turned Buck to the gate.

Desiree kept her chin up and showed no emotion as they rode out of the compound. All of the servants stopped what they were doing to watch her go. After they were twenty minutes past the main gate, she leaned into Beth's back and began to softy cry. Sam looked at Beth who was deep in thought.

She shook her head as she stretched out her bruised hand.

"How's the hand?" Sam asked.

"Oh, it hurts, but it is a good hurt. I have wanted to do that since I was four."

"Which, smash his mouth or kick him in the crotch?"

"Yes." They both laughed.

A soft, "Gracias," came from the girl. "I will be no trouble. Jist drop me in Smith, and I will be fine."

"Oh, senorita, you have no idea how fine you are going to be. You have just been rescued by the white knight, and you will soon be a guest at his castle," Sam said.

"What?"

Eli said gently, "Desiree, my cook Maria always needs more help than I can find. Please come and work for me."

"Si, I think I would like that."

Beth turned in the saddle to Sam. "I have always known how hateful Quentin was, but the colonel just sat there. How could I have missed it? Quentin comes by his hatred honestly. The more he said, the more the colonel seemed to approve."

"It was hidden behind the manners. As soon as a little pressure was applied, the mask slid off."

"Do you think Quentin killed Amos?" Beth's mind was spinning, trying to figure out the puzzle. At this question, Desiree began to cry again.

"Senorita, do you think Quentin killed Jeff Amos?" Sam asked.

Through the tears came a soft, "Si. Mr. Quentin hated Jeff because of me."

Sam softly pressed, "Why?"

She said nothing.

"Did Quentin know you and Jeff were courting?"

Beth looked questioningly at Sam, wondering where he got his information.

Forcing back the tears as she spoke, Desiree said, "No. Not until the night before Jeff was killed. Jeff came out to the ranch to see me. Only my papa and mama knew we were courting. My papa knew Mr. Quentin had other plans for me and dat he would be furious if he knew I was planning to marry. Jeff and I had to keep it secret until we could elope. That night I was to meet 'im by the barn after my work was done. It was late when I finally met 'im. He had seen something while he was waiting and was very excited. He told me he had to get back to the Running J to tell you, Mr. Eli, what he had seen and heard." The tears started to come, and she took a moment to regain her control. "Mr. Quentin caught Jeff kissing me good night. He was very mad. He cussed at Jeff and told 'im to get off the ranch. Jeff said he wasn't going nowhere until I was in my parent's cabin. Mr. Quentin let me go. I could hear them arguing, but I could not make out what they were saying. That was the last time I saw Jeff." She fell silent, leaning into Beth with her head turned away from Sam and crying softly.

Beth looked over her shoulder and back to Sam. "Where does this piece fit?"

Sam shook his head, "I don't know, but it is a big piece. I don't believe a word Quentin said. He said he was with Jenny that night."

"That is what she did for a living," Beth said.

"Yes, but Rowdy Larson told me *he* was with Jenny that night."

Beth, a bit shocked at the reality of Jenny's work, said, "She was a very popular girl."

Sam smiled. "I am sure of it, but I can't see those two following each other into Jenny's bed if they could help it."

A small tremor of disgust rattled through Beth. "Well, I know someone who will know the truth."

Sam began thinking out loud. "If Quentin was with Jenny, he could have had someone shoot Amos for him. Quentin obviously hated the young man, but whoever is behind this is really after the Running J, not just killing out of anger. The question here is: what did Jeff see that he was all fired up to tell you about, and is that what got him killed?"

They turned south back toward Smith, both quiet now and enjoying the company. Desiree had stopped crying and rode easy behind Beth. The morning was warming, and Beth's thoughts started to swirl around a dress and a dance.

✦

It was mid-morning, and the heat was beginning to build when they rode up to Jon Rockport's house. The farm, which sat just northeast of town, was alive with work and play. Everyone over the age of eight was hard at some chore. Two of the five sister wives were up on the porch mending clothes with the help of three girls who looked to range in age from ten to twelve. Elma was also on the porch teaching a lesson in sums to a group of four children who were about five or six years old. In the yard in front of the house, smaller children played while a teenaged sister read a book and watched them.

Beth had always liked coming out to the Rockport farm. Elma would invite all the leaders of Smith out her place a couple of times each year. This huge Mormon family drew her in with its love of children and home.

Elma greeted the riders, "Mornin', Samuel. Mornin', Elijah. What a pleasant surprise to have to such handsome men ride up. I'm guessin' you haven't come all the way out here for another cup of my good Dutch coffee."

"Good morning, Mrs. Rockport," Eli replied.

And then all three women responded, "Good morning," then chuckled to themselves about the joke they liked to play on folks who were not accustomed to greeting three wives married to the same man.

Sam joined them. Even though he lived and worked in the Utah Territory, he was still a Texan. He never got used to working in this fairytale land of harems. "Elma, I have thought of little else but your girlish company for the past hour."

"Don't let Jon hear you talk like that, you rogue," she said, pleased with the tease.

"The man has five wives. Surely he can spare one." The younger two wives both giggled at this flirting. "But if he can't, I will settle for a cool glass of water." Sam stepped off Buck, then came around and helped Desiree down from behind Beth.

"Elma, this young lady is Senorita Desiree Gonzales. Eli here just hired her away from the Seven-C. Could she wait out here with your sister wives while we talk in private?"

"How did you manage to take the senorita away from Quentin, Elijah?"

Beth held up her bruised left hand.

"Oh, I wish I could have been there. I am pleased to meet ya, senorita. Sister Lila, please get the senorita a cup of water. Samuel, Elijah, come into the kitchen. We can talk there." Suddenly, the twin ten-year-old boys appeared. They took hold of Belle and Buck. It was obvious the two boys could hardly wait to cool down the horses.

Together they said, "We'll take good care of them, Marshal. Don't worry."

"I'm not worried, boys. Just don't spoil Buck too much."

Beth watched them go, talking to each other in the way only twins could understand, and she longed for her brother.

Desiree was settled on the porch as Sam and Eli followed Elma into the house. Susannah was sitting in the front room, nursing her baby. Beth had never met Susannah and was a bit shocked by her lack of modesty. Sam just smiled and shook his head, and Beth blushed. Susannah, for her part, was happy to have two such important men seeing her ample gifts.

"Oh, Marshal, how good it is to see you," she cooed.

"Mrs. Rockport, it is a pleasure to see you."

"Oh, good golly, girl, cover up or it is out to the barn with the rest of the cows for ya." Susannah ducked her head and pulled a blanket up over herself. "That girl will be the death of me," Elma said as she pushed through the door into the kitchen.

They sat at the table as Elma brought three glasses and a pitcher of cool water that had been sitting under a damp cloth.

"Elma, we have a story for you, the likes of which I'll bet even you have never heard before."

Elma pulled the reporter's pad and pencil out of the front of her apron. "I'm not a gamblin' woman, but that is a bet I'll take, Samuel McKnight. Will I be able to print this one?"

"Yes. Do you have room for five columns in tomorrow's paper?"

Surprised, she said, "Five columns? Well, yes, but I will have to spend all night settin' type. It had better be some story."

"Madame reporter, you have no idea. I can guarantee you will sell every paper, but we can't give you the go ahead to print until Friday morning," Sam said.

Elma shook her head at this deadline then smiled and said, "Fire away. I'm ready." The reporter in her was so excited she could hardly contain herself. She sat down next to Beth, put her pad on the table, and leaned in, ready to scribble the story down.

"Eli, may I introduce your fairy godmother." Elma looked at Sam, wondering if she had accidently put something medicinal in his water. Sam turned to Elma and looked into her eyes. "Elma Rockport, may I introduce Miss Elizabeth Kennedy."

"Who?"

Slowly he repeated, "Miss. Elizabeth. Kennedy."

"But please, call me Beth," Beth added.

"Beth? Elizabeth? What are you talking about? What are you up to, Samuel? You're pulling my leg." But Sam could see the wheels in her head were turning.

Sam leaned toward her, locking eyes, and said, "As God is my witness, I am telling you the truth."

"I know you are His man, so if you say it is true, it is true, but..." Elma leaned forward in her chair, taking a more observant look at Beth. Elma's close scrutiny started to make Beth uncomfortable.

Beth began to protest, "I'm not sure this is a good idea—"

Sam gently interrupted her. "Let the reporter gather her facts. You can trust her, Beth."

Beth steeled herself and let Elma continue for now. Elma pulled her chair up close to Beth's. She reached toward her and cupped Beth's face in her hands, feeling Beth's tan, freckled cheeks and studying her eyes, nose, throat, and mouth. Now her hands moved to Beth's shoulders. "Whoever you are, would you please take off your vest?" Beth looked at Sam and got no help, so she stood and did as she was asked. Elma stood in front of Beth and felt her shoulders and arms. The look on Elma's face told Sam she did find what she was looking for. Beth's body was hard and strong, but not the well defined, chiseled muscles of a young, working cowboy.

Elma's hands moved to Beth's sides. Beth, being ticklish, began to giggle. The tone was a little higher than she usually would allow, but it was her true tone nonetheless. As Elma's hands slid down to Beth's slim waist, Elma began to smile. The clever way Beth dressed concealed her twenty-four-inch waist.

The truth began to twinkle in Elma's eyes as her hands started moving upward. This time the tickling was just too much, and Beth laughed out loud. Then her eyes widened as she realized what Elma aimed to do. Of course, for a young, immodest man who took his shirt off on a hot day, this probably would not be embarrassing, but for Beth, who had never had her shirt off in front of anyone, the prospect was mortifying.

In almost a panic, Beth said, "Now, wait just a minute. I think this has gone just about far enough."

Elma saw her fear. "It's all right. Don't be afraid. I'm the midwife in this town, darlin', and I tend to the medical needs of more than dozen men and boys on the place. There is no part of any man or woman that I have not seen or touched."

The use of the word *darlin'* calmed Beth. This sweet sister wife would not harm her or embarrass her without cause. Beth nodded yes to Elma as her ears and then her face turned red.

Elma's hands moved up the sides of Beth's shirt and pulled it tight across her chest. Definitely not muscle, but the softness of a young, childless woman.

Elma's smile widened with new recognition. "Hello, goddaughter." She stood and pulled Beth into her strong embrace. All this hugging was new to Beth. Men did not hug, did not touch. It was new, but she liked it, she needed it, and she gave herself to it.

Elma released Beth and reached for her pad as she brushed away a tear. "My brave daughter, how did this thing happen?"

◆◆◆◆ ——— ◆ ——— ◆◆◆◆

Beth retold the story to Elma much as she had done the night before to Maria, but this time it took longer because the reporter kept interrupting the story with her questions. Finally she put down her pencil and said, "I have the story now. How can I help?"

Sam poured a new class of water. "We want to draw whoever is behind this trouble out into the open. Force his hand. I figure the way to do that is to let the truth about Beth come out in your paper just before the dance."

"Yes. Yes, I see," Elma said, smiling as the plan began to become clear. "And ya came to me because Cinderella here needs someone to tell her story *and* find her a dress."

Sam picked up her pad and gave it to her. "Elma, you are the best storyteller I know."

Beth looked at Elma Rockport and saw a strong, bright woman. With her help, maybe this truth of Sam's could work. "Will you help me?" Beth asked, starting to get used to those strange words.

"With all my heart, daughter. It will bless me as much as I hope it will bless you. I spend my time writing other people's stories, but now I will be part of yours. Let's get started. Stand up."

Again she began to poke and prod Beth. She put her hands around Beth's waist and clucked her tongue. "You, my girl, are a clever one. The way you have hidden this girl's body of yours under all these man's clothes, it's a wonder. Turn around, Elizabeth." She ran her fingers though Beth's hair, eyeing the whole of her up and down. "Well, there is nothin' we can do about your hair, but your blue eyes and sweet face will more than make up for it, daughter. You are such a pretty girl." Beth's ears began to turn pink again. Those words had not been said to her by a woman since she was five. She had no idea how her woman's heart had longed to hear them again.

Elma continued, "I saw just the dress in town at Edward's store. I think he had it brought up from Salt Lake, hopin' someone would be willin' to spend a little more for the dance, but I think God's savin' it just for you."

"How do we get her into town to try on the dress?" Sam asked.

Rubbing her hands together, Elma said, "I have the perfect plan."

Elma walked to the back door and called out to the henhouses. "Sarah!" There was some squawking; then a lovely young woman stepped out holding a basket of eggs and brushing away a few feathers. Sam guessed she was about fifteen or sixteen. He had met her once about three years ago. She had been all arms and legs back then. The three years had grown her into a beauty. She was the image of her mother.

"Yes, Mama?"

"Come here, sis." The girl crossed the barnyard with the confidence and grace that you see in eldest children. "Samuel, I believe ya have met my oldest girl, Sarah."

"Hello, Marshal McKnight, Mr. Kennedy." She had a sweet, fresh smile and looked both of them in the eye as she spoke.

"Get cleaned up, sis. We are going into town."

"Yes, Mama." She moved into the house.

As the kitchen door swung closed, Elma said, "Sarah is just about your size. We can use her as a decoy while we try the dress on Elizabeth. We will have to tell her what is happening, but she is a good girl. I would trust her to run my house long before I would leave it to that Susannah. Sarah will keep your secret."

For Beth, the words "try the dress on" just kept turning over in her head. They tied her stomach in knots.

+++——◆——+++

On the ride into Smith, Sam and Beth rode behind the Rockport women as Elma filled Sarah in. Sam enjoyed watching the mother and daughter relate to one another. They had the same gestures and the same smile and frown. Sarah's voice was younger, but there was just a hint of Elma's strong Dutch accent. Sam looked at the long braid hanging down Sarah's back and couldn't help but think of all the long rides with Charlie in his youth. The memory was a sweet ache. How could he ever move on? He looked at Beth. *Oh, Father, what do you want me to do? This girl is strong, is smart, and has such a heart for people. She inspires me. She is also wounded and hurt so deeply I don't know if she can heal. She needs me, and my heart is beginning to need her, but I still love my Charlie—always will. How can this work?*

Sam could sense a peace coming over him. He could hear the words his granddaddy had given to him a year after he had lost Charlie. The first terrible pain of grief had begun to ease. Granddaddy had done nothing but love Sam through that dark year, but then as the light of dawn had started to appear, he'd said, "Boy, the hardest thing to do is trust, but if ya can, He'll get ya through it. Don't push, just wait."

They left Desiree in good hands at the farm and would pick her up on the way back to the Running J. Sarah turned back to take a good look at Beth. She nodded her head and smiled. "Good morning, Miss Kennedy."

"I'd like it if you would call me Beth, Sarah."

The young woman was outraged by what had happened to Beth, as the young and idealistic often are. In her righteous anger, she was ready to do anything or fight anyone. Elma assured her eldest that the best way she could help was to help Beth buy a dress. This did not seem heroic enough to Sarah, but it did sound like fun.

It was hot and dusty as they rode into Smith at noon, but the heat had not managed to put a damper on the buzz of excitement that filled the air. Folks were out and about, hurrying from here to there. The riders could piece together conversations of passersby as they rode. All of the talk was about the dance.

"What do you think Miss Laurie will wear?" one plump woman said to a gal so thin she could have been a general store advertisement for a broom.

"Somethin' from Paris, France, I'd guess," the broomstick replied.

Sam turned to the women he was riding with and said, "Ladies, I need to check for messages at the hotel. I don't think you will need me for your button and bow work. After you are done, meet me at the hotel, and I'll buy you some lunch."

"You are right. We don't need your help, Samuel McKnight. This is women's work and if we have any trouble, we have strong Eli here to protect us from the shiftless gun hands who have been showin' up lately in Smith." Elma said this loudly as if she were in a church play. Sam shook his head, winked at Beth, and turned Buck toward the hotel. The Rockport ladies, escorted by Eli, crossed the street to Ed's general store.

✦✦✦✦ ────── ✦ ────── ✦✦✦✦

Sam stepped through the double doors of Smith's only hotel and was greeted by the aroma of pork chops fried to golden perfection.

The dining room was hopping. George, the proprietor, was serving Maggie's famous chops with a side of her canned applesauce. The long ride had worn through Maria's large breakfast, and Sam was ready to sample some of Maggie's handiwork. "George?" he called out.

"Yes, Mar—Sam?"

"Could you set back four plates of your wife's delicious chops for me?"

George knew Maggie's pork chops where good, but four plates? He asked, "Of course, but how hungry are you?"

"Elma and Sarah Rockport are going to be joining Eli Kennedy and me."

"Of course," he said as he placed three plates in front of some hungry town folks.

Sam could feel someone's eyes boring into him. *Damn.* He knew better than to drop his guard.

✦

Elma led the way into Ed's store. Beth trailed behind Sarah, not knowing just what she was supposed to do. She was used to taking the lead, and she did not like all this being told what to do, but she decided the best course of action for now was to keep her mouth shut and follow Elma's lead.

Ed was finishing the pork chops he had just had delivered from the hotel. He wiped his face with a large napkin and said, "Good afternoon, ladies, Eli. How can I help you?"

"Edward," Elma said, motioning to Sarah, "we are lookin' for the perfect dress."

Just then Vickie Larson came laughing loudly into the store, her redheaded personality overwhelming the room. She was followed by a slick-looking gambler Eli did not recognize. The man was tall—over six feet—clean-shaven, and well dressed. His freshly barbered, light-brown hair and gray, tailored suit gave him the look of southern gentry.

Vickie spotted Eli and went right to him. "Oh, Eli, isn't this nice? I would like ya to meet my friend. This is Victor Holland of New Orleans. Victor"—she motioned to Eli—"meet Eli Kennedy, the one I have told you so much about."

"Pleased to meet you, sir," the gambler said in a deep, rich voice.

Vickie's attention moved to Sarah. She looked Sarah up and down, decided the young woman was a threat, and turned back to Eli. "What are ya shopping for, Eli?" she asked, pointedly ignoring the Rockport ladies.

Elma, always the observant reporter, saw Miss Larson's worry over a possible new rival for Eli's affections and could not help herself. "Elijah here has asked if he could take my oldest to the dance. Of course she is a mite young, but I was married at fourteen." She decided to lay it on extra thick. "Eli is very persuasive. He has generously offered to buy her a new dress for the occasion."

Ed slapped the counter and said, "Well, I'll be damned. That is the best news I've heard in a month."

◆

Sam's feelings for Beth had caused him to lose focus. He could hear Granddaddy saying, "That'll get ya dead, boy. Most of the good guns I've known died with lead in their backs. Ya'll got to be aware of what evil is around ya at all times." Sam looked toward the sensation.

He saw the source right off. Quentin Dunhill was staring right at him. He looked to be feeling better than when Sam had last seen him. He was wearing a brown suit with a brocade vest, and he had a new hat. The swelling in his lip had gone down a bit. Sam smiled at the memory of Beth's two blows.

The man sat with two gun hands from the 7C. One was a short, wiry, little rooster. He had a pinched, angry look that made Sam wonder if his boots were too tight. It was the gunman to Quentin's right that got Sam's attention. He was over six feet three, with some of the broadest shoulders Sam had ever seen. He was well muscled and hard; Sam guessed he was two hundred thirty pounds if he was an ounce. *Those arms have "steel mill" written all over them.* He had a proud, red mustache waxed to hardened perfection resting upon what appeared to be a permanent smile. Despite himself, Sam liked the man right off.

Maggie came from the kitchen with a pitcher of tea. Sam could see there was something wrong. She steadied herself then moved to Quentin's table.

"Would you gentlemen like any more tea?"

"Yes, darlin' girl," the big mick said. "I need one more drink to wash down that heavenly berry cobbler."

"No, we're done," Quentin interrupted, never breaking his gaze with Sam. "Let's go, boys."

The big mick shrugged, winked at Maggie, and gave her a swat on the rump for good measure. He broke out into a broad, happy laugh. Now Quentin broke his gaze with Sam and looked at Maggie. "Yes, Maggie makes some fine pie. I used to come to town and have a piece of her on a regular basis, didn't I, Maggie?" Quentin laughed and Pinched-Face joined him, but Big Mick was silent at this comment.

Maggie slapped Quentin's sneering face hard, knocking off the new hat. *Hit twice in five hours. I like these Smith women,* Sam thought.

George had been watching all this from the corner of the dining room. He said, "I knew it," and started to Maggie's aid just as Quentin slapped her back hard, knocking her to the ground. He had wanted to hit a girl since he missed his chance with Desiree. Sam was ready. He eased the thong off his Colt. He would not let his friends get hurt, but he wanted George to take the lead. It was his wife's honor.

George reached Quentin a moment after Maggie hit the floor. He hit Quentin with a right cross that bounced him off the wall.

Quentin wiped his bloody mouth and smiled at Sam as if to say, "What's keeping you, Marshal?" Sam watched and waited.

Pinched-Face took a swing at George, who ducked and stepped in with a punch to the man's gut. Pinched-Face staggered back and clawed at his Colt.

Then the most surprising thing happened. Big Mick backhanded Pinched-Face, knocking him to the ground. His Colt came loose and skittered across the floor, coming to rest at Sam's feet.

———◆———

Vickie stepped between Eli and the ladies. "Well, Eli, I must admit, I'm jealous. I was the one who taught you to dance, remember? As far as I know you've never asked anyone to a dance before." She leaned close to him. "We've shared so much over the years. I'm a little hurt you didn't ask me first." She glanced at Sarah, taking inventory of her opponent, and smiled. Sarah stared right back, her Rockport jaw set and ready for battle.

Vickie sashayed back to Victor and took his arm. He had been observing each player, trying to learn their "tells" or weaknesses.

"Oh, I'll bet I know what's goin' on here," Vickie purred. "This is one of your famous 'good deeds.' You're takin' this poor, little wall-flower to the dance out of pity."

"Wallflower!" Sarah erupted.

Now Beth stepped into the fray. "Pity? No. I find her quite lovely and fresh. I've asked Jon if I can come a-courting."

Vickie's mouth fell open, but she couldn't manage to say a word.

———◆———

With one of the friendliest smiles Sam had ever seen, Big Mick grabbed Pinched-Face by the front of the shirt and lifted him back onto his feet. As the large man began to dust the dazed cowboy off, he said, "Now, there'll be none of that gunplay. It's too early on this blessed day. This is goin' to be a fair fight. No unpleasantness." He looked to the marshal. "I must admit I'm looking forward to it. I've heard so much about you, Marshal." He then threw Pinched-Face at George, and they both crashed into a side table.

Sam took off his hat and gun belt and handed it to Mr. Black, who had just walked in for some of Maggie's chops. "Shoot anyone who draws a gun. It'll be good for business."

The undertaker broke into a broad, yellow-toothed grin and said, "Marvelous."

Sam pulled on his leather gloves and headed for Quentin, but Big Mick stepped in front of him. "You'll have to go through me, Marshal darlin'." Big Mick had six inches and sixty pounds on Sam.

This is going to hurt, Sam thought. Big Mick threw a hard left jab that Sam could not get out of the way of, and down Sam went, right into a table. The folks in the dining room headed for the lobby so they could watch in safety, and some scurried out onto the street to watch through the front window. No one wanted to miss a good fight.

✦

"Victoria, you'll want to close your mouth before something flies in," Elma said.

Vickie clapped her mouth shut and cut her eyes to Elma, who was barely containing her laughter. Finally Vickie managed to say to Eli, "I think you're lyin'. Next thing you'll be telling me is that you've decided to become a Mormon."

Eli put his arm around Sarah's waist and said, "I can see the advantages I must admit, but I'm no Jon Rockport. One wife is all I can handle." Both Elma and Sarah chuckled, knowing the truth about the young woman in Eli's clothes.

"Miss Vickie," Ed said as he walked over and put his hand on Eli's shoulder, "K here is a paying costumer with big plans and I need to help him and his young lady. So if you aren't buyin', skedaddle."

Vickie could not control her redheaded fury any longer, so she let fly.

Sam was back on his boots in an instant. He ducked the Irishman's right and pounded his own right into Big Mick's gut, followed by a left into his kidney. The blows felt like hitting an oak barrel, and sounded like it, too.

Grabbing his back, Big Mick said, "Marshal darlin', you hit like a mule."

Adjusting his jaw, Sam replied, "That sledgehammer you call a right isn't bad, either."

The sound of cracking wood made them both look to the back of the dining room where George and Quentin were fighting. The two men were hard at it. Sam admired the way George was attacking, but Quentin was giving back as good as he got. They both had their hands full.

Turning back to Big Mick, Sam moved in. The Irishman smiled and welcomed the attack. Sam jabbed with his left, and Big Mick blocked it, leaving an opening for Sam's right, which landed squarely on Big Mick's granite chin. He staggered back, and Sam followed, but the big man caught himself and landed a left to the side of Sam's face. Sam felt his teeth slap together and tasted blood. He fell to his right into an empty chair.

Shaking his head to clear it, Sam could see Big Mick spitting out a tooth. With a smile of pure, Irish pleasure he said, "Marshal darlin', it has been a joy bein' hit by a fighter like yourself, but me boss's worthless son is in a wee bit of trouble, so I'll be needing to knock you out now."

This is not good news, Sam thought.

Vickie screamed at Eli with no pretense of hiding the inner wild animal she was. "I hate you, Eli Kennedy! I hate you! You think you are too good fer me? Well, you ain't! Our daddies were friends.

We played together as children. I loved you then, and I was willin' to put up with Laurie Dunhill and you putitn' on your high and mighty ways, but no more. We are through! To hell with you and your fresh, little virgin!" She turned on her heel and charged out the door, Victor following. He stopped before leaving the store, turned back, and said, "There is a raging fire in this one."

"Be careful, Mr. Holland, or you might get burned," Ed said.

Through the window, Beth watched Vickie stomp out to Holland's buggy. Beth did love her childhood friend but did not love what Vickie had become. Of course, if Vickie knew the truth about Beth, she wouldn't want anything to do with her. Beth could never love or hold Vickie the way Vickie wanted.

"Now, Miss Sarah," Ed said, "let me show you a dress that will turn every head in the valley."

<hr />

As Sam struggled to his feet, trying to avoid the horseshoes Big Mick called fists, he heard a bell ring. He could not place the sound, but it was a bell. Sam looked at Big Mick and saw his eyes roll back; then his knees buckled, and like a giant ponderosa, down he went, taking a table with him. Standing behind him on a chair was Maggie with a number-ten cast-iron frying pan in her hands. She was hopping mad and ready to hit him again if he didn't stay down.

George's righteous anger was also winning out. He caught Quentin with a left uppercut that knocked him right into the chair Maggie was standing on. She was thrown into Sam's arms.

Sam, nodding to the pan, said, "Maggie, I have always said no one can handle a frying pan like you."

Through her anger, a smile broke out on her bruised lips. "It's a gift."

Quentin had landed on the floor next to Sam. He was beaten, with none of his men to help him. Sam knew what would come now that his Irish bodyguard was out, and Big Mick's warning about "no unpleasantness" was out with him. Quentin glared at George, pushed himself up with his left hand, and pulled his pearl-handled Colt with his right.

Sam had to act, but he had no gun, and his arms were full of Maggie.

◆

Ed pulled out a beautiful cream-colored dress covered in light-blue flowers, with blue ribbon trim and a matching sash.

"Edward, you have outdone yourself. This is perfect! We will go into the back to try it on, and since Elijah is footing the bill, we want all new underthings too. Bring us corsets, petticoats, and pantaloons," Elma said.

"Yes, ma'am," Ed said with joy. He pulled Eli aside. "I'm so proud of you, boy."

She looked into her old friend's face, suddenly tired of lying to him and said, "I hope you still will be tomorrow, Ed."

Ed cocked his head and with a furrowed brow said, "Little K, is something wrong?"

"No. Just know that you are one of my best friends. I would never do anything to hurt you."

"Well, I know that, boy. What are you talking about? If you are going to become a Mormon, it won't bother me."

"Good to know, old friend." And Beth left it at that.

Ed brought Elma all of the "underthings," and Beth just stared at them, unsure of all their purposes.

"Elijah, we would like you to come in with us so you can see what you're paying for."

Ed looked at Eli with a surprised expression. "These Mormons gals do things a bit different, but I like it. Go on, boy."

Ed did not know that he was ushering Beth into a world she had dreamed of. A world she had never been part of but longed for and, if truth be told, was afraid of. A world of women, of wives, of families, and yes, of babies. It was also a world of lost freedom and submission. Entering this would have a cost Beth was not sure she could afford.

Once in the room, the two smiling Rockport women stepped over to Beth. "It's time for Elizabeth to try on a new dress," Elma whispered, then she took off Beth's hat, and the women began to gently undress her.

Beth pushed Elma's hands away and said, "Really, I can undress myself,"

Elma straightened herself up and put her hand on Beth's shoulder. She gave her daughter a knowing smile and looked back to Beth. It looked to Beth as if they were sharing some secret code only those initiated into the sisterhood of women could know. Beth wanted to know the code.

"Darlin' daughter," Elma started, "let us serve you, girl. You have been striving your whole life to serve others. Let us bless you with this small gift of care. I know it'll be hard for ya. In truth, we will be blessed by serving ya, so do us a favor and let us do our work." Beth dropped her hands to her sides, and against her better judgment, let them do their work as she gazed at the beautiful dress.

Beth had dressed as a woman before—at the cabin and once in Salt Lake. But even in Utah's one city, she was so afraid she would run into someone she knew, she decided not to risk it in public again. On her way back from the cabin earlier in the week, she had decided to give up on the hope of dresses and give herself wholly to Eli, but Sam McKnight was changing all of that. Now her mind was spinning in a blur of white cotton, ivory buttons, and lace.

Sarah and Elma would not let her do anything. She was four the last time someone else had dressed her. She remembered it clearly. Her mama was getting her ready to go to one of those dances the colonel was talking about. Beth had been so excited. As Sarah and Elma slipped her new camisole over her shoulders and began to button it up, she could see her mama's hands buttoning up her little dress on that spring afternoon. Small twinges of grief pricked her heart. How she missed her mama.

Shaking her head, Elma reached into a box and pulled out a corset. She held it up to Beth and said, "Oh, darlin', now you are goin' to find out how foolish we women are. We are so determined to have a man think we're lovely that we would wear this instrument of torture. It's not something you have to wear every day. Lord knows I don't, but when I want to look fine for my Jon or on Sundays, I suffer it. You already have a lovely figure, but you'll be amazed at how this can enhance even you."

Beth had never worn a corset because she had no idea how to put one on by herself. The ladies wrapped it around her from the back. There were hook and eye clasps up the front. Sarah began putting each hook through each eye while Elma began to tighten up the laces in back. Sarah moved around her to help her mother, and they began lashing Beth into the corset in earnest. As they tugged and tightened, Beth looked at herself in the mirror, watching as Eli slowly disappeared and Beth emerged. Sarah tied the laces into a bow while Elma retrieved the dress. They both slipped it over the corset and began to button the back of the dress. The result was stunning. Seeing herself standing there before the mirror in that beautiful dress, attended by women friends who knew the truth about her, was almost too much to believe. She began to think Sam's plan might work.

✦

It had been another day of losing for Quentin. Once again someone he considered beneath him had quite literally beaten him.

Sam knew Quentin would kill George if he did not move quickly, so he attacked the closest thing to him. He stomped on Quentin's left hand, feeling several small bones breaking under his boot. The Colt fired, grazing George's arm. Quentin screamed in rage and pain and tried to turn the gun on Sam, but by this time, Sam had put

Maggie down and pulled a knife from his boot. The point was now pressed up against Quentin's throat.

Their eyes met. The depth of hatred, shame, and brokenness that Sam saw in those eyes shook him. He had not seen eyes like this since he had looked into Ewell's on that spring night four months ago. He recognized what he saw. Evil.

"Drop it." Sam pressed the point just a bit harder against Quentin's jugular. "Quentin?"

Quentin dropped the Colt, and Sam picked it up. He stood up, holding the revolver casually at his side. Big Mick had come to and sat up. He was chuckling to himself and rubbing the back of his head. Sam just waited to see if the fight was truly over.

Big Mick looked Maggie up and down. "Patrick O'Rourke brought down by this wee slip of a girl. Well, saints preserve us." He took in the sight of Quentin holding his smashed and swelling hand and his Colt in the marshal's hand and guessed the rest. "You just couldn't do it, boy-o. You just had to bring the unpleasantness." O'Rourke got to his feet. He took a pitcher of water and splashed Pinched-Face with it, who was out cold.

George had joined Maggie, and he was holding her close. She was examining his sleeve, which was soaked with blood from the .45 graze.

"I am so sorry, lassie. Mr. Dunhill will pay for all the damages," O'Rourke said.

"The hell I will!"

Without taking a step, O'Rourke reached down, grabbed Quentin by the collar, and lifted him to his feet. He then reached into Quentin's vest pocket, pulled out his money clip, and handed it to George. "You take what you need, sir, and return the rest to the colonel, bless him. I'll take this sorry excuse for a man home."

Quentin, struggling to get free from O'Rourke's grasp, said, "You can't talk to me that way, O'Rourke."

O'Rourke smiled, grabbed him by the pants, and threw him into the lobby as bystanders scattered in all directions. To Sam, he said, "Marshal, darlin', it has been a pleasure, a real pleasure. I wish I could say it was over with the boy, but we are both men of honor, and I won't want to lie to ya."

Sam offered his hand, and the big Irishman took it.

"Wait a minute, O'Rourke. He'll want this." Sam reached down and picked up Quentin's smashed Stetson. It was covered in applesauce. He tossed it to O'Rourke. "See you tomorrow night."

◆◆◆◆————◆————◆◆◆◆

Elma and Sarah came out of the back room, talking and laughing, arms full of the dress and "underthings."

"Edward, she looked lovely in the dress. I've always said you have an eye for fashion. Now," she said as she and Sarah set everything on the counter, "we'll take the dress and all of this and five more of all of the underthings and one more corset. Elijah also wants Sarah to pick out a few skirts and blouses and maybe shoes and boots."

Ed could not quite believe what he was hearing. "Good lord, Little K, what did these women talk you into back in that room?"

Without missing a beat, Elma said, "Elijah liked what he saw back there, and he has decided to buy his betrothed a trousseau for a honeymoon in Denver."

Ed could not help but laugh. He came around the counter and gave Eli's hand a good shaking. "Congratulations, boy. Your daddy would be so pleased. Finally we are going to have some new little Kennedys running around here."

Sarah continued to play the role of the sweet, young thing and took Eli's hand. Elma winked at Beth and went on with her fairy godmother duties. "When they're done pickin' everything out, please box it up and send the bill to Elijah here. Oh—and Edward, we will be needin' to borrow your buggy until tomorrow." Elma was having a little too much fun with the make believe.

"Of course. I'll have it hitched up and loaded by the time you get through with lunch."

Ed slapped Eli on the back. His eyebrows were alive with questions, but he was too much of a gentleman to ask. All he could say was, "Damn, Little K, I'm happy for you. And Elma, if you know of any Mormon widows, I just might be in the market."

After their work was done, the ladies joined Sam for lunch. They were more than a little surprised at the condition of the dining room. It looked like two bull buffaloes had come to try the pie. After all the commotion, Sam thought they shouldn't trouble the innkeepers for lunch, but Maggie wouldn't hear of it. So Sam and George brought a table and chairs out on to the boardwalk. A grateful Maggie brought golden, fried pork chops out in her number-ten cast-iron frying pan that had been put to such good use earlier, and George set out a large bowl of applesauce.

While they ate, Sam filled them in on the "unpleasantness" that had happened while they were busy at Ed's. Elma laughed so hard she almost spilled her tea. Sam finished with the description of Quentin's applesauce-sodden hat.

As soon as he was through, Sarah and Elma started in on their fairytale adventures at the general store. They began with jealous Miss Vickie and her friend Victor. "That woman was spitting mad at the idea of Elijah here marryin' my Sarah. And you should have seen the look on Edward's face when we invited Eli in to watch Sarah try on clothes. Old Edward almost converted to the church on the spot."

"I wish I could have seen it, but my hands were full at the time. I met Miss Larson yesterday by the river. Pardon me, Miss Sarah, for being so blunt, but she had just been lifting her skirt for some-one moments before I arrived—might have been Mr. Holland." Sam paused to think. "I have heard of Victor Holland. He's made a name for himself as a gambler, but he is even better known for almost beating William Cody in a long-range shooting contest. The US Marshal's office had their eye on him down in Arizona for a back-shooting murder, but his alibi was rock solid. Have you ever seen him here before?"

"No, Samuel, never, and I would know if a stranger had come to town," Elma said.

"Well, I don't like it. You are going to need to watch yourself, Eli. Just because those two gunmen didn't manage to kill you at the lake last week doesn't mean that whoever sent them has given up. Someone wants you out of the way," Sam said.

"I can take care of myself," Beth said.

Elma put down her fork. "Missed him at the lake? What are you two talking about?"

"We left out a few details about how we met last week," Sam said.

"It sounds like it," Elma's pad and pencil came out. "Now tell all."

"There is nothing to tell," Beth started. "I just ran into a little trouble with two gunmen down near Salt Lake, and the marshal used his Winchester to help me sort it out."

Sam smiled. "That's about right. Eli is leaving out the part about how he was not himself at the time, and that the gunmen had more than killing on their minds. Let's just say that when we first met, I could clearly see the truth about Eli."

Beth looked at the women, smiled, and shrugged. "One of the killers had a well-drawn map on him giving the details of where I would be. I thought no one in Smith knew about my little property down south. Someone worked hard to find me and sent those two to murder me."

Elma mulled over the new information. "Samuel is right. You need to be far more careful. Shooting those three yesterday only made it worse. You are stirrin' the pot."

"Yes, I am. I want this over one way or another," Beth said, taking a drink from her glass.

Elma, seeing Beth's mood was turning dark, changed the subject, substituting Sarah's name for Beth's. "Wait until you see Sarah in that dress. The blue ribbons make her eyes glow. It is just right for her. Not too frilly or young. It is simply and beautifully made. In fact you'd think it had been made just for her. I tell you, Samuel, when we had Sarah finally buttoned into that dress, she took our breath away."

Beth too had been stunned by the transformation. She longed for Sam to see her in the dress. At the same time, the anxiety in her was steadily growing. Finding the dress had been a fantasy she had longed to fulfill. Now the reality of becoming Beth in full view of everyone she knew was weighing on her. How would her ranch family react?

She worried about Jake most of all. He was proud to work for a man like Eli. She knew he had a tender heart when it came to women, but no matter what Maria said, working for a woman would be a whole other thing. Jake had been raised in the man's world of ranching, and working for a woman was out of the question. She had heard Jake say just that on more than one occasion.

As the others ate and laughed, she looked at the people of Smith walking by, nodding to Eli with respect. When they found out she was a woman, would that respect still be there? What would happen to her place here in Smith—or in Utah for that matter? Yes, women had the vote in Utah, but they were still second-class citizens, an afterthought in most decisions. Was she willing to give up her place in this man's world so she could live the truth? If she wasn't, was she willing to give up Sam? The truth was…she did not know.

✦

Sam watched her looking at the folks on the street. The joy had gone out of her. He could see the weight settling on her, and he wanted to help lift it off, but there was nothing he could do right then. "Hey," he said, "I am with you." He smiled, and she smiled weakly back.

After lunch, they escorted the Rockport women home. It was a far quieter ride than the ride into town. When they reached the farm, they retrieved Desiree. She got into the buggy with Eli. As they said their good-byes, Elma said, "I know more than most what the road ahead of ya looks like. It can be hard and painful for strong-willed folks like you and me, but no harder than the road you've been traveling, child, and this new road is full of joy, too. Be not afraid, for He is with ya. Sarah and I will be praying."

"Thank you," Beth said.

<hr />

The ranch was alive with activity as they rode through the main gate. Slim and Jesus passed them on the way in. The two cowboys were heading out to stand watch on the herd. Jesus knew Desiree and was surprised and pleased to see her. "Buenos Dias, senorita. Excuse me for asking, but what are you doing here?"

"She's decided to come work for the Running J," Eli said.

"Welcome! My wife Maria will be 'appy to see you." Both men tipped their hats and loped off to their duties. Beth watched them go. How loyal would they be when they knew? As they approached Jake's house, they could see Jenny tying Free to the hitching rail. She was talking to Jake, who was stepping off of his tall dun. He pulled his Winchester from its scabbard and stepped up to the porch. Jenny's face shone, and even though they could not make out what Jake was saying, Beth was sure it was the most words she'd ever seen him string together.

"Afternoon, Jake, Jenny. What have you two been up to?" Sam asked.

"Jake took me for a ride around the northern range like Eli asked him to. It's so beautiful up there," Jenny said.

"Yes, it is. Good thinking, taking her up there to get the lay of the land," Sam said with a wink and a nod.

"Well, I—I was just doin' what you asked me to, Eli, and I just thought it—it would be, well, important for her—I mean Miss Jenny, to start up north and—well, work her way down." Jake turned red.

Sam could not help himself and laughed. So did Jenny. Poor, innocent Jake realized what he had said and tried to recover. "I mean, starting north and going south." The laughing continued. Jake quit while he was ahead, looking like a schoolboy caught with his hand in the cookie jar.

Beth's heart warmed at her friend's obvious affection for Jenny. She loved Jake. He was the brother she had so missed. In less than twenty-four hours, he would have to make a choice about her—whether to follow a woman who had been lying to him or set out for Wyoming to start his own place. She knew he had the means. Jake had only stayed all these years because Eli needed him and Jake was loyal above all else.

Stepping in to end his misery, Eli said, "Well, you were right to take her to the northern pasture. That's where I would have started. Miss Jenny is going to have to be familiar with every acre of this ranch if she is going to be my secretary. Before we talk any more business, let me introduce our newest employee. Desiree Gonzales, this is Jenny Richards and Jake Brown." Everyone smiled and said hello. "She'll start with Maria in the kitchen."

Jenny stepped to the back of the buggy. "Looks like you've cleaned out Ed's ladies' department. Did you buy Desiree a new wardrobe too?"

"Yes, we spent some time at Ed's, and we ran into some trouble. Jake, Marshal McKnight will fill you in while I take Desiree up to meet Maria. Oh, and, Jake, I want to meet with all hands tomorrow during lunch here at the old house." Beth looked at Sam and said, "Don't get your hopes up yet. We'll talk."

"I'll set it up, Eli," Jake said.

Eli snapped the reins, and the buggy pulled away. Sam watched her go.

Sam turned to Jake and said, "Jake, someone has hired a real killer, Victor Holland. Have you ever heard of him?"

"Ya, somethin' about him and a long gun."

"That's the one. We need to make sure everyone is working in groups of two of more. No one works alone out in the open."

Jake stepped back onto the dun. "I'll grab a couple of boys from the bunkhouse and start spreading the word." He nodded to Sam and was gone.

Beth sat in her bedroom surrounded by boxes of femininity. She stood and stepped out onto her balcony. The sun was low in the west. Her father's ranch—her ranch—lay before her. From there she could see the whole valley. Groves of ponderosa opening into pasture stretched all the way to the river. Would it look the same tomorrow? Could she put on those dresses she had always wanted to wear and risk losing her home? Of course she would not lose it, but it would never be the same. The worry pressed heavily down upon her, causing pain in her chest.

Sam stood outside her door, wanting to help her but not knowing how. He knocked—no answer. Looking around and seeing no one was near, he softly called, "Beth?" Again, no answer. He tried the door. It was open. He pushed it, not knowing what he would find. As he entered the room, he saw her standing on the balcony. She looked so alone with her whole ranch before her. Her responsibilities surrounded her.

The room was almost Spartan. It had none of the color or detail that filled the cabin on the lake. The whole room focused on the large window and French doors that looked out over the J. A small, functional desk sat before one of the widows, so whenever Beth looked up from her work she would see her ranch spread before her. *With that view, who needs color on the walls?* Sam thought. The boxes from the general store were stacked around her bunkhouse-sized bed, and on the bed lay a beautiful dress. No other box had been opened.

"Beth," he said softly. She did not turn. "Beth." No response. He sighed and tried once more. "Eli."

"Yes," she said, not turning to him.

He walked around the boxes and joined her on the balcony. He wanted to take her in his arms and hold her, but every hand on the ranch could see them on the balcony if they looked up, so he just stood, sharing the beauty of the view, and waited.

"Sam, I can't. I can't risk it."

Sam waited again.

"You don't understand." She stepped back into the bedroom, looking at the dress. "I would be giving up so much, too much. To become Beth, I would be giving up my place in the world. Every day I see how women are treated. A woman is little more than a child or a valued slave you can sleep with. My men won't respect or follow me. To be honest, I don't even know if *I* would follow a woman."

Sam stood in the doorway and said, "You might be right. I know it will take an extraordinary woman to pull it off, a woman who could run a ranch on her own, a woman who could kill when killing was needed, a woman who loved and cared for her friends with the kind of loyalty that would make her consider denying her own life for them."

"No, no. I am not going to be pulled in by your talk again. People don't see things the way you do, Sam."

"Elma does. Maria does."

"They are women. They have no choice. I do."

"The choice to live your life as Eli?"

She stepped away from him and to her bed. "Yes."

"To never know love? To never have a real family? Who will this ranch go to when you are gone? When the murderer who killed your father kills you, what will happen to this place? If you manage to survive, are you going to grow old as Eli, always longing for the life at the cabin and not the life here at the J? That sounds like hell, not life."

She sat on the bed in anguish over what to do. "Stop! I can't think. Let me think! It is so easy for you. You're a man. Sam, you will never understand." Although she hated to cry, she started to weep. "Damn these tears."

"You are right." He sat behind her as she kept looking at the dress. "I will never truly understand. I will always be on the outside of the world of women, but I can see. I see strong women cleverly leading men."

"Where?"

"Victoria, in England. She came to the throne when she was younger than you. Now she governs and guides an empire that stretches around the world. Her people love her. She married a man who loved her deeply and bore him children, all while ruling Britain. I think you two are cut from the same cloth. Both of you have had great responsibility placed on you from the time you were young children. When the queen's husband died of cholera, she mourned him like no monarch before her. Did you know she still lays out his clothes every day?" Putting his hand on her shoulder, he said, "She allowed herself to love and live. That is a life well lived, full of joy and pain."

"Joy and pain? I have seen plenty of pain, and I want no more of it."

"I'm sorry, Beth, but you can't have one without the other. This world is at war. Evil occupies the land, and pain reminds us of that. But joy reminds us of what the world was meant to be, what is right and good."

She turned to him. "All I have that is right and good is here on this ranch, and you are asking me to risk losing it and the people I care for who work it. It is too much."

"The problem is the loss, the pain of losing Eli and Mary, of losing your mother and finally your father. When your father was killed, you became an orphan, and your inheritance was his promise and the responsibility of this ranch."

Beth could feel the tears coming again, and she forced them down. She was tired of all the crying she had been doing; besides, it did not help, but when Sam used the word *orphan* it hit home.

"Beth, I have known pain"—he grew quiet—"and great loss, believe me. To know great joy and love, you have to take a risk."

His admission of weakness caused her to stop and look to him. He stood and walked to the great window in her room overlooking the Running J. He spoke, looking out over the ranch into the past. "When I came home from the war, my Charlie was waiting for me. She had been staying with her mama, and my granddaddy was watching over both of them. Charlie had received a letter from me just days before I arrived, telling her I was on my way. She had spent the week preparing a little farmhouse we had bought just before I left for war." He paused as the memory he seldom dared touch came flooding back. "Beth, we loved each other so much. Six months later, she was gone, and there was nothing I could do to save her. No one to save her from, no one to beat to death, and no one to blame but God."

"You blamed God?" she asked.

"More than blamed. Hated Him."

Shaking her head in disbelief, she said, "You? How could you hate God?"

"He took my Charlie. We had two glorious months in the fall. We spent every moment we could together. Finally, it was time for me to start making a living, and Granddaddy had saved a place for me in the rangers.

"About a week after I started work, Charlie's mama came hurrying into town to tell me Charlie had taken a fall and was hurt. I was on a horse in moments and headed back to the house while Charlie's mama went for the doc." Sam paused, reluctant go into the deep waters of these memories.

"When I got to the house, I was off the horse before he came to a stop. Charlie's mama had gotten her inside onto the sofa in the parlor before going for help. She had been crying but was putting on a strong face for me. Her leg was broke just below the knee. She said it hurt like hell. I asked her how it happened. She said she had been heading down the back steps to go for a ride and her knee had just given way, and down the steps she went. Her mama found her at the bottom of the stairs about an hour later.

"While we waited for the doc, I got her up to her bed. Granddaddy, Charlie's mama, and the doc soon arrived. Granddaddy stayed in the parlor while Charlie's mama and I helped the doc.

"He gave her some laudanum to ease the pain, and she was out. He set and splinted her leg. Then he spent an hour feeling the bones in her other leg and her arms. He then moved to her spine. I did not like the amount of time he spent there. She had just broken her leg. It happens all the time. She was a strong, young woman, and in a month or two, she would be up on her feet, back to normal." Beth watched him as he became lost in the memory.

"The doctor was a kind, young man, fresh from the battlefield and on top of all the latest discoveries in medicine. He asked me to come out on the back porch with him. I felt like he was walking me to the gallows, and in a way, he was. He told me Charlie had fallen because there was a tumor in the bone just below her knee. It was bone cancer. He had found another tumor on her right forearm and two on her spine." Again he stopped, gathered strength, and went on. "By this time, I could barely hear what he was saying. My mind was swimming. He said the usual treatment would be to amputate the leg but that there was no need to now. I told him I wanted him to do anything he could to save her. Amputation would be unbelievably hard to bear, but I loved her too much to lose her. He just looked at me. He was a good man. His chin quivered, and as gently as he could, he told me, 'You are going to lose her, Sam. The only reason to amputate is to stop the spread of the cancer. It has already spread. There is no stopping it. Charlie is going to die soon, and I am sorry to say it is going to be painful, extremely so.'

"My legs wouldn't hold me up. I sat down hard on the steps and asked, 'How long?'

"'She will not see the new year,' he said.

"He was right." Through tears now, he kept going deeper. "Early on the morning of December ninth, my childhood friend—my lover, my wife—died in my arms. I wanted her to go. She was in so much pain that the laudanum didn't help, but I wanted her to take me with her." Sam looked at Beth and gave her a weak smile. "I don't have to tell *you* how painful it is to lose someone you love. The day I buried Charlie, I threw my kit together, got on my horse—Buck's father—and ran from the pain, cursing the God who would take my love. My future was gone, our life was gone, the children we would have had all were gone. Yes, I hated God.

"I did nothing but ride for six months. I rode to the Pacific, up to San Francisco, and into Oregon country. It was in the high Cascades I began to remember all the joy and pure pleasure I had had with my Charlie. All of that was a gift. A hint of the way life is supposed to be. The cancer was an evil, the kind of evil you find in this fallen land occupied by the enemy. The enemy had taken my girl and knocked me out of the saddle. The question was, would I stay down or get back into the fight? I hope you can see I chose to stand."

Beth stood and moved away from the dress. She said to him, "But you would not choose the pain again if you could avoid it."

Stepping toward her, he took her in his arms. "I'm choosing to risk that very pain again for a chance to have that joy with you." He kissed her. She struggled, pushing at his shoulders, but the fire of passion rose in her. Before she could think, she was not pushing him away but pulling him in.

What am I doing? No, no! "No, Sam!" She was crying now. She pulled away from him, grabbed her hat, and ran. Down the stairs and out the front door she went. Maria called after her, but she did not stop. Beth ran to Belle, mounted up, and galloped north.

Sam stood at the hearth of the fireplace smoking one of Beth's cigars. It was quiet except for Jenny's soft mumbling. She was going over the ranch's ledgers for the last few months, trying to understand how the money flowed in and out of the ranch. Finally she shut the book in frustration.

"This would be a lot easier if Eli were here. Did he say when he was comin' back?"

"No, Jenny. He didn't saying anything when he left."

"It just seems so strange for him to leave without a word. I'm worried."

Sam moved to the couch and sat beside her. "He'll be fine. There is nothing out there in the dark he can't handle. Jenny, you know this territory is about to blow wide open. The only person who has managed to keep that from happening until now is Eli. The pressure on him to grow this ranch and keep the peace would overwhelm anyone. He is only a couple of years older than you. I marvel at what he has accomplished."

"I know. I want to help him, but I don't know how."

"Your chance to do just that will come tomorrow. He is going to talk to all of you about what is really going on. He will need all the support he can get." She looked at the marshal, fearful. Sam sighed. "I said not to worry. He is just out there on the land he loves, working it through tonight."

"I'll pray. In my former profession we all did a good deal of prayin'."

"Jenny, I do have a question for you about your old line of work."

She cocked her head, ready for what always came from men, a business proposal. "Ask away."

"Did you know Jeff Amos?" Sam asked.

She shook her head. "Well, not professionally, but I knew who he was."

"On the night before Jeff was killed, were you working?"

She leaned back on the couch. "Marshal, the only night we got off was Sunday, and if the Double L was in town, we didn't get that night either."

"Do you remember who you were with?"

"Of course. There are some men you never forget. He was one of those. He liked to leave his mark on me; it was Rowdy Larson. He kept me busy all night and into the morning and left me with a black eye and a cracked rib. I couldn't work for a week." She looked like she'd spit if she weren't trying to be a lady.

Suddenly, Sam wanted to run into Rowdy again. Since Jenny's bed had been full that night, it meant Quentin was lying about what he had been doing or at least who he'd been doing it with. Sam put his hand on Jenny's and said, "That is all behind you now. Eli has seen to that. All we have to do is stop someone from the Double L or the Seven-C from killing him."

Jenny earnestly took his hand in hers. "And you'll protect him, won't you?"

"That is what I intend to do."

The front door to the great room opened, and the sound of boots on the wood floor could be heard. Sam and Jenny looked toward the sound, and Jake appeared out of the darkness. He was wearing a clean shirt and his best belt buckle, and his hair was all slicked back. Jake had a shy smile on his face, but as he entered the room, it changed into a worried question when he saw Jenny holding Sam's hand. Jenny saw his concern and pulled her hands back.

"I just came by to see if you wanted to go for a walk before bed. It is a fine, warm night, full moon just hangin' there, and I—I—well, I have a question. I'd like to ask ya somethin', but if you're busy I'll just see ya in the mornin'," Jake said.

Jenny stood and stepped toward him. "I'm never too busy for you, Jake. I can think of nothin' I'd like better than to walk under the moon with you." She took his hand, and Jake was so surprised and happy that he dropped his hat on the spot. Sam chuckled to himself.

Not knowing what to do next, Jake picked up his hat, offered Jenny his arm, and said, "Good night, Sam."

"Now, you be careful out there, Jenny. Don't let Jake talk you to death."

She smiled at Sam as she took Jake's arm. "Oh, don't worry, I wouldn't. Good night, Sam." And out the door they strolled.

Sam stared at the closed door. He looked up to the high windows and could see the edge of the moon rising through them. Where was Beth? The house was quiet, too quiet, and he was restless. He knew he would never sleep. *Beth is out under that moon. Keep her safe,* he prayed. He wanted to be with her, to hold her hand and walk with her under that moon without the shadow of Eli following them. He moved back to the hearth, relit his cigar, and threw the match into the fire.

Things were starting to spinning out of control. He had never been one to fear a little chaos; in fact, he often welcomed it. Chaos brought the opportunity to bring order where it was needed. But not when it came to his heart. He had protected his heart since it had been so wounded by the loss of his Charlie, and now his heart was in danger of being wounded again. He could not control what Beth would do, and he did not want to; he wanted her to choose him on her own. To add to the chaos, someone was trying to kill her, and a back-shooting murderer had just come to town. He could feel his frustration building into a slow burning anger. He was a man of action, and there was no action to take, so a ride into town on Buck would have to do. Maybe he'd try a hand of cards with Mr. Holland. He had a few questions for him anyway.

In moments, he was ready. As he headed for the barn, he shifted the cross-draw holster he had just added to his belt. He wasn't quite sure what he was walking into, and he wanted to be ready. He had spent time cleaning the guns before Maria had served a dinner to Jenny and him that could have filled up four cowhands.

These guns were trusted tools. Granddaddy would say, "Son, I seen many an old boy in trouble because of a misfire or some malfunction of their piece. If they lived through it they'd cuss the gun, maybe get a new one. But the truth was the misfire was rarely the gun's fault. It was the lack of care given to a tool that can save your life or take someone else's. That is the kind of tool that deserves a little extra time. You care for your gun, and it'll care for you, boy." Sam crossed the grounds to the barn.

Buck saw Sam as he entered the stables. He stomped and threw his head. When Sam reached him, Buck pushed his head against Sam's chest. "I'm glad to see you too, boy. It's a little lonely without our girls, isn't it?" He ran his hand down Buck's back and began to saddle him; soon he was in the saddle and headed for Smith.

✦✦✦✦ ———— ✦ ———— ✦✦✦✦

Beth sat on the edge of the cliff overlooking the meadow where Jeff Amos was killed. The moon was bright behind her, casting a blue light that caused the trees and bushes to throw sharp shadows on the ground around her. Beth loved these late, summer nights. The woods were alive with game, and as a young teen, she would quietly move out among them, seeing how close she could get to deer and elk. She also knew this was a dangerous light. While she was moving up quietly and slowly on a fawn, a cougar might be moving quietly and slowly up on her. Everything about this light made her senses come fully alive so that she could think of nothing else but the woods themselves, their beauty, and their danger. This brief escape from her life of responsibility was what she longed for.

Even with the full moon, the night sky was bright with stars. The vast ceiling of bright beacons felt like a warm quilt. In August, the night was usually full of falling stars, and tonight was no exception. As a child, each time she saw a falling star, she imagined her mother was saying, "I love you, darlin' girl," from heaven, or that her brother was winking at her. She found comfort in thinking they were watching over her. Over the years, she had often come to that very spot as she struggled with the demands of the life. Up there at night she had found peace and the will and strength to go on. She was looking for that peace now. Gazing up, she saw a bright, blue star streak across the sky, and before its tail had faded, an even brighter star followed.

Beth smiled and said, "I love you too, Mama," and, "Hello, Eli." She was comforted, and peace began to wrap around her.

Beth had never spent much time in a church made by men, because this was her church. This is where she felt Him—who or whatever "Him" was. Tonight she felt Him strong in the trees, in the moon, and in that sky.

She sat listening, searching for direction. All was quiet; then she heard a bull elk bugle for his harem. Hearing him caused her to drift back to the new sensation that had come to life in her: her physical desire to be with this man, Sam. These new senses were powerful and distracting. As she thought about their last embrace, she was surprised at how strongly her body responded to the memory even now. Mixed with this animal response was an aching in her chest for his tender words, his deep, kind looks, and the peace that seemed to radiate from him. She wanted that peace almost more than she wanted him. But there was no denying she wanted him more than the ranch, even more than her overwhelming desire to protect her family. She wanted all of it at the same time: the power of being a man, the family, the ranch, and a life as a woman with Sam McKnight, but how could she choose?

The town was quieting down after a day of anticipation. *If they only knew what was coming next.* Sam smiled to himself. The lights were still burning at the hotel. Riding by the restaurant windows, Sam could see George and Maggie sitting at a table, talking. Maggie was gently touching her hero's swollen cheek, loving him with her every word and gesture.

Down the street, the saloon was still full of action; the sound of drunken laughter was spilling out into the street. Sam stepped off Buck and tied him to the rail. Buck's ears were up, and he was looking into the saloon. Sam knew this look. He thought Buck was sizing up the door to see how hard it would be to get in there if shots were fired. Sam put his hand on the big chestnut's jaw and said, "I'll be fine. Just wait, boy." Sam pulled his Winchester from its scabbard and pushed through the batwing doors.

Outside it was still warm from the heat of the late August day, but the saloon was just plain hot. Smoke filled the air with a smell of good tobacco and bad. There was a fella playing a piano in the corner. He was singing to one of the working girls, who was leaning on the upright, no doubt on a short break between customers. Every table was full of cowboys from all three spreads playing cards and drinking. Sporting gals were sprinkled throughout the room, some standing behind cowboys, some sitting in others' laps, and some leading men upstairs to spend some of their winnings. It looked to Sam that each crew was mainly keeping to themselves, but the 7C table and the Double L kept eying each other. The smallest spark could start this night on fire.

Despite himself, Sam liked the place. The fact was he loved a good saloon. A shot of whiskey, a good cigar, and a hand or two of cards suited him just fine. His shoulders began to relax. *This is going to help,* he thought. He walked to the bar and handed his Winchester to the barkeeper.

"Hello, Jim. You're looking well." Sam was admiring the forty pounds of belly Jim had put on since he last saw him three years before. "Business must be good."

Jim patted his belly with pride. "It is good to see you too, Marshal, and yes, business is good. Town is a-growing. You could do me a great favor, though, if you could keep these old boys from shootin' the place up tonight. All that blood and broken furniture does cut into the bottom line."

"Now, we wouldn't want that, would we, Jim? I'll see what I can do," Sam said, turning to the tables.

"What'll you have?" Jim asked.

"I'll let you know."

In the far corner of the saloon sat Victor Holland at the table with the Larson crew, his back safely to the wall. Victor's eyes were on Sam. He was smiling. Everyone else at the table was looking at Vickie Larson as she reached forward and pulled a considerable pot toward her. Usually men are frustrated to see their money leave the table, but these boys weren't looking at the money. Sam moved a little closer to the table so he could hear what was being said.

Vickie sat to the left of Holland, and Sam could guess what was going on. Vickie had a large stack of coins and bills in front of her; Holland's stake was smaller yet still ample. Holland was showing Vickie a good time by cheating these poor boys.

Johnson, the gun slick Sam had met at the 7C that morning, threw down his cards and said, "Holland, I don't like the way this game is bein' played. I ain't saying there's cheatin' goin' on, but Miss Larson has been mighty lucky when you deal." No one moved at the table; they just watched and waited. An accusation of cheating could turn into gunplay, and stray bullets could put a real damper on a cowboy's fun.

"Oh, I would say I have been the lucky one with Miss Larson." He turned and winked at her, and she leaned over and kissed him.

Miss Vickie leaned back in her chair and smiled. "I've been called a cheat before, but never at cards." She laughed, and all but Johnson joined her.

Sam knew that Johnson was itching to prove himself, but Sam did think Johnson knew who he was up against in Holland. Holland would not back down, and he had proven it all along the Mexican border country.

Pushing his chair back, Johnson stood, and everyone suddenly moved away from the table except Holland and Vickie.

"I ain't sayin' Miss Larson is cheatin', Holland."

"You are wiser than I thought, Mr. Johnson, because if you were questioning Miss Larson's spotless character, I would have to defend it," Holland said.

"Why, Victor. How can I ever thank you?" Vickie purred.

"A gentleman never asks for payment from a lady, my dear."

Johnson interrupted their foreplay. He was worried Holland had forgotten him. "She ain't no lady, and you're sure as hell no gentleman."

Sam couldn't care less if the young gun hand ended up in the ground or not. He had sent men like him or better to hell this week, but he was a US marshal, and he was duty-bound to save this poor idiot if he could. Besides, Jim had asked him to try to keep blood off the floor. He stepped up behind Johnson and asked, "Is this chair open, son? Because I sure do have a hankerin' to play with Miss Larson."

✦

Beth needed to cool off from her thoughts about Sam so she could think straight. The Juniper River was right below her. She stepped on to Belle, and they started down.

Bathing in the river was something she loved to do, but here on the ranch, she could only do it at night. How she had envied Laurie and Vickie when they were younger and it was hot. They would slip away from her and swim. Slipping off to another private swimming hole was out of the question because Vickie would always be sneaking back for a peek. Of course, it was no better around boys or men. If they did bathe, they had no trouble stripping down around her, and she often saw far more than she wanted to. She managed to stay on the shoreline by pretending she had a fear of water.

It was just after her thirteenth birthday that she slipped away on a hot summer night and swam in this very spot on the river. Like most things in her life, she had had to teach herself to swim. She watched the men swimming and picked it up as best she could. The cold water of the river thrilled her. On hot summer nights, these treks to be near her mother and Eli had often ended in nocturnal swims.

When she reached the river, she tied Belle off near the water so the mare could drink. She sat on a log and pulled off her boots then stood and undressed. The day had been hot, but with the sun down, the heat had eased to a pleasant warmth. There was a slight breeze that felt like a gentle caress on her bare skin.

She stepped into the water, and the coolness surrounded her feet as slight ripples moved out across the glassy surface. The moon was beginning to set behind the cliff she had been sitting on moments before. It was huge, hanging just feet above the cliff's edge. Beth stood there—her feet tingling in coolness, taken with the beauty of the night sky. She had never seen an artist come close to catching this kind of glory. Before her, the reflection of the moon was captured perfectly in the still water of her swimming hole. It took her breath away. She wanted to remember this moment, this picture of the two moons standing before her, one in the water and one in the sky. She followed the reflection back across the water, looking at each star in the reflected sky until she came to her face. Her face surprised her.

Her gaze moved down the reflection from her face to her neck, to the swell of her breasts, the slimness of her waist, and the curve of her hips. *I am a woman. There is no denying it.* She continued looking upon her femininity for a moment longer, then looked back to the moon now touching the cliff's edge. A brilliant star blazed through the night sky. Beth said, "I love you too, Mama. Thank you." She ran forward and dove into the water. She came up far out in the swimming hole from under the fresh water, took a deep breath, and stared up at the sky. Suddenly, the sky was full of shooting stars. Beth was overwhelmed by the love she felt and her tears of joy mixed with the water of the Juniper.

<hr/>

Johnson spun around, reaching for leather as he moved, but as his hand got to his holster, he found his Remington .45 missing. Sam held it up. "Why, look here. This is the new 1874. You know, I do like these new Remingtons. I just don't think they are proven yet." Johnson's eyes were wide with surprise and anger. He had heard about the beating a gunman had taken on the street the day before once the marshal had disarmed him. Johnson had bragged to his friends how McKnight had better not try that with him. Now it had happened, and many of the friends who had heard the boast were waiting to see what he would do. First thing he did was to step back out of the reach of those fists. Sam locked eyes with him, hoping he would play it smart. Sam asked, "Could I ask you a favor, Johnson?"

Surprised at this question, he said, "Yeah, sure. What?"

"Could I borrow this until tomorrow morning? I haven't had a chance to really test one of these, and this one seems to be hardly used. I will buy you a box of shells for your trouble." Sam wondered if the young idiot would be smart enough to take the gift Sam had just offered him. Johnson's eye raced around the room, trying to see his outfit's reaction to the marshal's words. He was still puzzling over just how fast the marshal had had to be to pull his gun before he could touch it. One thing was now clear to Johnson: McKnight could beat him in any fair fight. Finally, he said, "Sure, marshal, you keep it 'til morning. I can understand why you would want to know what the good, new talent is using."

"Oh, I do boy. What are they using?" The cowboys at the table broke into laughter. Without a second thought, Sam tossed the Remington to Jim at the bar. Johnson worriedly watched it sail through the air. Jim caught it almost without looking and stuck it under the bar, and Sam called, "Keep that for me, and bring me a bottle of the good stuff Mr. Kennedy was telling me about—oh, and a new deck of cards." Jim nodded. The other card players eased back into their seats as Sam took Johnson's chair and sat down. Johnson just stood there, not knowing quite what had just happened. He decided he needed time to think it through, so he headed for the bar.

Miss Vickie gave Sam a less-than-wholesome smile. "Marshal, I am so glad you have joined our game. I do admire the way you handled Johnson's gun. I had heard you were fast, but even I was surprised by that move." She turned to Holland and caressed his hand. "Have you seen anything like that?"

Holland, still staring at Sam, said, "No, darlin', that was fast—very fast." He gave Sam a small nod of respect. Victor would not challenge the marshal tonight, with pistols at any rate.

"I will take that as a compliment, Miss Larson, coming from you. I hear you are one of the fastest women in northern Utah." Miss Vickie's honor was not ruffled. She took Sam's comment as praise and an invitation. Then one of the saloon girls arrived with a bottle, a glass, and a new deck of cards. Sam laid his money on the table, poured himself a shot, and drank it. Sam could see his granddaddy sitting by the fire, his arm around his young wife, saying, "It gives the good Lord pleasure to see His children enjoyin' savory food, hard drink, and bein' with the women we love. He doesn't want us to be ashamed of enjoying His good creation. That's old Satan tryin' to shame us into thinkin' we're sinnin'. Now gettin' blind drunk, eatin' like a pig, and sleepin' with anything in a skirt—that is sin, but enjoyin' in moderation—that ain't."

At the poker table, Holland said, "Welcome to our game, Marshal," and reached for the deck of cards, but before he could pick it up, Sam put his hand on it.

"I think I'll deal, if no one minds." He broke the seal on the deck, poured another shot, and began to shuffle the cards. The other hands at the table all seemed to think a new dealer was a good idea. "Five card draw, one-eyed jacks are wild. Holland, I have a few questions for you. Do you mind?"

"No, it would be my pleasure to answer your questions, Marshal."

As the last card landed, Sam looked up at Holland and asked, "Were you through here last spring?"

Holland picked up his cards. "I do believe I was through here in the spring. I had met Miss Larson in Salt Lake and could not resist her charms." He kissed her hand, and she smiled coyly. "I even played some cards at this very table."

So he was here. I wonder if he was Vickie's swimming partner yesterday, Sam thought. He looked at his hand. He had dealt himself two kings and a one-eyed jack. His expression never changed. Everyone began to lay their bets. Sam looked at Vickie and said to Holland, "I can see why you would follow the beauty of Miss Larson up to Big Bear Country, but did you see any of the other sights? Why, just yesterday I was down by the Juniper River, and I was real impressed with the cold, clear water. It was so hot I was tempted to take a swim."

Holland smiled and said, "This is grand country, but I prefer a young, strong city. Denver or San Francisco have the kind of beauty I desire. The only bathing I do is in a hot bathtub if I can help it. If it is no trouble, I will take two." Vickie looked to Holland, knowing the marshal had gotten a new piece of information. She smiled wryly at Sam.

So she wasn't skinny-dipping with Holland yesterday, Sam thought. "How many, Miss Larson?" Vickie, not sure what he was asking her, paused. Sam clarified, "Cards."

"Two," she said with a playful smirk.

The other four cowboys and gun hands at the table drew cards. When it came back around to Sam, he took two. This time he dealt himself a queen and a ten. Sam looked at Vickie and Holland. Victor gave no sign of what was in his hand, but Miss Larson was not as smooth. As bets were placed, she began to twirl a loose curl of hair by her ear. Sam could tell she was about to bluff.

Bets were placed, and only one older cowboy folded. When it came to Vickie, she pushed the pot up. This time one of the gun hands from the Double L folded, but everyone else called until it came to Holland. He eyed Sam and made a choice, "I think you are bluffing, Marshal," and he pushed the pot higher.

Now the other two cowboys folded. "Too rich fer my blood," said a crusty, old cowboy Sam had seen at the Running J.

The bet came to Sam, and he called by throwing in two Golden Eagles. "Call."

Victor grinned as he laid out his cards. He had a full house—three queens and two aces. The pride of a hand well played without cheating was on him like a boy in a schoolhouse. Miss Larson was next. She gazed directly into Sam's eyes and laid down three sevens. Then down came an eight and a one-eyed jack.

She purred, "Can you beat four sevens, Marshal?"

Sam just shook his head and said, "No ma'am." He watched her as once again she scooped up all the winnings. He had learned a great deal about her. She could lie about lying. She had a gift for it. Sam had rarely been fooled, but she had done it; she had sucked him in with a twirl of her hair. Sam was impressed. He also knew that someone who could lie without a drop of shame was dangerous. He now believed she was somehow a part of the Amos murder.

Sam poured himself another shot of the good stuff and watched Miss Larson put his Golden Eagles in one of her stacks. She winked at him as she did it. Losing the coins was a small price to pay to learn so much about her; besides, the night was young. Sam was confident the coins would come back his way. He winked back at her with an assured knowing that caused her to look uncomfortably away.

<hr />

Beth pulled on her boots and stood up. The moon had gone down now, and it was darker, but the stars of the Milky Way silhouetted the cliff edge and the treetops. There was enough light to get home safely. She buckled on her gun belt, put her hat onto her wet head, and stepped onto Belle.

Before leaving, she took one last look at the river. She could hear it more than see it. The stars were still reflecting in it, but the cool surface was as black as obsidian. She thought back to what she had seen in that surface. Coming out there, she was determined not to give up the life she knew, but that water had brought her to a cross-road. If she took one more step down the road Sam had laid in front of her, there would be no turning back. The truth was she may have taken a step too far by bringing Maria, Elma, and Sarah into her real life. *My real life? My real life?* she thought. She turned Belle toward home. She would make her decision in the morning when she decided what to wear.

Sam came in late, well after the moon had gone down. He was relieved to see Belle in the barn when he brought Buck in after cooling him down. Of course Buck was glad to see her. He pushed Sam over to her stall, and the working horses touched heads and got quiet. Sam just let them stand for a moment. He had seen how Buck behaved when he wanted to breed with a filly, and he had known Buck to enjoy the company of other horses, but there was something different here. These two seemed to have a true affection for each other. The stall next to her was open.

Sam walked Buck in and brushed him down, all the while talking to his partner. "You got it bad, don't you, boy? I know, me too. I hope I can work it out for you, my friend." Buck looked back at him and threw his head twice.

Sam stepped out of the barn and looked up to Beth's bedroom window. No light. She was sleeping—or trying to. Sam would do the same. As he walked to the main house, he thought about how hard he had pushed her today—now yesterday; maybe too hard. The only thing he knew for sure was he wanted to look into those amazing, aqua eyes again and touch her soft cheek.

He opened the door and stepped into the great room, hoping to see her by the fire, but the fire was out, and the room was empty. *Just gotta trust,* he thought. *Tomorrow is a new day.*

＋＋＋＋ —— ◆ —— ＋＋＋＋

Sam did not sleep much. If thoughts of Beth weren't keeping him up, turning over Jeff Amos's murder was. So as soon as he heard the kitchen coming to life, he headed down for a cup of coffee. He knew the kitchen would be the first place Beth would come after she woke up, and he wanted to see her and talk to her. Besides, he liked kitchens. They were often the center of everything that was happening on a spread. The truth was he enjoyed the company and conversation of women. He had had many enjoyable mornings talking to or listening to a gal over a good cup of coffee while she cooked or cleaned up. He had found if he did a dish or two, he was her best friend for life. He had seen his granddaddy do many a dish, not because he had to, but because he liked to serve a gal that way. Sam had learned the lesson well.

This morning Maria was at her wood stove working her breakfast magic with cast iron. Desiree was at her side. Maria was teaching her how thick she liked the biscuit gravy to be. Desiree was listening intently, trying to make a good impression. Something apple was filling the room with a sweet aroma Sam could almost taste. Kate Young was working on buttermilk biscuits, and Angelica was carefully slicing bacon. Angelica never stopped talking. "Kate, how is your dress coming for the dance tonight?"

Kate smiled at her young friend who could think of nothing but the dance. "I finished it last night. I'm afraid I look like a cow in blue gingham, but there is no hiding my little friend here." She lovingly rubbed her belly as if the baby was already in her arms.

Angelica cocked her head and asked, "What did Dobb say?"

Looking coy, Kate said, "That I was going to be the prettiest gal at the dance."

Sam chimed in. "Dobb was right. You are shining, gal—just shining." Kate blushed and went back to work. Angelica just could not help herself; she impulsively put down her knife and ran over to hug her Kate. Maria gave her a stern look, and she rushed back over to her bacon. Kate and Desiree stifled giggles.

Sam could hear someone on the stairs and turned to the door, hoping to greet Beth and not Eli. The door opened, and in came

Jenny. Her brown hair was pulled back into a ponytail. She wore a light-blue blouse, dark-blue shirt, and a smile she could not wipe off if she tried. She announced to the room, "Jake Brown is taking me to the dance," and the kitchen erupted into rapid, female chatter. Maria wiped her hands on her apron and walked to Jenny. The girls fell silent as Maria embraced her.

Maria pulled back, narrowed her eyes, and said, "Jake is a rare man. He has taken a shine to you. Don't take dis wrong, but have you been honest with 'im?"

Jenny was not hurt by the question. She knew what she had been. "Yes, he knows. Everybody here knows. He told me it doesn't matter to him. He said what he likes about me is how smart and kind I am. He also said my past makes me a survivor."

Maria laughed. "He said all dat? He must be in love."

Jenny looked warmly at Maria and said, "I think I am too," and the two women hugged again.

Yes, morning in a kitchen can be an entertaining place, Sam thought.

"Back to work," Maria said. "You will have time to cluck with each other like chickens later." Maria poured Jenny a cup of coffee. "Sit. Eat. You have a big day in front of you."

Thoughts of Beth and how the day might play out filled Sam's head. He was so preoccupied he did not think he was hungry—actually wasn't that hungry until eggs and bacon were placed in front of him. Then out came Maria's Dutch oven. This time it contained a cake she called an apple coffeecake. It was so delightful that, for a moment, all he focused on was the pleasure of a well-cooked meal. He was so distracted by the good meal and fine company that he did not hear the footfalls on the stairs. When the kitchen door opened, he was so surprised he almost dropped his fork. He spun around to look at the door.

Beth stepped into the kitchen. Avoiding eye contact with Sam, she grabbed a coffee cup and headed for the pot on the stove. Sam could see that there was something different about her, but at first he couldn't quite put his finger on it. Whatever it was, Beth did not seem to be happy about it. Maria looked to Sam and shrugged her shoulders. The young women all greeted her, but only Jenny gave Beth a second look.

Before Beth could pick up the coffee pot, Maria had it in her hands and was waiting for Beth to hold out her cup. "Good morning," Maria said as she began to see the subtle changes Beth had made to how she was dressed.

Beth glanced quickly at Maria. "Good morning." She took her cup and sat at the head of the table across from Sam. "Good morning, Sam."

Sam watched her as she found her place at the head of the table. Her customary vest was gone. He had never seen her dressed as Eli without a vest or overcoat. Her jeans were still on the baggy side, but she had used one of her beautifully tooled belts with a silver buckle to pull the jeans down to her actual waist size. The new light blue work shirt she wore fit her better than the shirts she had been wearing.

"Good morning," Sam replied. "You look fine this morning."

She looked up and gave him a small, grudging smile. "Thanks."

Sam pressed ever so gently. "Does this mean we are going forward?" Maria put a plate of eggs and bacon down in front of Beth and then just stood there, waiting for Beth to answer Sam's question. Beth reached for the coffeecake and dished a piece up for herself. Feeling Maria's stare, she glanced up at her and said, "Can I help you?"

"Si, you can answer the marshal's question."

Finally, speaking directly to her food, she said, "Yes, for now." Looking to Maria and then to Sam, she added, "But a lot could change by noon."

Jenny was watching the three of them, not understanding what she was seeing or what they were talking about. She picked up a piece of bacon, took a bite, and asked, "What is goin' on here?" She pointed the bacon strip at Eli and continued. "Eli, pardon me for sayin' so, but you're actin' strange."

Beth put down her fork and leaned forward to reassure Jenny everything would be all right, but she didn't manage to get out a single word before Jenny leaped back, knocking over her chair in the process. "You—you!" she stammered, still pointing the bacon at Beth. "You got breasts!" Jenny covered her mouth and just kept pointing. The banging of the chair as it hit the floor along with Jenny's declaration caused everyone in the room to turn toward Beth and freeze. Beth too was frozen in place, stunned by Jenny's words. Sam looked at Beth and could see what had tipped Beth's hand. As she had leaned forward to reassure Jenny, Beth had leaned against the table and pressed her new shirt back just enough to reveal the truth about what had been hiding beneath the cloth.

Beth pushed back in her chair, but it was too late. She looked from Kate to Angelica to Desiree to Maria, and every one of them was staring at her chest. Maria just shrugged. Finally, Beth looked at Sam, who smiled and said, "The cow is out of the barn now! Or should I say, 'the *cows* are out of the barn?'" He stifled a laugh.

Beth did not like this one bit. Besides the embarrassment of having everyone staring at her chest, this was not how she wanted to tell these women. Sam finding humor in the situation just made her mad. Trying to wipe the grin off his face, she said, "This is not funny. Now what do we do?"

Jenny, still in shock, took another step back. "Oh my Lord, oh my Lord!" she cried and began to babble. "Eli, if those are what I think they are…then you're a woman. If you are a woman…well, to think I wanted to kiss you, to have you! This is wrong. What is goin' on here? I demand to know what is goin' on here!" By this time she had backed herself up to the water pump.

Maria looked at the four young women, then to Sam and finally to Beth. "You should just tell them."

Suddenly Kate moaned, and Angelica caught her by the elbow. "I need to sit down," Kate said. Sam jumped up and righted the chair Jenny had knocked over in her panic. Angelica and Desiree brought Kate over to the chair while Jenny pumped her a glass of water. As soon as they had her settled, they all looked back to Sam and Beth.

Sam gestured to the table and said, "Ladies, I think you all should have a seat," and they all pulled chairs up and sat. No one said a word; they just kept staring at Beth, giving her a more critical looking over. Sam gave Beth a wry grin and said, "The floor is yours."

Beth did not want to begin, but what could she do? There seemed to be no going back. She felt cornered. Then a peace started to grow in her. She turned to Sam, and he was gazing at her. It was a warm, steady gaze that seemed to say something, but she couldn't quite make it out.

Taking a deep breath, she said, "You're right, Jenny. I have been deceiving you, all of you, and I am so sorry." Then in a clear tone she added, "I am a woman." Jenny started to stand up again, but Beth, with a voice of command, said, "Jenny, sit down, and please—hear me out." Jenny sank back into her chair. Angelica crossed herself, and Kate just shook her head in disbelief. Desiree, who had seen much sorrow, just waited.

Beth took a drink from her coffee cup and began telling her story, starting back on that black day when the monsters in burlap masks rode into her life. Sam and Maria quietly watched as the four young women heard for the first time from Beth's lips about the horrors of that day. Of course they had heard the story before, but that was more of a legend. This was truth.

As they listened to the tale of a father's decision to transform his little girl into a little boy for her safety, they began to make small, sympathetic sounds. Angelica reached for her mother's hand and held it. When Beth came to the part where her father began to see only Eli—and seemingly had forgotten about Beth altogether—Jenny got up and came around to Beth and sat next to her.

++++——◆——++++

Sam remembered his granddaddy talking about fathers and daughters. They had been sitting together one fine spring evening. Sam had just begun to court Charlie and had arrived home after a ride with her. They had been talking about Charlie and how she had grown up into a beautiful woman. Out of the blue, Granddaddy said, "Ya know, boy, Charlie grew up without a daddy. There will be a wound in her heart because of it." Sam remembered starting to protest, but his granddaddy cut him off. "Oh, I know she thinks of me as her daddy, but it is not the same thing. A father is the most important person in a little gal's life. If he adores her, he can give her a strong start in this world, but if he ignores her or abandons her, he can wound her heart in a way only a loving husband can mend. Ya got some mending to do with Charlie. I'll be right here to help if you need me." With that, he had put his pipe back in his mouth and kept on rocking.

Sam knew that Beth had really been abandoned by her father when she was only five, and he could guess from Jenny's line of work that she had also been abandoned long ago. The wounding they had in common turned Jenny's outrage into sympathy.

As Beth recounted the years of her childhood and on into her teens, Angelica blurted, "But Mr. Ken—I mean, Miss Kennedy, how did you—" She stopped short and looked embarrassedly at Sam. She moved up close to Beth and sat across from Jenny. She asked, with worried concern, "How did you manage the curse?"

"Angelica," Maria scolded.

"It's all right. I don't mind," Beth said. She glanced at the other young women, and from the concerned looks on their face, she knew they all had the same question. Beth smiled and put her hand on Angelica's. "There was a girl I used to play with. Luckily for me, the curse hit her first, and she wanted to tell Eli all about it. If she hadn't, I don't know what I would have done. If it had come without warning, I'm sure I would have thought I was dying. It has been the hardest thing to hide." Knowing glances passed from woman to woman.

By the end of the telling, all of the women were at Beth's end of the table. Sam sat at the foot of the table alone, drinking his coffee. He studied the scene and liked what he saw—his girl, Beth, answering all the questions coming from these young women who had just been let into the biggest secret of their lives. Beth was smiling.

"Back to work, we have a hungry crew to get fed," Maria commanded. As the girls headed back to their work, Maria came over and squeezed Beth's hand and then headed for her stove.

Beth looked up at Sam with a warm smile. He returned the smile and winked at her, thinking, *This has gone well, but these were women. The ranch hands will be another story.*

The sun was high, and the day was already getting hot. Off to the east, thunderheads were beginning to build over the Bear Mountains. The men and women of the Running J who waited for Eli out in front of the old main house to make his announcement were looking for shade. Twenty years earlier, Mrs. Kennedy had planted fruit trees at the southeast end of the house. Now the trees were mature and heavy with apples, pears, and shade. As they waited, the Running J folks were enjoying everything the trees had to offer.

Work for the day had ended early so the folks who were going to the dance could get ready. Jake had asked his crustiest, old, bachelor cowboys to stay behind tonight and watch the Running J and its herd. He had planned to stay himself before Jenny had come onto the ranch. These old boys had no intention of going to the dance anyway. One of them commented, "Hell, I cain't dance, and even if I could, there ain't a gal who would dance with this old, broken-down saddle tramp, and I don't blame 'em."

There was much conversation about what Eli was going to tell the folks who worked and rode for his brand. Most of the talk centered on the rumors that had come back with the cowboys from Smith the night before. Everyone in town had heard about Eli spending time in a dressing room with Sarah Rockport. Slim's wife, a plump gal who was built more like an apple than an hour glass, was talking to a few of her friends in the shade of a pear tree. She spoke with the authority of inside information, said, "Why, I heard he went right into the room with those Mormon women while young

Sarah, wearin' nothin' more than her birthday suit, was tryin' on new underthings. Those Mormons have no shame." Dropping into a more secretive tone, she added, "When he got back to the main house yesterday, he and Maria's boy carried the clothes he bought for Sarah right up to his room. Why, I wouldn't be surprised to see him bring her home within the week." This comment was met with murmurs of agreement and concern. Encouraged by her audience's attentive faces, she voiced her own worry. "Well, he'll just have to become a Mormon himself if he is going to marry that Rockport girl. I'd do anything for Eli Kennedy. Why, workin' for a good, honest young man like Mr. Eli is a pleasure. But if we have to start workin' for some Mormon gal barely outta braids, I don't know. Never liked working for women. They can be mean and spiteful." This was met with a chorus of, "You have got that right," and "Amen, sister."

At eleven fifty-five, the door to the main house opened, and Eli emerged with Marshal McKnight, followed by Maria and all the young women who knew Eli's secret. The Running J folks started to quiet down, anxious to see if they had guessed right.

✦

Beth and Sam had spent the morning in Beth's room talking through how her story would be shared. Beth had just wanted to tell them straight out, and she didn't really see any other way, but Sam argued for coming at the news from the side. He leaned against her desk as she stood at the window gazing out at the ranch, watching all of the hurried activity below. Folks were rushing to finish their chores so they could get ready for the dance. Sam couldn't help but stare at her lovely form. How he wanted to take her into his arms.

They had been going back and forth about how to start and who would do the talking. As she watched the people she had known most of her life, Beth said, "They work for me, Sam. I know them. I care about them. They need to hear this from me. I'm the one who's been lying to them."

Shaking his head, he said, "It took Elma, a keen observer by nature, some time and some touching to convince her you are a woman. Jenny figured it out by accident when she saw your true shape. Being women, they were the easy ones. How are you going to convince the men who have been riding with you for years? They have it in their minds that you're a man. What are you going to do, come out wearing a dress? They will just think that you are Eli gone crazy and that they had better shoot you and put you out of your misery."

Sam came up behind Beth and gently placed his hands on her waist. He said softly into her ear, "There was a powerful king in the ancient world who had committed adultery and murder. His most trusted adviser needed to confront him with the truth before the king's sin destroyed the king and his kingdom." Sam's touch and his breath on her neck had her so distracted she could barely stay focused on what he was saying. Sam whispered, "The adviser knew if he came at the king with the plain truth, the king would fly into a rage and probably kill him." Sam kissed her neck, and she leaned back into him. "So the adviser told the king a story that had the heart of the truth in it, but it was about another made-up man." Beth's body responded to Sam's touch, to his lips. His words began to fade behind a curtain of pleasure. Sam kissed the short hairs at the back of her neck and went on, "The king did fly into a rage. He wanted the man in the story dragged before him so he could punish him. It was then that the wise adviser told the king that the man in the story was the king himself. The king was broken by the truth and did his best to mend what he had done."

Beth turned to him and leaned back against the wall. Sam leaned into her, their faces just inches apart. Looking into his eyes and back to his mouth, wanting to kiss him, she said, "Who will be the adviser, and who will be the bad king?" She crossed the last inch and found his warm lips. This was the passion they had both been forcing down since yesterday morning. The need they felt for each other was strong and growing.

Sam broke from the kiss but not the embrace. "I'll be the adviser, and you will be the heroine."

Pulling reluctantly away, she said, "I don't need you to talk to my folks for me."

"Yes, you do. There is only one way to convince those men without getting shot."

Turning back to him, she said, "And what way is that?"

"Well, darlin', you have to stand right up in front of them and say, 'Boys, I know you thought I was a man but I'm not—and to prove it, I will now strip naked.'" Sam smiled broadly at her, and she started to laugh.

Stepping back to Sam, she put her hand on his chest and said, "There is only one man I intend to get naked for," and began to kiss him again while starting to unbutton his shirt.

"Whoa, gal. You are making me feel like the woman here," he said as he backed up.

"Good. I've been feeling like a man my whole life. It's about time I made a man feel like a woman." There was a mischievous spark in her eyes as she leapt onto Sam, knocking him onto her small bed amidst their laughter. They tickled each other and wrestled, finally spending time kissing. All of these feelings and desires were new to Beth, and she wanted to learn more about them. Sam on the other hand, had learned the art of the lover long ago with his sweet, young wife. He knew the passion building between them could get out of control within moments, and he wanted to be out of control, but this was not the time. There was a straight way and a crooked way, and in Sam's life, there could only be one choice.

At eleven-thirty, Beth stood up, trying to catch her breath, "All right, you can be the adviser, but if I need to, I will step in."

"Fair enough," Sam said, watching her tuck her shirt back into her jeans.

Now they walked together down to the old house that was the hub of activity on the J. The flush of the physical excitement on Beth's face had been replaced by worry. Maria and little Jose trailed right behind them, followed by the softly whispering, young women. Beth was dressed as she had been at breakfast, but she had added a large, dark-blue bandana and her hat. As they were greeted by her hired hands, Sam could feel the tension in her increase.

They stepped up onto the west end of the covered porch and met Jake. Jake was all smiles, thinking he knew what the boss was going to say and looking forward to a night of trying to dance while holding his new gal. They walked to the center of the porch, and folks got up from under the shade of the fruit trees to hear from the employer they respected and rode for. Slim's wife moved to the front of the crowd, waiting to hear her prophecy confirmed.

Eli stepped to the edge of the porch, and all got quiet. Even now Beth did not know where to start. The folks she cared for were all looking up at her, smiling and waiting. "I want to start by thanking you. You are what make the J something special. I am proud of all of you, of your hard work." She paused. "What I've got to say is hard," she began, and she could feel emotion starting to take her. This was not the time or the place to do any of the crying that had become such a bother in the last ten days. She forced it down and looked out at each face. Their expressions had changed. The light-hearted anticipation was gone, replaced by worry and concern for the boss they would do anything for. Beth pressed on, "My good friend, Marshal McKnight, and I have been talking about how to share this news with you, and I have asked him to say a few words." She stepped back, waiting for the axe to fall on her life. This was something she could not fight or run from. She had to stand in the path of this truth and let it crush her life as Eli if she had any chance for a life as Beth.

Sam took Eli's place, and all eyes turned to him. Slim's wife, her authority all washed away, was now convinced that the Running J had been sold out to Dunhill or Larson and they were all out of a job. Sam said, "I want to start by telling you a story about a Scottish highlander."

Sam looked at each face. The crew of the Running J had known trouble was on the horizon ever since William Kennedy had died. They had been ready to fight the Larsons or the Dunhills with just a word from Eli. Now Sam could see a new fear in their faces: the fear of losing the fight before the first shot had been fired. They were worried their young boss had sold out the J after hanging on for so long. Sam wanted to relieve their fear, but for now he figured a little concern was a good thing.

Sam knew cowboys. One of their favorite pastimes, other than pretty gals, riding a good horse, or playing a hand of cards, was storytelling. These men spent a good part of their time out on the range, pushing cattle or sitting around a campfire. Stories were more than a way to pass the time; they were an art form. Sam pushed his hat back and started. "About six hundred years ago there lived a tough, fighting man in Scotland who loved freedom. His name was William Wallace, and he knew no fear. Now, Wallace was not the kind of man who'd go looking for a fight, but if he were pushed, he'd push back harder. Well, the king of England, Edward, was pushing. He wanted the Scots to know that he was the new king of their land. To prove his point the king decreed that his British warlords could sleep with the young Scottish maidens on the night before they were wed to their Scottish bridegrooms."

Slim's wife said, "Do you mean to say that on the night before their weddin', the brides got raped by the redcoats?"

The old cuss who did not want to go to the dance spit tobacco in the dirt and said, "Damned British. Always thinkin' they can do anythin' they want."

Sam continued, "That's right. Well, Wallace and his highlanders weren't going to put up with that tyranny, so they began to strike back. Now remember, this was a time of swords and archers. They fought like the Sioux—small raids at night or an ambush that caught the warlord out in the open alone. Then they would take their time making him pay for his violation with his life or worse." Sam paused here, smiling, and readjusted his jeans. Everyone caught on to his meaning, also smiling and nodding their approval at Wallace's justice. "In no time the warlords who still had their manhood intact were afraid to leave their castles.

"King Edward was furious and, in his anger, made a fatal mistake. He thought if the warlords went to Wallace's villages and killed a few of the women and children, it would take the fight out of the highlanders. The warlords and their soldiers came into the villages while the men were off raiding." Sam got quiet. "The soldiers brought out Wallace's young wife and took turns with her then slit her throat." There were gasps at the frankness of his words. Young Angelica moved into her mother's arms.

"The soldiers worked their way through the village, torturing and killing the womenfolk, young and old, while the old men and young boys who were left in the village were forced at knifepoint to watch. A few of the girl children were saved by the brave acts of their mothers.

"One such brave lassie was Bess Duncan. She had prepared a hiding place for her baby girl if the British or anyone else came raiding. She tucked little Millicent into the hiding hole and prayed that the little baby girl would sleep and not cry. God answered her prayer. The soldiers dragged Bess out and did the work of the devil. All through her torture, Bess listened for her sweet baby girl, but little Millie never made a peep." Sam looked to Beth.

"Seeing the smoke from the village, Wallace and his men rode hard, praying they weren't too late. As they reached the rise above the village, they could see the carnage—women and children's half-naked bodies lying dead in the dirt and old men kneeling by them, wailing in grief. Down the hill they rode into the midst of the suffering, leaping from their horses to embrace the bodies of the loved ones they were too late to rescue."

All of the ranch folks had fallen silent now. "Liam Duncan, Wallace's right-hand man, searched for his Bess. He found his beloved's body thrown facedown over a crate. The brave young Scot pulled off his cloak and covered his lass's nakedness. He held her small frame in his warrior's arms as sobs of grief rocked him. How could he go on when the one he lived for was gone?

"The cry of a baby girl brought him back to the present. There was another life that gave him the breath he needed. Liam gently carried his beloved into his small cottage and laid her on their bed. He kissed Bess's face, knowing her last act in this world had been to save their baby girl. He went to the hiding hole and found a very hungry and wet little Millie. Cradling his precious baby girl, Liam marveled at how God had spared her. She smiled up at her daddy and reached for his face. At that moment he swore to God that the fate of her mother would never touch Millie. A plan began to form in Liam's mind. Before he avenged his wife's blood he had to make sure his daughter would be safe, even if he never returned.

"After meeting Millie's immediate needs, he took her and rode to his clan in the hills. His grandmother lived tucked away by a mountain stream. She was a hearty lover of life that could stand up to anything or anyone. Liam didn't doubt she could still give him a good thrashing if she put her mind to it.

"Through tears of unimaginable loss, Liam told his grandmother what had happened to his Bess, of his oath to God, and of his plan to keep Millie safe. 'From this day forward,' he said, 'Little Millie will become Micah. You will raise her as a boy to keep her safe from the English.' His grandmother argued with him, but in the end, not wanting to make him suffer more, she gave in." Listening to Sam's words brought Beth back to that night, where, in love-crazed grief, her father changed the course of her life. She knew Liam Duncan.

"The next day, Liam joined Wallace's men, and together they rode into the camp of the British lord responsible for the deaths of their wives and children. The British were caught by surprise. Wallace and his men showed no mercy, killing all down to the last man and sending a message of defiance to King Edward. Brave Liam, sword in hand, fought like a lion, cutting down a dozen men himself before an archer's arrow found his broken heart. In moments, he was back in the waiting arms of his Bess."

Slim's wife spoke up, "But what about Millie?" Everyone wanted to know. So far the story had worked.

"Liam's grandmother raised Millie as a boy. Millie was a hard worker, strong, and fit. When she was nine, she could outrun every boy in the village. Her great-grandmother treated her as Micah during the day, but in the evening when the two of them were alone, Great-Grandmother welcomed Millie back into her arms." Beth listened to Sam's tale, wishing she had been welcomed into her father's arms each night as herself. Sam said, "But as Millie grew into the lovely image of her mother, it became harder to hide the truth, so Great-Grandmother kept her close to home up in the highlands.

"By Millie's sixteenth birthday, things had changed in Scotland. There was an uneasy peace with the new British king, and the Scottish lords were in charge of the country. The danger had passed for the time. So Millie's great-grandmother made a decision. Her beautiful great-granddaughter would be reborn.

"A festival was to be held celebrating Wallace's victory some sixteen years before. There would be dancing and song. On that night, Great-Grandmother brought Millie down dressed in a spring skirt with flowers in her long blonde hair instead of the warrior's ponytail she and most of the young men wore. There were gasps and shocked murmurings, but dressed in her peasant's blouse and skirt, there was no denying she was a lass. A young highlander, who had been beaten by her in a race as a boy, came up and took her hand, leading her out to the center of the dance. He fell in love with her that night, and she with him for being the first to accept her. They would later wed and have a basketful of children. Their first was a beautiful girl they named Bess, followed by a brave little buck they named Liam— Liam McKnight." Sam glanced to Beth, whose eyes had grown wide at his use of the name McKnight.

Slim's wife was too busy wiping away tears to speak, so Slim took this rare opportunity and said, "You oughta write that down, Marshal. It's a better story than most of the penny dreadful stuff in Ed's store." He took off his hat and scratched his bald head. "But what I don't understand is, what has Scotland got to do with Smith and the Running J?"

Sam took his opening and said, "Slim, you and your dear wife like this story because the wild and dangerous land of old Scotland has nothing on northern Utah twenty years ago or even today."

Jesus said, "Hell, we all know what 'appened right here."

Pointing to where they were standing Sam said, "That's right Jesus, seventeen years ago, men in burlap masks rode up to this house to do evil. I'm sorry to be so blunt, ladies, but I must. They raped Eli's mother and sister." Once again, Beth could hear the screams of her sister. "These monsters shot and killed a five-year-old child. Finally, they spilt the woman's blood on the ground beneath your feet." The women who were standing with their husbands clung to them as they pictured the terror that had happened where they now stood.

"I didn't know William Kennedy, but most of you did. From what I've heard in the last few days, I know he was a good man. I have also heard he was never the same after he returned to find his family slaughtered on that dark day." Nods of quiet agreement moved through the crowd like a breeze over grass.

Sam took off his hat. "I know the pain of losing a beloved wife, but I cannot imagine adding the loss of a daughter and son." He let the word *son* float out across them. There were a few fleeting looks back and forth between folks who were not sure they had heard him right. Cutting his eyes to Beth, he could see her body stiffen, getting ready to take the blow he hoped the story had been able to deflect.

Sam's granddaddy had always said, "When yer workin' with folks, it's best to just wait and say nothin'. Never worry about too much silence." Sam had had great success following this advice. He would let them ask the question.

Slim's wife, always ready to correct a man, obliged him. She said as if she were correcting a five-year-old boy, "Pardon me, Marshal, but you meant to say daughters."

He took one step down the front stairs and calmly said to her, "Mary and son, Elijah." Slowly the light of the truth began to dawn on the folks of the Running J, and all eyes began to turn to Beth. Being a shy person by nature, all of this staring made her ears begin to turn red. Never one to turn from trouble, she stepped forward into the intense scrutiny and stood beside Sam.

Sam, impressed by her courage, said, "William Kennedy was crushed by his loss that day. After burying his wife and two of his three children, he sat in this house and made the same choice Liam Duncan made. He would protect his little girl from the torture only women can suffer by hiding her in plain sight as a boy." By this time Maria, Jenny, and the young women from the kitchen had moved in behind Beth and Sam. "Kennedy here cares for you folks, and *her* greatest fear today is that you will not be able to accept the truth about her. Yes, *she* has been lying to you folks every day for the past seventeen years. The truth is, it has not been some tough, young buck who has been leading this spread through tough and dangerous times. It has been the courageous daughter of William Kennedy, Elizabeth, trying with all of heart to do what her daddy asked her to."

Beth took off her hat. "I am so sorry that keeping the promise to my father meant lying to all of you. Please forgive me." She paused and then firmly said, "But if you can't, I will understand." Turning her hat in her hand and biting her lip, she went on. "Just so you know, I intend to keep right on going where I have been going with the J, but now I will do it as Elizabeth Kennedy." She looked out on their stunned and confused faces and saw doubt and some anger. "If you can't abide working for a woman, I will understand. Frankly, until recently, I felt the same way. You can come by the main house, and I will settle up with you. No hard feelings, but it is my hope that you will all stay. The fact is, this...*gal*...needs your help."

Soft whispering started at the back of the crowd and moved forward. Beth gave Sam a discouraged look. Little knots of cowhands and women formed. They were talking with quiet intensity. Beth and Sam could see some finger pointing and headshaking going on in each group.

Maria moved up beside Beth and took her hand. "We, the girls and me—you know we are with you."

"Thank you, Maria," Beth whispered. She turned and gave a grateful glance to Jenny and the girls, but the conversations out in front of them were not as reassuring. Jake stepped off the porch and motioned for Jenny to follow him. Beth watched them as they began to talk. Jake was deadly serious. He said a few words, and Jenny protested. Jake glanced up at Beth and saw she was looking at them. He turned his back to her and continued talking with Jenny.

Watching her ranch family, Beth said, "Oh, Sam, this is what I was afraid of." She took a moment to recover her control. "Jake and my crew won't follow Elizabeth."

Sam looked out across the crowd and then turned to her. With quiet confidence he said, "Just wait. These are good folks, hand picked by your father and by you. They just got some unbelievable news. Give them some time and have a little faith."

Slim's wife elbowed Slim hard in the side. "Ouch, stop it, Myrtle," he said.

Myrtle pushed him forward. "Well, get up there, husband, and tell her what you just said."

Slim took off his hat. Beth braced herself for the worst. "Boss—I mean, ma'am...uh...miss...oh, hell..." There were snickers behind him. He looked back at Myrtle and got another threatening glance followed by an encouraging nod. "Me and most of these boys have been workin' for your father and the Runnin' J most of our working lives. Hell, Jesus over there was with your daddy on that terrible day." He looked back at Myrtle, and she was smiling, so he began to relax into this unfamiliar land of public speaking. "Miss Kennedy, I've known you since you were a boy...uh, girl of twelve." To Beth's surprise, Slim paused here.

Slim coughed to hide his emotion and went on. "From that day forward, I have admired you, and I know the boys have too. Hell, most boys of twelve are lazy and no 'count, but you were always a hard-workin' little buck. Damn, even then you was as honest as the day is long. If you said you were goin' to do something, you did. That was true then and it is true now. We"—he motioned to the folks standing behind him—"have been proud to ride for you. You are the smartest, toughest boss I know of, but more important, Miss Kennedy, you are kind. Hell, you got a heart o' gold. The way you treat our families, like they was your own kin."

Myrtle had her hand over her mouth, stunned and proud of what she had started.

Slim motioned to the boys to step up, and they did. "Damn it, the J is our home, and you, Miss Kennedy, are our boss. We owe you everything, and come hell or high water, we are the crew of the Runnin' J."

Myrtle grabbed Slim and gave him a big kiss.

"Damn, Slim. You should run for office," Jesus said. Everyone laughed, and the weight of Beth's fear began to lift. Then Jake stepped up onto the porch.

He had Jenny by the hand, and she had been crying. Jake walked right up to Beth, and Sam stepped back to let them face each other. The man she trusted with her life, who had been Beth's right hand for the last four years, stared deep into her eyes. She could not tell what he was thinking; she had no idea what to expect, but she thought the worst. Maybe he would strike her for her lie; she felt she deserved it. Jake shifted his stance, and Beth was ready to accept the blow. His hand did come up, not to strike, but to offer. Jenny smiled with a reassuring nod at Beth. Beth grabbed the offered hand and shook it as Jake's face broke into a broad smile.

Jake said, "So, boss, when are we leaving for the dance?"

As Jake turned and shook Sam's hand, Beth faced the people of the Running J and said, "We'll head out at two, dressed for fun, but arm yourselves for trouble." Whoops and hollers went up, and everyone started off to get ready for a night that promised to be full of adventure, at the very least.

After lunch Sam went up to his room to change and found a new suit laid out for him with a note in Beth's handwriting. Sam picked it up as if it were laced with dynamite; after all, the last note he got from her knocked him on his tail.

He unfolded the paper and read:

> Dear Sam,
>
> Thank you for today and for everything. I begin to see a new road before me—a road of hope, and I want to go down it. I am wondering if you are now that road, but for now I will follow the advice of the wise, old Texas Ranger and be patient.
>
> The suit is from my fairy godmother. She said to tell you, "Samuel, the prince must look his part. Don't worry about the fit. This fairy godmother knows her men's sizes." Should I be jealous? See you at 1:45.
>
> Yours,
> Elizabeth

Elma was right. She knew her men's sizes. The rich, brown suit fit him perfectly. The pants were his exact waist and length, the tan vest fit his chest like a glove, and the frock coat accommodated his broad shoulders and well-muscled arms. Elma had been paying attention to the details of Sam's rig because the suit matched Sam's hat and boots.

Looking in the mirror, he thought, *I haven't looked this good since my wedding day.* After dressing, he headed out to the stable to hitch up the buggy. When he entered the barn, the buggy was already hitched up to a glossy, black gelding. Jake stood by the gelding's head, tightening down the last buckle.

"Thank you, Jake," Sam said.

"Oh, you don't have to thank me. It blessed me to do it," Jake said, a little embarrassed. "This here gelding is named Rowdy, but he's a far sight smarter than his namesake." He smiled.

"Jake, I think you're having just a little too much fun working this horse." Sam chuckled.

"Not possible. Oh, and I figured you might want to take Buck, so he is all brushed and combed. You just need to saddle him."

"Why, Jake, thank you again." Jake began to protest, and Sam said, "I know, I know. It blessed you to do it. Well, thank you anyway, friend." Sam offered his hand. Jake stepped forward and took it.

"I'm in this to the end," Jake said.

"I know you are."

Sam stepped to where Buck was stabled. Buck looked like he was ready for a parade, and he knew it. He was stomping his hooves, anxious to be on the move.

Smiling to himself, Sam said, "Boy, you are almost as vain as me. We make a dandy pair." Then he saddled him.

Now the buggy and Buck were out front waiting. Sam had put his gun belt and both .44s on the floorboard of the rig. His Winchester was in the scabbard on Buck.

At 1:44 p.m. the door to Beth's bedroom opened. Maria and Angelica had been with her for the last hour. Angelica came out first, dressed in a lovely, white skirt and blouse, the perfect match of innocence and beauty. Maria came next in a dress befitting a good wife but with just enough color to have a little fun. Then came Beth.

Angelica watched Sam to see his reaction, and she was not disappointed. As Beth came out onto the landing, the sight of her took

Sam's breath away. His face reflected his appreciation for the beauty before him. The dress amplified everything feminine about Beth: the blue sash around her slim waist, the lace framing the swell of her breasts, and the blue flowers that matched those eyes he could not get enough of. The only thing that seemed out of place was the gun belt that hung from her left hand, but Sam was not at all surprised to see she wasn't leaving her twin Colts behind.

Sam took three steps up the stairs and offered her his hand, saying, "Cinderella, you are beautiful. Our carriage awaits."

She blushed. Mustering all the grace she could, which wasn't much, she started down the stairs to Sam. He took her hand and her gun belt and led her out to the buggy.

The rest of the folk of the Running J had gathered around the front of the house to see their boss in a dress. When she came through the front door, she was met with gasps of pure delight and surprise. The surprise then broke into spontaneous applause. Sam came around to her side of the buggy and offered her his hand. She looked at it and back at him. Reluctantly she put her hand in his and let herself be helped into her seat. Beth hadn't been helped into anything since she was six. Sam climbed up beside her, grabbed the buggy whip, and gave Rowdy a little snap on the rear.

✦

The closer they got to the 7C, the more anxious Beth became. *The Smith Herald* would have come out at noon. Elma's stories were eagerly awaited every Friday. The good articles often spread like wildfire. Beth imagined her story had created some heat. She had been overwhelmed by how her own people had accepted her, but she did not expect the same from the townsfolk or the crew of the 7C. She looked at Sam and her crew riding behind her, and a peace started to settle over her. *Sam and my friends accept me as I really am. To hell with the colonel and his folks. The only opinions I care about are those of the folks around me right now,* but then she thought, *What about Ed?*

As they rounded the last bend before the main gate of the 7C, Beth could hear shouts of, "There she is," and, "Look, here she comes!" Apparently Elma's edition of *The Smith Herald* had done its work. There were stares and fingers pointing, and everywhere she looked, people were talking about her. Standing at the hitching rail in front of the stable was Ed with a look of disapproval on his broad face.

Ed took Rowdy's lead and tied him off then stepped to Beth's side of the buggy. He offered his hand to help her down and said, "Miss Kennedy." She warily put her hand into his, but as she leaned forward, he suddenly swept her off her feet and into his arms. He spun her one- hundred and twenty pounds around as if she were a little girl on her first day of school. Holding her in his arms he said, "Little K, I always knew there was something wrong about the way Bill treated you, I just couldn't put my finger on it. Seeing how lovely you are, I don't know how I could have ever have missed it, but I am so sorry I did. Can you ever forgive me?" He set her down.

Barely able to catch her breath, she said, "Ed, old friend, it is I who need to do the apologizing. Of course I forgive you."

"Thank you, little K. 'Course, you could've told me." He was now smiling from ear to ear as he asked, "Can this crusty, old man give this pretty girl a kiss?"

Not knowing the right response to this question, she nodded yes. He kissed her like an uncle would, on the forehead. George and Maggie had stepped up to greet her next as a crowd of townsfolk gathered to welcome Miss Kennedy. There were many more hugs and kisses. Sam stayed in the buggy, happily watching, awestruck by how his Father had worked things out.

Elma stepped up beside Sam, smiling. "Looks like our Elizabeth is doin' just fine."

"That must have been one amazing story you wrote for the *Herald*."

"The story wrote itself. I hardly had a thing to do with it. Oh, and, Samuel, you were right. By two there wasn't a paper left in town. I should have printed one hundred more."

Sam jumped out of the buggy and hugged Elma. Kissing her on the cheek, he said, "Thank you. We couldn't have done it without you."

Blushing, she said, "I hope John saw that. It would be good for him to be a little jealous for once."

Not everyone was happy to see Elizabeth Kennedy. The crowd around Beth began to break up as folks followed the sound of a fiddle into the barn. Laurie Dunhill had been standing on the veranda with her father watching all of the happy greetings. She turned to her father and said, "The nerve of that, that…"—she spat the word—"*woman*. Showing up here after all of her lies." She slammed the glass of tea she had been drinking down on to the table and marched down the front stairs of the house to confront Beth and Sam at the barn doors.

＋＋＋＋———◆———＋＋＋＋

The colonel watched her go, admiring his daughter's strength and wishing his son had an ounce of the same power. His gaze moved to Beth, and memories came flooding back to him. She was the image of her mother, with the added strength she had gained from life as a man. How he missed her mother—dancing with her, the feel of her, the smell of her.

＋＋＋＋———◆———＋＋＋＋

With barely concealed fury and a forced smile, Laurie said, "Welcome, *Miss* Kennedy, to the Seven-C."

"Thank you, Laurie. I hope you can forgive me for deceiving you all these years."

"I suppose I'll have to. Everyone else seems to have done so once they read that degenerate woman's paper."

Beth winced at the insult to Elma. She was taken aback by Laurie's venom. In childhood, she had seen Laurie be mean to the girls in their schoolhouse, but that anger had never been turned on Eli.

Laurie stepped in close, and Sam got ready to break them apart if a fight broke out. "Was it fun for you, toying with me all those years, making a fool out of me? Everyone knows I had my cap set for Eli, and now you have made me into a laughingstock."

"No. I never meant to hurt you. I cherished our friendship, and I hope we can be friends again."

"Hah." Laurie scoffed. "That will be the day. So far, Elizabeth, you have managed to make this evening all about you. Well, this is *my* night, and I'm not going to let some ugly, little saddle tramp spoil it."

Before she could turn to go, Sam said, "Oh, you are right, Miss Dunhill. There is some ugliness here, and it is dripping from the center of that spoiled, little heart of yours. Now, if I were you, I'd shut my filthy, little mouth."

"Well, you're not me and—"

Sam cut her off. "Shut your mouth, or your daddy is going to find out about you and young Mr. Johnson 'riding' on the way into town yesterday."

Laurie's eye widened, and Sam knew he had guessed right, so he pressed on. "Now, I'm sure he is not the first, and if the US Marshal's office in Boston did a little digging, I'll bet they would find other men your daddy would not approve of, but if you play nice and pretend to be a lady, I'll be happy to let the illusion stand." Sam stared directly into her eyes, waiting for her to deny his words. Laurie stared straight back, unwilling to back down but not wanting the truth about herself to be revealed to anyone, let alone her daddy.

Finally, she flashed a mock smile. "I hope you both have a lovely evening." She turned and walked away to greet other guests.

Beth leaned into Sam, looked up at him, and said, "I guess I always knew how mean she was. I saw her torment the girls in our schoolhouse, most especially Vickie Larson. She was a bully, but the teacher never caught her at it. In fact, she was the teacher's pet. And I didn't see it because I was in her inner circle—and I was a boy."

Sam gazed down at her and touched her face. "Darlin', you were never a boy, and I praise God for that. Now, forget that poor, unhappy woman, and let's go dancing. And remember, the man leads." He kissed her softly.

Holding him tight, she said, "Lead on, McKnight."

Thunderheads were climbing high in the south as Sam and Beth entered the barn. The large structure had been cleaned and polished for the occasion. Colorful sashes and summer flowers adorned every post. A small band was up in the hayloft at the north end of the barn playing the strings off their instruments. The ground floor was already filled with folks dancing and laughing, but no one seem to be enjoying themselves as much as Patrick O'Rourke.

He was whirling around the barn floor with the very girl who had laid him out with a frying pan the day before. Being knocked out by Maggie must have made her a challenge to him. O'Rourke's waxed mustache was resting on one of the jolliest smiles Sam had ever seen. When he saw Sam and Beth, he released his out-of-breath partner and bowed to her. Maggie curtsied back.

"Ah, thank ya kindly, darlin'. Ya're a marvelous dancer. Now don't go far. I'll be lookin' for ya later."

Maggie, enjoying the giant Irishman immensely said, "Sir, if I am not in my husband's arms, I am yours."

O'Rourke strode up to Beth, came to attention, clicked his heels together, and bowed to her. As he rose, he took her hand and kissed it. To Beth's astonishment, she could see a tear rolling down the big man's face. He said, "Oh, lassie. I read yer story in the paper. And to tell ya the truth, I soaked two handkerchiefs in the readin'. I never read a story I liked more."

Beth, not knowing what to say, said, "Thank you?"

Never releasing her hand, he said, "Ya'er welcome, darlin'. Will ya do me the great honor of dancing with this broken-down, old soldier?"

She looked to Sam. He shrugged and said, "I'll be over by the punch."

Beth nodded to O'Rourke, and he whisked her out onto the dance floor.

Sam walked to the east side of the barn where Maggie's pies and the rest of the food had been laid out. The spread smelled and looked delicious. Sam poured two classes of punch, knowing Beth would need something to cool her off after her workout with the whirling dervish. He sipped his and immediately knew there was a little more than punch in it. Just then O'Rourke came spinning by with Beth and asked, "Do ya like the punch, Marshal, darlin'?" and winked as he spun away to the other end of the floor. Sam liked this Irishman.

While he waited for his turn to dance with the lovely Miss Kennedy, Sam took the opportunity to scan the barn to see where a threat might come from. There were men stationed at the doors, front and back. Sam could see Laurie talking to one of them. The gunman was Johnson. The barn looked secure enough. Sam would have put someone in the loft to make sure, but the colonel had done more than a good job securing the entire compound. It would take a small army to breach his defenses.

The music ended, and O'Rourke brought Beth back to Sam. "Ah, thank you, Miss Kennedy. It was a true pleasure." With that said, he took the two glasses of punch out of Sam's hands. He gave one to Beth and drank the other glass in one gulp. "Thank ya, Marshal, darlin'. That's just what the doctor ordered."

Taking Beth's hand, Sam asked O'Rourke, "May I?"

O'Rourke bowed. "Be my guest, but be careful. She wants to steer the ship."

As the fiddler began to play a waltz, Sam led her out onto the floor. He put his hand on her waist, and she put hers on his shoulder. He took her free hand and began leading her around the floor. Soon she fell into his rhythm. The two of them were in the moment, holding each other and moving to the music.

The thunderheads continued to build, and the late afternoon grew dark. The breeze began to pick up with light rain starting to fall. The sweet aroma of a summer shower blew through the barn. Smelling the rain, Sam thought the colonel had made a good choice to have the dance in the barn. At that moment, eight cowboys from outside stepped into the barn wearing slickers with their hats pulled down against the rain. They pulled the large barn doors closed, front and back.

Sam and Beth continued to dance. His heart was full. He needed to tell her what he knew was true. "Beth?"

She looked up with an openness to him he had not seen from her. "Yes?"

"Beth, I…" Something was wrong. Movement caught his eye. He followed it to where Johnson was standing. The movement had been Johnson being knocked to the ground by one of the cowboys who had come in out of the rain. The cowboy now had a bandana tied around his face. He was tall, and the slicker could not hide his powerful build. Sam knew at once it was Rowdy Larson, and he was holding the scattergun he had just taken away from Johnson.

Beth, seeing the sudden concern on Sam's face, said, "Sam, what's wrong?"

At that moment, the deafening crack and roar of the scattergun brought screams and confusion.

The shotgun blast had been Johnson meeting a bloody end at the north end of the barn. After Rowdy knocked him down, Johnson had struggled back to his feet and reached for his new Remington. Before he could clear leather, Rowdy proved to the young gunman that he wasn't as fast as he thought. The scattergun had almost blown him in half.

Blood had sprayed onto Laurie, who had been standing near Johnson. Another gunman, Roland, Sam thought, now had Laurie by the waist with his gun pointed at her defiant head. This had put a clamp on the colonel's mouth, as he now stood in barely controlled fury at that same end of the barn. Rowdy and Roland shared a look of amusement at the damage done to Johnson's body by the scatter-gun. Sam could see Roland snickering. The other gun hands had spread out and had everyone covered.

Two of the men who had been guarding the doors had joined Rowdy's crew. *So someone on the inside got Rowdy past the colonel's defenses,* Sam thought. They had disarmed the colonel's one-eyed foreman and tied him to a chair. Two of Rowdy's crew had climbed into the loft to cover the crowd. Guns were trained on everyone who could make a fight.

In just a moment, the eight men had taken control of the barn. The attack was well planned, so he knew Rowdy wasn't responsible for it. Sam was frustrated at himself for not being armed. He had felt trouble coming but could not imagine gunplay at this dance. Wrong again, and now his .44s were stored out in the buggy, and his Winchester was still on Buck. The only weapon he had on him was the knife in his boot. He pulled Beth close to him. She too was longing for her Colts, and she also knew the gunman who had just committed murder was Rowdy.

Laurie yelled angrily at the men who had been guarding the doors, "Traitors! My daddy's been good to you, and you repay him with treachery. You will hang for this!"

Roland pulled the hammer back on his Remington. "Oh, shut up!"

"I will not!" Laurie struggled to break free.

"Baby girl, be quiet. These men do not care who you are. I will handle this." The colonel turned to Rowdy and said, "This is an outrage. How dare you come on into my home and…"

Rowdy nodded to a gunman wearing a muddy, black hat and a black bandana pulled up to just below his eyes. Black Bandana holstered the gun he had been holding in his right hand. He stepped up and pounded his right fist into the colonel's gut. The colonel doubled over, staggering back against the doors of the barn, but did not go down. There were screams of shock and fear from the women in the crowd. Black Bandana grabbed the colonel by his tie, straightened him up, and pulled him over to Rowdy. He then pushed the colonel to his knees and in front of Rowdy and, with a flourish, bowed as if he were making an offering.

What is going on? I have not seen this outlaw with Rowdy before, Sam thought. It was all Sam could do to just stand, but for Beth's sake, he would hold his ground. He looked at O'Rourke, knowing how loyal he was to the colonel. The big man's jaw was set, and his fists were clenched, but for now, he too was waiting for an opening.

Rowdy lifted the colonel's chin with the barrel of the scattergun. "We will just have to beg yer pardon for this outrage, 'Dunghill.' Ya can get back to yer little soiree if you give me what I want."

Still gasping for breath, the colonel said, "What do you want?"

With smug glee, Rowdy said, "Now, that was more like it, 'Dunghill.' Ya asked that real gentlemanly. Didn't he ask real gentlemanly, boys?" There were laughs and hoots from his crew. Then Rowdy said flatly, "We want Eli Kennedy. Now where is he?"

A smile began to form on the colonel's face, and then he began to laugh. "If you are looking for Eli Kennedy, you are too late. He is dead, shot in the back."

"What are you sayin'?" Rowdy sputtered, dumbfounded by the news. "When did this happen?"

"Seventeen years ago."

Rowdy, impatient with the nonsense coming from the colonel, smacked him alongside the head with the flat side of the butt of his scattergun. "What the hell're ya talkin' about?" The rain was coming down hard now—lightning then a thunder crack.

Pushing himself up on one elbow, apparently more than happy to give Beth up, the colonel said, "Eli Kennedy has been dead for seventeen years." Rowdy raised the butt of the scattergun again. "But— if you are looking for his lying twin sister, who has been impersonating him all these years, *Elizabeth* Kennedy is somewhere near the marshal."

Not knowing what to do with this strange information, Rowdy said to Roland, "Let her go and come here." Roland released Laurie, who then headed straight to her father. Rowdy motioned Black Bandana to join him, and the three of them talked over this new information. Beth closed her eyes at the colonel's words. So much for considering the 7C as her home.

Sam took Beth's hand and leaned near her ear. "Stay close. They are here for you. Play it smart. The important thing is to stay alive. Being a woman might help."

She looked at him with confusion, "What?"

"If they came to kill you, they would have killed Eli right off, but now that they know you are a woman, I'm betting Rowdy will want to toy with you." Turning his back to Rowdy and pulling her into a tight embrace, he continued whispering in her ear. "I know you will want to fight and that you could probably hurt him, but if you do, he will kill you." He pulled back and met her eyes. "Beth, I love you. Stay alive for me. I'll be coming." He kissed her.

"I will stay alive."

Rowdy's voice boomed across the room. "Now, if no one does anything stupid, they won't get killed like this dumb piece of crap. Now where is *Eli-za-beth* Kennedy?" He began scanning the guests for Beth.

A gruff, mean-eyed Mexican yelled to Rowdy, "Hey, look what I found!"

Rowdy pushed through the crowd to Mean Eyes, who had Jenny by the arm and his pistol pointed at Jake. Rowdy, delighted, said, "Well, my God, Colonel. I had no idea you invited whores to your *home*." Looking at Mean Eyes he said, "Now this is my kind of party." He grabbed Jenny by the hair and pulled her to him. Looking her up and down with greedy eyes, he said, "Oh, we have had some fun, ain't we, Jenny girl?"

She spat in his face. Rowdy raised the scattergun to strike her.

Jake, not able to see his Jenny harmed, charged at Rowdy.

Jenny screamed, "No, Jake!"

Rowdy's scattergun leveled at Jake. O'Rourke, who had been standing behind Jake, grabbed him by the shoulder, spinning him around. He hit Jake with a right cross that most likely broke his jaw. Jake bounced off the floor in an unconscious pile. Rowdy pointed the scattergun at O'Rourke. "Who asked ya to stick yer big Mick nose in?"

"It's just my nature to be helpful, sonny."

"We don't need yer help. So stay out of it." Rowdy still had Jenny by the hair, and he pulled her in close. "So ya like that saddle tramp. Well, ya can have him, whore. Lord knows there is hardly a man in this barn that hasn't had ya." He and his crew laughed as he released her hair, back-handing her hard in the mouth. She fell next to Jake.

"That's if he can stand the sight of ya when I'm through with ya."
He raised his boot to stomp her face with his spur.

That was enough. Sam and O'Rourke began to move. No matter how outgunned Sam was, he would rather die than stand by and watch an animal like Rowdy Larson do his pleasure. Apparently O'Rourke was of the same mettle, but before either man could get himself killed, Beth's voice rang out loud and clear.

"Stop!" Beth shouted. "If beating a woman makes you feel like a man, here I am—unless you're afraid I might hurt you."

"Beth?" Sam said, begging her with his eyes to go easy.

"Why, looky here, boys. Eli is wearin' a dress." Rowdy started to laugh, and his crew joined him. He turned to Mean Eyes and Black Bandana, "Keep yer guns on the marshal and this big, dumb Mick." The men both stepped in closer to Sam and O'Rourke, easing back the hammers on their guns.

Rowdy walked to Beth, chuckling to himself. "My, my…you do make a fine girl. A little lackin' upstairs, but I bet the rest is choice." He circled around her, taking a good look. "Yes, fine indeed. Boys, I believe we're goin' to have a little more fun than we had planned." Hoots and catcalls were followed by a thunderclap. Sam's fury was building with the storm.

In front of her once again, Rowdy pounded her chest with the same forefinger Beth had made him pull back just two days before. "You been actin' pretty high and mighty, ridin' around here in your britches all these years." He hit her hard enough with his finger to push her back with each poke. "Hell, all the time ya was nothin' more than a damn, lyin' woman! How the hell did ya kill three good men this week? Maybe you ain't a girl. I heard of men who like to wear dresses. Maybe you're one of them. Let's find out," and his finger began to slide to Beth's right breast.

Beth had had enough of that finger. With the same lightning speed she had used to kill Rowdy's three men, Beth's right hand came up and grabbed Rowdy's finger, bending it back. Rowdy screamed like a little girl as Beth broke his finger at the base at the same time as she used her left hand to pull off his bandana.

＋＋＋＋————◆————＋＋＋＋

Lightning flashed, and thunder clapped as time stood still. The action of tearing the mask off Rowdy caused Beth's memory to spin back to the monster in the burlap mask. Once again she was running with Eli to the hiding place. Eli was pulling her along, but she had looked back to see if her mama was all right. She remembered her mama had said to the monster, "You can't hide behind that mask. God and I both know who you are!" Her mother had reached forward and pulled the mask off the monster. Then she slapped him. For the first time Beth could see the face clearly. The monster had looked to her at just that moment. He knew she had seen his face. That day when Eli was killed trying to save her, the bullet was meant for her.

＋＋＋＋————◆————＋＋＋＋

Sam watched Beth break Rowdy's finger and just shook his head. If this was her idea of taking it easy, he couldn't imagine what her idea of fighting back might look like.

At that moment, Black Bandana's pistol came crashing down on the back of Beth's head, and down she went. Lightning struck near the house, rattling all the glasses at the punch bowl. Sam could see the blood begin to flow from the back of Beth's head.

Oh Lord, please don't let this happen again. Use me. Take me, he prayed. He sensed a whisper in reply. *Wait.* He did not like it, but there it was. He had learned to follow this gentle guiding, so he waited.

Rowdy was whimpering in pain. He pushed his finger back into place and tied his now- discarded bandana around his hand to hold the finger in place. He reached down and grabbed Beth by the front of her dress hoping to strike at her and make her pay for his ruined

• 225 •

finger, but she was out cold. She dangled at the end of his arm like a rag doll. All he managed to do was tear free a few of the buttons in the front of her dress, exposing her corset.

He yanked her up on her feet and threw her over his shoulder. He shouted to his crew, "Boys, we're goin'!" And the gunmen started to make a covered retreat. Rowdy turned to Mean Eyes and Black Bandana and said, "Kill the marshal, Dunhill, and the big Mick now. I don't want them on my trail." He turned to the door and started out.

Black Bandana stepped up to the marshal and placed the barrel of his high-grade Colt against Sam's forehead. "This is for my hand."

Big mistake getting this close to me, Sam thought. Lightning struck the windmill in the center of the compound. The crash was deafening. Sam's left hand swept up, grabbing the Colt and yanking Black Bandana off balance. Sam slammed him with a head butt, pulled the gun out of the stunned gunman's hand, and shot Mean Eyes in the forehead before the sound of the thunder died away.

As Mean Eyes's dead body fell toward the floor, his .45 swung in Sam's direction. Knowing the gun might go off reflexively in the outlaw's death throes, Sam pulled the dazed Black Bandana in front of him as a shield. The .45 boomed, and Black Bandana's body jerked. Sam felt a searing pain in his side that he recognized all too well. He looked down, and sure enough, the bullet had blown through Black Bandana about kidney high and still had enough energy to graze Sam. He could feel the trickle of blood starting down his side.

Black Bandana started to go limp in Sam's hands. The wound was mortal and would take the outlaw quickly. Sam eased him to the floor. He needed information from the dying man and he did not have much time. Sam pulled off the gunman's hat and bandana, knowing who he would find.

Fear and pain filled Quentin Dunhill's eyes. There were gasps of shock and surprise from those standing near the dying man. Laurie Dunhill, supporting her father, came close and began to cry.

"Quentin, how could you?" She turned to her father, not wanting to see the truth. The colonel just stared down with disgust at his dying son.

Quentin's eyes searched Sam's face, knowing he would get the truth from the marshal. "Am I dying?"

"Yes, Quentin, you are."

With smoldering hatred, Quentin cut his eyes to the colonel. "Well, Father, you are finally getting your wish." Thunder from another lightning strike somewhere behind the main house roared through the barn. Quentin's body shuddered.

Sam was running out of time as Quentin's life bled out. With kindness for the unloved son, he asked, "Quentin, where did they take Beth?"

Fear flashed in Quentin's eyes. "I'm going to hell. I'm going to hell. That woman lied to me. She lied to me."

"Do you mean Beth?" Sam asked.

Not hearing him through the delirium of blood loss and pain, Quentin said, "She said this would all be so easy." Again, his body spasmed. "Kill the colonel at the dance." He would not last much longer. "Kill...Rowdy, Roland, and the old man at the Double L." Now he forced a mocking tone through clenched teeth. "We say we were trying to save Eli, but he got killed in the crossfire. We would have it all, simple." His eyes began to fade, but he wanted his father to hear his treachery. "My part to kill father." He smiled as his eyes closed. Sam shook him awake.

"Quentin! Quentin! Where did they take Beth?"

Quentin just whispered now. "To the...Double..." and he exhaled his last breath.

Sam looked up at the colonel with contempt. The colonel looked away. Sam stood and scanned the room. Maria was tending to Jenny's split lip, and O'Rourke was walking to the unconscious Jake with a bucket of water. O'Rourke threw the water on Jake, and he sputtered awake.

Grabbing Jake by his shirt, O'Rourke lifted him to his feet. "Now there you are, my lad. Right as rain."

Jake grabbed his jaw and worked it, making sure it was still working the way it should. Then he reached back and punched O'Rourke hard in the face. The Irishman hardly flinched.

Wiping a small trickle of blood from his mouth, he said, "I had that one coming, lad, but if you want more satisfaction it will have to wait. The Larsons have Miss Kennedy."

Sam came up behind Jake and clapped him on the back. "To the end."

Jake nodded. "All the way." He looked for Jenny and found her with Maria. Relief at seeing her in one piece spread through him like a warm breeze. Stepping to her, he asked, "Are you all right?"

"Yes, silly man. Rowdy's done far worse to me before, and he would have tonight, but Beth saved me." Knowing what Larson was capable of, she said, "You and the marshal have got to save her."

Jake cupped her cheek. "We will," he said and gently kissed Jenny on her bruised lips.

She said, "Go." And he ran to catch up to Sam and O'Rourke, who were already out in the storm.

Sam stepped out into a driving rain. The collapsed windmill still smoldered from the lightning strike, but the downpour had put out the fire. Sam went right to Buck, relieved to see he hadn't spooked in the storm. "At-a-boy, Buck," he said, leaning his head against the chestnut and stroking the warhorse's neck.

Throwing his ruined frock coat into the buggy, Sam retrieved his .44s and strapped them on. Tightening down the belt, he felt the tear in his side talking to him. He liked the pain. It reminded him he was alive and kept him sharp. Seeing Beth's gun belt, he pulled one of her .36s and pushed it into his belt. Jake and O'Rourke had found their mounts and rode up just as Sam stepped onto Buck.

As the colonel and the rest of guests came streaming out of the barn, the colonel called after them. "Wait, my men and I will come with you!"

Sam, Jake, and O'Rourke exchanged glances. Sam shouted to Buck, "Hah!" and the big horse broke into a gallop, followed by the only men Sam thought he could use. *We are yours, Father. Guide us. Use us. Let us be the sword in your hand.*

<hr />

Beth had started to wake up as someone threw her off Rowdy's saddle into Roland's arms. She knew she must have been riding laid over the front of a saddle, because her ribs ached. They had tied a bandana so tightly over her mouth that her jaw was stiff. As Roland put her up in another saddle, she became dizzy and almost threw up, but she forced it back. The pain in her head boomed with every beat of her heart.

Now her hands were being tied to the saddle horn. She was almost grateful she was so dizzy she wasn't sure she could stay in the saddle. The wind and hard rain in her face slowly brought her back to the reality of her situation and the danger before her. She was in bad shape. Taking advantage of an opening would be difficult at best. It was so dark she couldn't see a thing. Cold and wet, she tested the leather bonds, but the gunman who had tied her knew his work. She was so tightly secured that the leather was cutting off her circulation, and her hands were already starting to hurt.

Trying not to show concern, Roland asked Rowdy, "How fer back do ya think they are?"

"Not fer."

"I thought Quentin and Pete would have caught up by now. I heard the shots." He looked into the darkness down their back trail.

Rowdy shook his slicker and stepped back onto his horse. "Ya heard shots, did ya, stupid? How many shots?"

Roland thought back and counted out loud. Counting was not one of his strong skills. "One, two—only two."

"That's what I counted. Unless Quentin was a better hand with a gun than I thought he was, the last time I checked ya need three bullets to kill three men. I figure they got the drop on that useless dandy. So they're comin' right into the trap. Let's move," he said.

Beth's heart leaped. *Sam is still alive. He is coming.*

Roland stepped onto his horse, never letting go of Beth's reins. Rowdy's crew moved out at a trot. The darkness would not allow them to proceed any faster. Even in the darkness, Beth could see Roland looking over his shoulder past her at the back trail, trying to see into the darkness and rain.

Sam, Jake, and O'Rourke rode through the night, staying off the road to the Double L. Sam had no desire to catch them in the dark on the road. Even a half-wit like Rowdy could set an ambush in the dark. A gun battle in the dark and rain would most likely get Beth killed.

He would trust the whisper he had heard. Beth was safe for now. If Rowdy was going to play with her, he would be looking for some place dry. Sam believed Beth would be safe until Rowdy got to the rock fortress the Larsons called home.

Of course there was Victor Holland to worry about. He was out there somewhere, probably covering the stronghold from high ground, but he would not be a problem until dawn. Back shooters need light to do their work.

Jake knew the country. He told Sam, "If we stay off the road and stick to the game trails across the scrub, I think we can reach the ranch when they do. If we get some light, maybe before."

Sam clapped Jake's already soaked shoulder and said, "Lead the way."

Jake took them out through the ponderosa at a good pace. It was dark with just a slight glow from the August moon that had risen behind the thunderheads, but Jake knew the way. The map of every gully and hill was in his head.

Sam had experienced this himself dozens of times. He'd get up long before the sun to hunt deer and walk through buck brush and trees in the pitch black with nothing to guide him but the scouting he had done. He'd sit down at the tree he had picked as his stand and wait. Sure enough, when the light began to come, he was right where he thought he was and the buck, Lord willing, would be standing out in the meadow.

As the night wore on, the thunderstorms diminished. Breaks in the clouds would let brief shafts of moonlight illuminate the nightscape before them. These breaks were often followed by intense showers. Jake moved confidently ahead.

They crossed the Juniper River around midnight. The storm faded, and the full summer moon from the night before broke through the clouds. Now the men were able to push hard, and they made good time. They soon were on the Double L and headed for the stronghold.

✦

For hours the full moon had led Beth's captors. All night they had been looking to their back trail, stopping now and then to listen and then pushing on. They had ridden their mounts to exhaustion, and now their lathered mustangs were faltering. Beth's head was still pounding, and all she wanted was sleep, but she forced herself to stay awake.

Now in the high desert of the Double L, Rowdy picked a small knoll to pull up and check his back trail. It was a good spot for an ambush if one was needed. As soon as his crew was past the rise, they dismounted. Rowdy said, "Roland, watch her. I'll be right back." He headed back to the crest of the hill for a look-see.

Beth's hands were aching, and she wanted off of the saddle. She had seen men defer to women her whole life if they just said they needed to relieve themselves. If they just mentioned they needed a moment to themselves, men stopped whatever they were doing and waited. So Beth thought she would try it. "Roland, I have to relieve myself," she said. The words felt awkward coming out of her mouth.

Roland almost peed himself when he heard her request. He did not want to make Rowdy mad, but Rowdy was not there to ask what to do.

In the girliest tone she could muster, she said, "Roland, I need to go. Now." Beth was not used to using her feminine wiles, but she gave him the most pathetic, little-girl look she could. "Please."

Beth could almost see Roland's small brain working. This was a no-win for him. He knew he would get yelled at or punched for letting her down, but he would get the same for letting her pee herself. Finally Roland decided to get her down. "Jimmy," he said to one of the gunmen, "cover her."

"Rowdy ain't goin' to like this," Jimmy said as he levered a bullet into his rifle.

"Well, Rowdy ain't here right now," Roland said, scratching the back of his neck.

The wet leather strap around Beth's hands had gotten tighter as it dried. Roland could not work the knot loose, so he finally cut it. Then he stepped back and pulled his Frontier Remington. This woman had killed three men just two nights before, and they were men who could handle themselves, men Roland was not sure he could have beaten in a fair fight.

Beth watched him quickly pull back and clumsily pull his gun. He was afraid, and she thought his fear might work to her advantage. The problem was her hands were still just a numb ache; she could not use them.

"I can't feel a thing," she said, "You'll have to help me down."

"The–the–the hell I will."

Trying her best to sound like Laurie, Beth said, "Now, don't tell me you're afraid of little, old me."

Jimmy laughed behind Roland and said, "I think you is afraid, Roland."

Roland holstered his gun and set his face in his meanest frown. He stepped forward and held his hands out. Beth swung her leg over the saddle horn and slid in his direction. He grabbed her by the waist and set her on the ground. If she had feeling in her hands, she would have disarmed and killed him, but as it was, she was just starting to feel a painful tingling coming into her fingertips as circulation was returning.

He stepped back and pulled his gun. "Now yer off the damn horse. Go pee. There is some sagebrush right there." He pointed to a clump of brush about eight feet off the road. The brush was no more than three feet high. Pointing the barrel at her nose, he said, "I want to see yer head the whole time."

Beth walked behind the sagebrush, rubbing her hands and trying to get some blood back into them. When she got behind the brush, she looked down at her dress. It was covered in mud and blood from the back of her head. Like the cabin, another dream ruined. She looked to heaven and asked, "Did I make the wrong choice? Sam says you whisper. This seems more like a shout."

"Come on. How long can it take?" Roland asked.

"Maybe she needs some help," Jimmy said. They all laughed.

While doing her business, Beth looked for a way to escape. Her hands still had the pins and needles feeling, but they were now useable. Suddenly she had the feeling she was being watched. Spinning around, she could see Rowdy silhouetted by the setting moon.

"Goin' somewhere, *Elizabeth*?" he asked.

She stared defiantly back at him and asked, "How is your finger?"

Rowdy had had enough of women making sport of him. He strode down to where she was standing and grabbed her by the elbow, almost lifting her off her feet. He pulled her close to his face, and Beth could smell the foul stench of chewing tobacco and feel his spittle as he spoke. He kissed her. She clamped her mouth shut tight but could still taste the tobacco juice. "Oh yeah, *Elizabeth*, yer gonna to have some fun with me and the boys, but I wanna do it right, and that will take some time."

Not wanting to give him the satisfaction of seeing how afraid she was, she stayed close to his face and whispered, "Could you see the marshal coming?"

Rowdy, furious that he could not shake her, threw Beth away from him toward the horses. She struggled to her feet as Rowdy came up behind her. He grabbed her by the back of her dress and threw her again toward the horse she had been riding. Beth knew her words had gone straight to Rowdy's fear: McKnight was coming. This small victory helped her cope with her own fear of what lay ahead.

As they put her back on the horse and began to tie her hands, she remembered Sam's last words to her: *"Beth, I love you. Stay alive for me. I'll be coming."*

The sky in the west was just turning from indigo to purple, and the edge of the great August moon was slipping behind the desert hills to the south. Sam and his comrades crawled up to the crest of a hill west of the Larson's stone house. Jake had taken a risk by coming in from the south through the Larson herd. He figured the majority of the good hands had gone with Rowdy on the raid. Only a couple of worthless gunmen would be left to watch the cattle. The few remaining good hands would be at the stronghold looking to the east for trouble. Sam had liked Jake's thinking. They had come quickly through the herd, skirting one sleeping lookout.

The three men were lying on their bellies in the dust. The thunderstorms had not reached this parched ranch. Sam was looking through his Union field glasses at the Larson stronghold. Four men stood casually guarding the house. Two were looking up the road to the east. One was looking south, and one was at the back of the house looking north. Movement in the barn to the south of the house caught Sam's attention. There was a man with a rifle in the hayloft looking down on the house.

Sam looked to Jake and patted him on the back. "Well done. We have beaten them here."

O'Rourke said to Jake with admiration, "You done yer dad proud, lad."

Jake, not knowing how to take compliments, said nothing. O'Rourke looked at Sam's field glasses and said, "I heard the colonel sayin' ya served as captain under General Sheridan."

Not taking his eyes off the stronghold, Sam said, "That's right."

"A finer Irish officer and gentleman never lived than Phillip Henry Sheridan."

Sam turned to him. "I would have to agree." He smiled. This Irishman just kept surprising him.

"Well, Captain darlin', how do we assault this company of worthless souls?" O'Rourke was itching for a fight.

"I'm guessing it's 'Sergeant-Major O'Rourke?'"

"You'd be guessin' right, there, Captain," O'Rourke said with pride.

Sam pointed to the road coming from the east up to the house. The stronghold had been built so Larson could see anyone approaching at a gallop for a good ten minutes before they got to the house.

"There are five men that I can see guarding the house." Sam pointed them out. "Four at the house and one up in the hayloft, and I'm guessing that is Holland. There are probably one or two more in the house with Larson. When Rowdy arrives that will bring the count up to twelve or so."

Sam continued decisively, "As soon as Rowdy and his crew break the horizon, everyone down at the ranch will relax. Everyone but Holland. That is when we will move. Jake, you will go for Holland. It will be close, wet work. Can you do it?"

Jake pulled his knife with skill. "Yes."

"From the loft, you will have a good field of fire. Sergeant-Major, you and I will assault the main house. Their guard will be at its lowest when Rowdy's crew reaches the house and starts to dismount. Larson will probably come out to greet his boys and get a report."

"How sad," O'Rourke said, "that he'll be so disappointed."

"I like you, O'Rourke. When this is done I'd like to buy you a drink. You too, Jake."

Jake nodded, and O'Rourke said, "It will be my pleasure to have a drink with you, lad."

Sam continued. "With the Lord's help, it will still be predawn. I'll take the south of the house, and, O'Rourke, you take the north.

We won't attack until we see you are in place, Jake. As soon as Beth has dismounted, I'll kill whoever is guarding her and kill my way to her. O'Rourke you do the same from your end."

"Oh, I like it, Captain darlin'. Outnumbered four to one. I do hope there are a few more wretches keeping Larson company in the house—just to make things fair, ya know. And if anything goes wrong, kill everyone and save the girl."

"Yes. That is plan B." Sam smiled. The men around the stronghold all shifted and looked to the east. The first horse had appeared on the horizon. Sam turned to Jake to tell him to go, but he was already gone.

Beth watched the last bit of blue-white moon go down and wondered where her McKnight was. She believed he was close. She thought she could sense him near, and this was a new feeling for her. It was a comfort that pushed back the fear. She had seen him kill, and she had read Elma's account of his gunfight with the Ewell gang down in southern Utah. Rowdy certainly hadn't read the story, because he hadn't read anything to speak of since the last day he went to their one-room schoolhouse in third grade. Carl Larson and his boys had no idea the amount of pain and death they had called down upon themselves.

It had been two years since she had ridden down this road to the Larson place, but she knew it well. As a child she had come here to pick up Vickie for their days of fun, but she had never stayed long. The Larson house was a house of anger. Rowdy was always picking at and fighting with Roland. If the two boys weren't at each other, Carl Larson was beating the both of them. Usually when Beth got there, Vickie was on her horse ready to go. Beth had rarely been in the house and only got to go to Vickie's room. So as they crossed this last rise, Beth knew the lights of the Larson place would be before them.

The stone house had only a few lanterns going inside and possibly one on the porch. Beth was not surprised Rowdy would choose guns to settle the long-standing feud between the Dunhills and the Larsons, but she was stunned that Carl Larson had struck first. Her father had always told her that despite his gruff bark, Carl was a man of honor. Come to think of it, she had never heard her father speak about honor and the colonel in the same breath. But her father had been wrong. Carl Larson had struck first.

There was no honor in the attack at the dance tonight. It must have been Carl who had had Jeff Amos killed, but that didn't make sense, and now they had kidnapped her and were going to kill her. What she could not figure out was why. She and Carl had always worked things out. She thought he trusted her. What had pushed him over?

＊＊＊＊——————◆——————＊＊＊＊

Sam moved slowly up to the back of the house. He could see Holland, who had come out of the shadows to watch the returning raiders, and Sam kept his eyes on him. Sam had taken off his blood-stained, white shirt and put the brown vest back on to tone down his white chest. Holland scanned the grounds from time to time, and when he did, Sam would freeze. As soon as Holland's attention was directed back toward Rowdy's crew, Sam would move.

Carrying his Winchester, two .44s, and Beth's Colt .36, he felt well armed enough to walk into hell to take Beth from Satan himself. The truth was that was exactly what he was doing, and he knew it.

Sam and O'Rourke reached the house at the same time and pressed themselves up against the back wall. Now it was a game of waiting and timing. Jake would have to pick the right moment to kill Holland, and he would have to do it without drawing attention. If Holland detected him early and a fight broke out before the rides reached the stronghold, the likelihood of saving Beth grew very slim.

Holland stood up and leaned against the frame of the hayloft door and lit a cigar. So far, God was smiling on them.

The stars were beginning to fade as Rowdy's crew rode up to the house. The predawn light was bringing the ranch to life. A rooster was crowing, and songbirds were letting it be known they were awake. There was a touch of September's coolness in the early morning. Beth loved this time in the morning. If Rowdy weren't trying to rape and kill her, she would be enjoying herself, she noted wryly.

She expected Carl Larson to be standing on the fallen-down juniper porch waiting to greet his boys. Sure enough, as the horses came to a stop, the front door of the house opened, but instead of the massive, oak-barrel presence of Carl Larson, a tough cowboy wearing a brown shirt and a two-gun rig backed out of the door. One of his guns was out, and he was pointing it at whoever was following him. To Beth's surprise, the gun was on Carl Larson, whose hands appeared to be tied behind his back. He was followed by another gunman who had a rifle pointed at Larson's head. Finally, out came Victoria Larson.

I should have guessed, Beth thought.

The predawn light was growing. Maintenance was not a high priority on the Double L, so the roof of the barn was not keeping much out, including the light. There was just enough illumination for Sam to see another man standing in the loft behind Holland. Holland was enjoying his cigar and watching what was happening on the porch. Sam was desperate to see if Beth was all right, but he had to wait for Jake to make his move.

Victoria Larson wore pants, a red shirt with the sleeves rolled up, and a Colt tied down. Her wild mane of red hair was tied back, and in her right hand she was carrying a double-barreled coach gun. She stood in her boots with a broad stance. All the men on the porch deferred to her, sheepishly bowing their heads. Beth glanced at Rowdy and was surprised to see him biting his lip, trying not to make eye contact with Vickie.

He is afraid of her. Well I'll be damned. Sam was right. Men will follow a strong woman, Beth thought.

Vickie scanned Rowdy's crew, and before Rowdy could say anything, her eyes stopped on Beth. Vickie's head tilted to one side. She squinted as if she must not have been seeing clearly. Beth met her eyes, knowing that her appearance must have been quite a shock to her childhood friend. Beth's dress was covered in mud, the neckline was torn, and her corset was showing. Even spattered in mud and soaked from the rain, Beth guessed she looked like a woman. Vickie shook her head as if she wasn't sure she was awake and said to Rowdy, "Who the hell is this?"

Rowdy, brightening at the chance to speak about something that was not his fault, said, "This is Eli, sis. Kin ya believe it? He's a girl!" Rowdy spoke as if he were a little boy trying to please his mother. His tone of submission stunned Beth. She realized her mouth was open, so she shut it.

Roland jumped in. "They said she was Eli's twin, Elizabeth, from before the massacre. She been pretending to be Eli ever since." He smiled at Rowdy, proud of his clear report. Rowdy returned a look of disgust.

Vickie stepped forward to get a better look. "Well, at least that explains why I could never get you to like kissin'. I was startin' to think you liked boys"—she laughed—"and it turns out I was right." All the men started to laugh at her joke. "I was worried I was losin' my touch."

"And what touch was that?" Carl Larson interrupted. "The fact that you are a whore just like your worthless mother?" He took a step toward her, and the two gunmen on each side of him pulled him back.

Vickie's eyes filled with fury as she turned to her father. She took two steps toward him and rammed the business end of the scatter-gun into his gut, screaming at him, "Shut up, old man!"

The pain sent Carl down to one knee, but he looked up at her defiantly and said, "A crazy Jezebel just like your mother." He gazed up at Beth and said, "Ah, little Lizzy. You came back from the grave."

Beth's mind raced. *Little Lizzy,* she thought. Her memory spun to the summer before the monster came. She'd been on this very porch. Her father had been sitting in a chair next to Carl Larson, talking. Rowdy and Roland were wrestling out front, and Eli, Vickie, and she were playing on the steps. She remembered Mr. Larson calling to her, "Little Lizzy! Come here and give me some love." She had jumped up and run to him. As a child, she had liked him very much, but after the monster, her father had not gone visiting, and she had forgotten.

"So Bill hid ya, did he?" Carl said, with a tenderness she did not know he possessed. Beth nodded with new compassion, sorry to see the proud, old rancher betrayed by his children.

Carl, undaunted by his daughter, said, "I'm sorry fer this. Ya always was honorable with me."

Vickie smacked him in the mouth with the butt of the scatter-gun. Her eyes grew wide and wild, and her face was red with fury. "I said shut up!"

Again, with blood dripping from his mouth, he stared back at his treacherous child.

Calming her contorted face back to a mask of sanity, Vickie straightened herself and turned to Beth. "So you've been playing 'boy' all this time?"

"Vickie, what are you doing?" Beth asked.

"What'm I doing? What have *you* been doing all this time? You, lying about yourself under those pants you were wearing. I always thought you were a straight arrow, that I'd know if you was lyin'. Turns out you're a bigger liar than me."

Beth knew she was right. All she could say was, "I'm sorry, Vickie. Please—"

"Oh, shut up," Vickie cut in. "I don't give a damn about your lyin'. And I sure don't need your apology. I wasn't bringing Eli out here to bed him. I brought him out here to kill him, and that is just what we are going to do with you." She turned to the men on the porch with her. "That is, after they have a chance to blow off a little steam with you first." Vickie let the words hang in the air. Beth was not going to beg for her life or try to make a deal. Vickie said, "Oh, you look sad—what is your name? Oh, yes—*Elizabeth*. Did you believe my little fit at the store? Me and Victor had a good laugh over that performance when we got to the bar." She cocked her head, looking for a reaction from Beth.

Beth just felt pity for her childhood friend, gone mad with the lust for land, but she did want one or two questions answered. She asked, "So who killed Jeff Amos, and who drew the map?"

Vickie, caught off guard by the questions, weighed her answers. "What map?"

"The map to my cabin."

Again, a smile broke out on Vickie's face as she saw a chance to reflect on her brilliance. "The cabin...the cabin. Surprised I found you down there by the lake? All those smart, little plans to hide away? You and Laurie always thought I was the dumb one. Turns out

I'm the one with the brains. The creator of the map and the marksman responsible for Jeff Amos's murder are one and the same." She leaned in with a girlish giggle, as if she were sharing a secret. "He is right..." She scanned the horsemen for her comrade in treachery, but he wasn't there. Her smile left, replaced by confusion. "Rowdy, where is Quentin?"

Of course, Beth thought. She remembered back to Rowdy and the other older boys teasing Quentin about his pretty handwriting in school.

Rowdy did not want to answer. He tried to form words, but his jaw just could not get going. As he hesitated, Vickie's eyes drilled into him, panic just behind her eyelids. Finally, Roland spouted it out, quickly: "We think he is dead. Pete too."

"What?" she screamed, and stepped forward, looking at the returned men as if she might find him still.

Rowdy found his voice and reluctantly said, "Sis, he wanted to be the one to kill his pa. Ya said to follow his lead. We was—"

Flying into a panicked rage, Vickie yelled, "I *knew* I should've gone! Ye're both idiots. How could ya mess this up? It was so simple! Ya kill the colonel and the marshal, and we kill Eli and Pa. Quentin takes over the Seven-C, and I take the Double L, and we combine them into one big spread by buying up the now ownerless Running J." She said it as if it was something she had memorized for school. Pacing back and forth in front of the horses, she said, "So they're comin' then, the marshal and probably the colonel. Ya idiots! I hope to hell they kill ya today."

Carl Larson, again standing with his head bowed, started laughing. He lifted his head to look at the children who planned to kill him, "What a worthless litter of cats ya'll turned out to be. I should've drowned you at birth. Saved the hangman a little work." He looked directly at his sons. "Since ya followed little sis, ya'll be hangin' by Christmas." Beth watched as Carl's face moved from bitter laughter to sorrow for the dreams he had lost.

Vickie's jaw clenched. She pulled her Colt and shot her father in the gut. "I told you to shut up!"

Carl looked down at what his girl had done and knew she had killed him. He sat hard on a small barrel the family used as a stool.

◆

When Sam heard the gunshot, it was all he could do to hold his ground. *Father, protect her and let me be the sword in your hand,* he prayed. Looking quickly to the hayloft, he saw Holland still leaning against the doorframe, but his expression had changed. Holland's eyes were wide with surprise. The cigar he had been smoking sagged in his mouth. His body jerked violently up, and his eyes grew even wider. The cigar fell from his mouth as the light went out of his eyes. Victor's body slumped to the side, and a smiling Jake appeared behind him, easing Holland's body into the hay. The gunshot had been the perfect cover for Jake.

Sam nodded to O'Rourke, and the two of them began to slide up to the front of the house. Jake knelt on one knee, taking aim at Rowdy's crew. To Sam's surprise, he heard Victoria Larson giving the orders. *So old man Larson wasn't behind the attack,* he thought.

◆

Vickie began to give orders. "Drag that old man off to the side of the house. I want him to die slow." She pointed her pistol in her brothers' direction and they both flinched. "Take Elizabeth in the house and tie her up." Both brothers brightened at this command, but Vickie spoiled it. "Ya idiots. Thanks to you, we got all of Smith riding down on us. Ya don't have time for your fun. Just tie her up and take cover. She might be our ticket out of here." To the rest of the men, she shouted, "Take cover, boys! The colonel's coming to pay us Larsons a visit, and we want to show him some Larson hospitality!"

Rowdy's crew began to dismount. Rowdy and Roland stepped off their horses and handed their reins off to Jimmy. Roland came up on Beth's right and reached for her waist. Beth took the open opportunity to plant her boot heel right in his mouth. Roland reeled back, grabbing his face.

She felt a brutal tug from behind her as she was yanked out of the saddle. She fell flat on her back, knocking the wind out of her. Struggling for air, not able to take a breath, she opened her eyes to see Rowdy towering over her, rubbing his wounded hand. He whispered, "Don't pay any attention to what sis says. We still got plenty of time to play." He spit tobacco juice in the dust next to her head.

Sam, crouched at the edge of the porch, watched as Rowdy yanked Beth off the horse and slammed her to the ground. He had stood by and watched helplessly as Rowdy had attacked the innocent without cost the night before. Well now it was time for justice. Rowdy would pay with his very life.

Sam's heart pounded in his chest, and as his heart rate increased, he could feel his senses sharpen, the dim morning brightened, and colors and shapes became crystal clear. He had put his Winchester down, and his .44s were in his hands. At this range, the .44s were all he needed. If he was alive two minutes from now, he could retrieve the rifle. He leaned forward, wanting to fight. God had built his clan to protect the innocent from evil, and evil was right here before him.

He stood ready to step onto the porch as two gunmen dragged Carl Larson around the corner of the house and directly into Sam's path.

At first Sam could not wrap his mind around what he saw: a wounded Carl Larson hanging between two of his men who were obviously not trying to help him.

Carl looked weakly up at Sam and smiled. Both of the gun hands had been straining to carry the weight of the old rancher and had holstered their pistols. Now, seeing their short lives flashing before their eyes, they did not know quite what to do. Finally, they dropped their old boss and reached for leather. Both of Sam's .44s went off as one, the roar silencing the rooster crowing in the barnyard.

Both sorry gunmen took the bullets in the chests and were blown off of their feet. The one standing to Sam's right crashed off the porch and the one to his left flopped lifelessly on his back, skidding to a stop on the floorboards.

Carl, now on all fours, bleeding from his gut and his mouth, lifted his head and said, "Save little Lizzy." Sam nodded and stepped onto the porch.

The fight was on. Rowdy and his crew had turned toward the gunfire and, seeing McKnight, were trying to move to cover. Old Haney, the man who had talked to the marshal about Jeff Amos, was at the north end of the porch with a young hand who looked like he'd been sleeping with the pigs. They both were heading around the edge of the house and ran right into O'Rourke.

"Are ya surrenderin', lads?" O'Rourke asked.

Haney's gun was already out of its holster. As he eared back the hammer, the Irishman shot him in the forehead, and he crumpled like a sack of potatoes. The pig boy was running to O'Rourke's left as his gun cleared leather. He fired, missing O'Rourke and hitting the house. O'Rourke returned fire, hitting pig boy in the left shoulder and knocking him off his feet. The gunman hit the ground, but up came with his gun. O'Rourke's second shot slammed him square in the chest, and pig boy fell back in a cloud of dust.

"Thank ya fer not surrenderin'," O'Rourke said, as he stepped past the bodies.

There were two gunmen to the west of Sam. One was in a Texas rig with well-made chaps and the other was a bandit from the south side of the border. Their guns were out, and they were running for the barn. The Texan got off a shot, and Sam felt the bullet graze his thigh, but before Sam could pay him back, the crack of Jake's Winchester broke the air. The Texan looked like he had run head-long into a brick wall. The bandit slid to a stop and raised his pistol toward the rifle he now saw in the hayloft, but he was too late. The next blast lifted him off his feet and out of one boot. He hit the ground and did not move.

Vickie and the two hired men with her were moving to the front door of the house. The man closest to the door had a belly on him that his belt could not contain. He turned to face O'Rourke and got off a shot that hit a juniper post next to O'Rourke. Not flinching, O'Rourke kept coming.

At that moment, Vickie fired off her scattergun in Sam's general direction. Sam dove off the porch, but a few of the buckshot caught him in his right calf. Ignoring the pain, Sam rolled into a firing position. A thin man in a well-worn derby stood between Vickie and Sam. He was drawing a bead on Sam before the round from Sam's .44 caught him high in the chest. Derby fell back into Vickie, knocking her off balance and away from the door.

Sam turned his attention to Beer Belly, who was staring at the blood covering his hands. The blood was pouring from his chest. Apparently O'Rourke had returned fire. Beer Belly grabbed Vickie as he began to fall, and she pushed him away. He fell against the door, blocking Vickie's escape. Vickie pulled two more shells from the bandolier she wore and started to reload the scattergun.

Where is Beth? Sam thought. Before him was pure pandemonium. Rowdy's crew was being fired upon, and they were returning fire. Spooked horses were bucking and trying to run. The dust was thick. In the middle of it all, Sam saw Beth. She was on her hands and knees, still trying to breathe.

For the moment Rowdy had turned his attention from Beth to trying to survive. He had grabbed a skittish horse and was struggling to mount with only one good hand. The two of them were spinning in an awkward dance.

Sam yelled to Beth, "Stay low! I'm coming for you!"

Rarely had Sam shot a woman, and he did not want to add Vickie Larson to his short list, but his throbbing leg told him he could not just ignore her. She would have reloaded her gun about now. Turning to her, he saw her barrels coming up, but not at him. Vickie's mad hatred was being aimed at Beth.

Vickie was close to Sam, no more than ten feet. With the confidence born from years of practice, he shot the scattergun rather than the woman. The bullet hit right in front of the breach just as Vickie pulled the trigger. As the gun was knocked from her grip, the bent barrel exploded in her face and knocked her back on top of the dead gunman at the door. The second barrel's volley escaped the scattergun, but instead of striking Beth, the eight-buck shot pellets landed in the back of the gunman standing next to Roland. Blood sprayed Roland as the hapless outlaw slapped face-first into the dust.

Sam's .44s covered Vickie for a moment more, but she was out cold. Her hair was burned back from her blackened face, and there was a deep gash on her right cheek. For the moment, she was no longer a threat.

Roland and the last of Rowdy's crew still standing now faced O'Rourke. Wiping the blood from the man who had been standing next to him out of his eyes, Roland fired off two rounds in O'Rourke's general direction and ran for the nearest horse. The other gunman did the same. O'Rourke never ducked but just kept on forward, firing his Winchester as he came. The bandit Roland was running with got to the nearest horse first, but before he could mount, his sombrero was blown off along with a large portion of his head. He bounced off the horse and fell to the ground.

Roland charged for the horse the bandit had just fallen from as something grabbed at his chest, and he started to slow down. He coughed, and up came blood. Seeing the blood in his hand, he cried, "Rowdy, I'm hit!" and fell to his knees. "Rowdy, help me!" He was crying now. Rowdy glanced in Roland's direction but did not respond. Rowdy had just managed to mount the spinning horse that now started to buck in earnest. Roland fell on to his side and reached out with his hand as his life bled away. The spooked mustang gave Rowdy a good pitch, and off he went, landing by Roland. Rowdy shook his head clear and looked at Roland. Roland's eyes were now blind, but he managed to say, "Rowdy...ya got to help...me." And then his hand fell.

Rowdy looked into his brother's dead eyes and flew into a rage of injustice. It was not his fault, but people were going to pay. He rolled up on one knee and shot O'Rourke high in the chest, breaking the big man's collarbone. The Irishman dropped his rifle and fell back.

By this time, Sam had reached Beth. She had caught her breath and moved to cover near the porch. Kneeling, he embraced her, kissed her dirty face and stroked her short hair. When Sam saw O'Rourke fall, he struggled to stand between Beth and the enraged Rowdy.

Rowdy had his Remington trained on Sam as he wiped the sweat from his mustache with the back of his broken hand. "Now, ain't that sweet, the marshal protecting that worthless, lying tramp. Marshal—ya look a little shot up."

Sam knew he was right. His leg was throbbing, and his vision was closing in. The loss of blood had taken its toll. "I'm here for you, Rowdy. I'm happy to send you to your daddy."

"What are ya talking about?" Rowdy said. "My pa is lying right over there."

"I'm not talking about your earthly daddy. I'm talking about your father below."

Rowdy's eyes flashed with anger, and the muscles in his forearm began to tense as his body instinctively leaned slightly forward, anticipating the recoil from his gun. That instant was all Sam needed. The only thing Rowdy saw was the flash of McKnight's Colt. The impact of the two-hundred-and-thirty-grain-long Colt staggered his huge frame, but did not send him down. He straightened himself and stepped forward. At first Rowdy thought it had been his Remington that had fired, but then he looked down to see that his hand holding the pistol had dropped to his side. Try as he might, he could not get his Remington to come up and aim. He took another step forward, trying to curse at the marshal, but suddenly the ground was coming up to meet his nose, and all was darkness.

Sam watched him fall, and relief washed over him. His body began to relax. *Thank you, Father,* he prayed as the sun broke over the top of the Bear River mountains. The gun blast from behind him caught him by surprise. He looked down and saw fresh blood on his chest from the bullet that had just passed through. He struggled to stand but could not. Down he went, onto his side.

"No!" Beth looked toward the sound of the blast and saw the freakish Vickie standing with her smoking Colt in her hand. Getting to her feet, Beth ran to Sam and knelt by his side. Rolling him on his back, she could see he was still alive. She kissed him and whispered in his ear, "I love you, Sam McKnight. Don't you dare die on me!"

"You! You ruined everything," Vickie screeched.

Beth turned to her childhood friend, protecting Sam's wounded body with her own.

Vickie's burned hair was swept wildly away from her face, blood dripped from the open cut on her cheek, and her wide, crazed eyes were framed by her powder-burned skin.

Vickie pointed the Colt at Beth's chest. "It all yer fault! Why couldn't ya just love me?"

"I did love you, Vickie."

"Not the way I wanted, Eli. Ya always loved Laurie best."

"It not true. You were my favorite." Beth knew this was the truth, but not the truth Vickie wanted to hear.

Shaking the pistol at her, Vickie said, "Then why didn't ya take me, Eli, and marry me?"

"Vickie, can't you see? I'm Beth, not Eli. I couldn't marry any woman."

"Liar!" she screamed. "Liar! Eli, ya always thought you was better than us Larsons. Well, if I can't have ya, no one will!" She eared back the hammer on the Colt.

She had nowhere to hide, nothing to defend herself with. Had it been worth it to put on the dress and tell the truth? She thought of dancing with Sam. The blast made Beth flinch and close her eyes, but she felt no pain. She heard something topple and then a man crying softly. Realizing she was still in one piece, she opened her eyes. Before her on the porch stood Carl Larson, standing over his daughter's lifeless body with what looked like Sam's Winchester '73 in his hands. Suddenly, Jake appeared and skidded to a stop, raising his rifle to shoot Larson.

"No, Jake!" Beth called, raising a hand. The old rancher sank down beside the child he had to kill.

"I didn't want to do it, sis. I didn't want to! Ya made me. I couldn't let ya kill Lizzy." He picked up his daughter's small, broken body in his strong arms. Her hundred-and-ten-pound frame looked like a small child against his massive body. He was weakened by the shot he had taken, but it took more than one body shot to kill the tough, old rancher. He carried her off the south end of the porch around to the back of the stronghold.

Jake ran to Beth's side, and they both knelt down next to Sam.

O'Rourke had dusted himself off and was holding a bandana on his bleeding shoulder. "How is he, darlin' girl?" O'Rourke asked.

"I don't know. Let's get him up on the porch out of the sun." Beth and Jake picked Sam up and carried him to the porch. Once she had Sam settled in the shade, Beth started to peel away the bloody vest she had bought him only the day before.

O'Rourke touched her shoulder and said, "Look, help's on the way, darlin'," and he pointed to the west. The colonel and his men had just ridden up over the horizon.

"I wouldn't be too sure of that," Beth said.

Jake brought water from the well, and for the next several minutes, Beth cleaned Sam's wounds, all while the riders from the 7C grew nearer. Sam had a deep gash on his side from the graze he had received from Quentin, and three buckshot had gone clean through his calf; how he had stood to fight Rowdy, Beth could not guess. Last but not least, Sam had been hit high in the back on his left side by Vickie's attempt to murder him. This bullet, too, had gone clean through.

Jake worked on O'Rourke's shoulder as the Irishman protested, "I'm fine, lad. Help the lass with the marshal." Jake paid no attention to him and continued cleaning and binding the big man's wound.

Beth kept looking up at the progress the colonel was making. When he and his men were still about ten minutes out, she said, "Jake, Mr. O'Rourke, reload and arm yourselves."

"Oh, lassie, it's just the colonel. He's come to help." The Irishman tried to reassure her.

She reached for her Colt .36 that she had taken out of Sam's belt and said, firmly, "Mr. O'Rourke."

"Now, I know he's your boss, but believe me when I say he has not come to help." She stared straight into his strong, Irish eyes and said, "Trust me and reload." She spun the cylinder on her Colt. Jake had already reloaded his rifle and was checking his pistol. O'Rourke reluctantly started doing the same.

"Jake, help me get Sam inside."

O'Rourke grabbed the Beer Gut's lifeless body and dragged it away from the door, and Beth and Jake carried Sam into the house.

"Jake, Vickie's bedroom is back here. We'll put him on her bed." Beth led Jake back to the only room in the stronghold she had spent any time in as a child. It was a woman's room with bed, mirror, and a large wardrobe. They laid Sam gently down on the bed. She kissed his forehead and stood, catching sight of herself in the mirror. She was covered in mud, and her dress was torn open at the bust line and at her back. It hung off her shoulders.

"Jake," she said, "tear this thing off me."

"What?"

"You heard me. We don't have time to unbutton the silly buttons that are left. Just tear it off."

Shaking his head, he said, "You're the boss," and grabbed the back of the dress and tore it open.

"Now cut the laces off this corset."

"But boss, ya'll…ya'll be naked."

"Cut. I won't drop the corset until you have turned away."

He pulled his knife and sliced through the laces. The corset opened up, and Jake found himself staring at the skin of her back.

"Turn around," she said, impatient with his maleness.

"Yes, ma'am."

Beth tossed the corset aside and stepped out of the remains of her dress and walked over to Vickie's wardrobe. Opening it, she found jeans and a shirt. She stripped off the muddy pantaloons and pulled on Vickie's jeans. Next, she threw on the shirt and buckled one of Vickie's belts around her waist. Beth pushed the .36 into the belt and said, "Jake," but he did not look her direction. "It's all right, I'm decent." He turned slowly to her, relieved to see her in more familiar clothes.

"Boss, I'm sorry. I ju—"

She could see him blushing through the dirt on his face. "Oh, Jake, be quiet. We're running out of time. When we step out onto the porch, follow my lead and be ready to kill."

"What? Ya can't mean that."

"That is exactly what I mean. Trust me, friend. The colonel is
not here to help. And keep an eye on Pat. I don't know if he can go
against his old commander." Jake just nodded and led the way out of
the room to the porch.

They reached the front door as the colonel and his troop reined
up. Jake stepped out first and walked to the south end of the porch.
O'Rourke was standing at the north end. Beth came out and walked
right to the center edge of the porch. She hitched her thumb into
her belt just inches from the butt of the Colt.

The colonel surveyed the aftermath of the battle, then looked at
O'Rourke's wound. He nodded to O'Rourke. "Sergeant, well done."

"Thank ya, Colonel," he said.

Turning to Beth, Colonel Dunhill said, "I am so glad to see you
are alive and well, Elizabeth. Where is the marshal?"

"He's in the barn, seeing to the horses," she said.

The colonel cut his eyes to the barn, but did not see a gun barrel
pointing in his direction. "So you wiped out the filth that's been poison-
ing this country for years. I see the two worthless brothers, but where is
the red-headed whore and the old boar who fathered this brood?"

"I'm right here," Larson said, stepping up on the deck from the
south end of the house, carrying a scattergun. His gut wound had
stopped bleeding. "Yer on my land, and ya might be right about my
children bein' worthless, but by God as long as yer on the Double
L, ya won't be speaking ill of them. Anyhow, my children weren't
anymore worthless than yer murderin' Quentin, and that hussy you
had to send off to finishing school."

"My Laurie was not mixed up in this," the colonel said.

"That's what yer prayin', ain't it? The way I see it is, the only child
out of our Dunhills, Larsons, and Kennedys with any honor is Bill's
girl here, Lizzy."

Looking at Beth with contempt, the colonel said, "Honor? How
can anyone who has been lying to both of us almost her whole life
have *honor?*"

"All I know is," Larson said, "she's kept to her pa's word and dealt straight with me on the water, which is more than you or our treacherous children would have done."

Beth cut in. "Oh, would you both be quiet! I'm so tired of trying to keep you two from killing each other! You're both so filled with hate. What happened last night and this morning is the result of it. Your hate for one another spread to your children, and it killed them. We are standing in Vickie's blood! There on the ground are Rowdy and Roland, and Quentin is getting cold back at the Seven-C, but they didn't hate each other. They hated the two of you. Your children died trying to kill the two of you *and* me."

Carl seemed to weaken with her words; he swayed and had to grab a juniper post to catch his balance, but the colonel's face grew red and the blood vessels on his face began to stand out.

Struggling to keep his voice calm, the colonel said, "You've fought well here today. Are you all that are left?"

Beth knew this is where he was going. Pulling her Colt, she yelled, "Jake!" and Jake leveled his Winchester at the foreman of the 7C. O'Rourke did not know what was going on, but if he had to choose between the colonel and Beth, he was with the lassie. His pistol came up, covering the hired gun on the colonel's right. Carl Larson, stunned by the turn of events, also decided to follow the daughter of his old friend William Kennedy, and aimed his scattergun at the men in front of him.

Outraged, the colonel shouted, "What is the meaning of this, Kennedy? We're here to help!"

Her gun pointed at his heart. "The way you loved to *help* my mother dance? The way you tried to *help* my father in his grief? I hear I look like her. Is that true?"

"There is some resemblance," he growled, "but Ellie was a lady—something you will never be!"

Her anger pushed her on. "Well, be that as it may, this must seem all too familiar. You, with armed men, ready to kill a member of the Kennedy family."

"What are you talking about?" he roared. "I loved your mother more than your father ever could, and she loved me!"

"Is that why she tried to kill you that day in front of our home?" Then Beth quoted her mother's last words. "You can't hide behind that mask! God and I know who you are!" Beth could see a large vein throbbing in the colonel's forehead.

The colonel raised his hand, and his men began to move.

"Don't make a move, lads. We'll cut half of ya down before ya fire a shot," O'Rourke said.

The colonel's foreman raised his scattergun anyway, and Jake blew him out of the saddle. The rest of the troop let their guns rest easy.

The colonel scowled at his men in fury. "Cowards! We outnumber them three to one!"

"Give us a moment, Colonel darlin'," O'Rourke said, "and we will even those odds."

"What, Colonel?" Beth asked. "Are you not used to the women and children you torture and kill fighting back? You claim to be a man of honor. What kind of monster rapes and kills their family friends?"

The colonel's eyes narrowed. "Ellie *made* me do it! All she had to do was come away with me, but she would not. I've never wanted anything so much as that woman, but she would not leave Bill. He was weak! He did not deserve her. She belonged to me and if I could not have her, no one could."

"Dunhill, ya evil bastard! Ellie Kennedy was the kindest woman I ever met. When my family came down with smallpox, she spent two week nursin' them. Lizzy, don't believe what he is sayin'. Never did a woman love a man more than your ma loved her Bill," Carl said.

Beth's breath had grown short, and her heart was pounding in her chest with wrath for the monster before her. Over and over she saw her mother tearing the mask off of Dunhill's face. "This reign of hatred ends today—with you and me." Keeping her eyes on the evil mounted in front of her, she said, "Jake, O'Rourke, Mr. Larson, if any of the Seven-C men move, kill them.

"Dunhill, I'll give you a choice. You can throw down your weapons and go back to Smith to hang for your crimes against my family, or we can end it right here."

The colonel smiled. "I am not going back to Smith with you."

"I was hoping that is how you'd want to play it." Beth slid her Colt back into the belt around her waist. The colonel unleashed his Smith & Wesson, sweeping his frock coat back and out of the way.

"Your move," Beth said, staring into the eyes of the man that had robbed her of so much: her mother, sister, and twin brother.

The blood vessel still bulging from his forehead, the colonel said, "Your father thought he was faster than me too. That day on the ridge he had finally figured out who Ellie really loved. He tried to brace me, but all the old fool managed to do was get thrown from his horse. Broke his leg falling on the rocks. I could have helped him, but if it wasn't for him I would have married Ellie, so I let him rot."

At Dunhill's words, the roar of blood in Beth's ears began to overtake her. Her hands tingled, and her lips grew numb. The thought of her father slowly dying in pain overwhelmed her, and for a moment she lost focus. Dunhill seized the lapse and drew first, firing as Beth's Colt cleared her belt. His sudden movement caused his horse to step left and his bullet grazed Beth's forehead.

Her head tugged right but she never took her eyes off the man who brought all of the pain into her life. Her Colt barked and barked again. Both slugs landed within inches of each other in the colonel's left chest. His horse began to rear, and he struggled to stay mounted. He slid off the back of the horse onto Rowdy's body. He tried to push himself off of this Larson he felt was so beneath him. But Dunhill's body would not cooperate, try as he might, and he just sank down onto dead Rowdy until their faces were touching.

Beth watched, her Colt trained on him as he took his last breath on this side of life. A voice came from behind her.

"Beth."

She spun around to see Sam standing in the doorframe. His .44 was in his hand. Her McKnight was there for her, just in case. She tucked her Colt into her belt as she moved to him. He gently touched the cut on her forehead, and she winced. He took her in his arms and sucked in from the stab of pain he felt. They carefully kissed each other, trying not to cause more damage than pleasure would allow.

"Elizabeth Kennedy, will you do me the honor of marrying me?"

She smiled. "Yes, Sam."

Epilogue

It was a fine, warm day. September had turned into October, and the fruit trees Ellie Kennedy had planted so long ago were glowing with red and orange. Northern Utah was experiencing Indian summer.

Over a year had passed since the day he had seen the beautiful girl with the short hair at the edge of his lake. Sam stepped off the porch of the Kennedy homestead and walked to Buck, who was tied to the rail. The big chestnut pushed against Sam's chest with his head, looking for the apple he knew was hidden somewhere on Sam. He found the apple slice in Sam's vest pocket, and Sam rewarded his friend with the fall treat.

Sam surveyed the Running J and thought back to how he had longed for the shorthaired girl that first night in the cabin, while not yet knowing a thing about her. He mused at how the Father had used him to save the girl Sam would fall in love with, and how God used the girl to save him. Sam remembered how the two of them could hardly wait for his granddaddy to make the trip from Texas to Smith so they could be wed. They had had a grand dance of their own right here on the J that day. O'Rourke must have danced with every pretty girl in Smith, and of course the punch was the Irishman's own recipe.

Granddaddy loved Beth right away, and she had loved him like she had known him all of her life.

And there was the sweet memory of their wedding night and all the nights after. Sam smiled; he knew there had been quite a bit of talk around the ranch about how the two of them could not get enough of each other. God had surely blessed him in the past fourteen months.

8

Jake ran up to the house from the barn. "Is Boss inside?"

"Yes, she is talking to your wife and Maria. How is Belle?"

Jake smiled with the excitement of a little boy at Christmas. "It's time."

Sam called into the house, "Beth! Jenny! Belle's about to foal." Sam rubbed Buck's neck and whispered in his ear, "Atta boy, Dad." Buck threw his head, and Sam laughed as Beth stepped out onto the porch. Her shoulder-length, blonde hair was pulled back in a ponytail, and she was wearing a blue work shirt and brown riding skirt. She ran to Sam and hugged him, smiling up with those sparkling, aqua eyes.

"I can't wait to see the foal." She gave Buck a hug around his neck. "With this handsome stud and Belle's bloodlines, this colt is going to be a smart, little beauty."

Seeing her excitement, all Sam could do was kiss her. "I love you, wife."

"And I love you, husband."

Maria came through the front door with an infant in her arms. She was followed by Jenny, who was great with child. Jenny walked to Jake and kissed him.

Beth looked at Jake expectantly, and he said, "Belle is doing fine, Boss, but we need to get in there."

"I'll be right there, Jake."

"I'll be in the barn." With his hand on Jenny's belly, Jake kissed her on the cheek and ran back to the barn.

Beth held her hands out to Maria for the baby. Maria smiled and brought the infant to her.

"Here, my sweet boy." Beth kissed the little boy's cheek. She turned to Sam, so in love with the son Sam had given her, and said, "This boy and this little colt are going to be fast friends."

"I was just thinking that," Sam said.

Beth kissed the baby boy one more time and said, "I've got to go be with Belle. Can you watch your boy?"

"I can think of nothing I'd rather do, Mrs. McKnight." He took the infant into his arms. He pulled Beth close and kissed her.

She looked up at him, smiling, and said, "Hold on to that thought for later." She gave him one last, quick kiss and ran for the barn, stopping halfway to look back at her husband and son standing next to the chestnut warhorse. She took a few steps backward, then turned and ran to Belle's side.

Sam watched her go. He looked down on the face of his sleeping boy. "I love you, Eli." Sam could hear his granddaddy saying, "Yer love fer yer children will give ya just a glimpse of how much our Father loves us."

"You are so right, Granddaddy, so right."

Citations

I have been blessed to grow up and live in God's country, the southern Cascades of Oregon. This meant as a boy I spent my time hunting and fishing with my family. I get to do what others only dream of. Good hunting and fishing are only fifteen minutes away.

I am also a nut about westerns, particularly John Ford western films. So when I heard you could compete with guns of the old west at cowboy action shoots, I jumped in. To handle and use a Colt Peacemaker or a Winchester rifle while wearing a cowboy costume is every little boy's dream (at least those raised in the 1960s.) I fell in love with the guns of the west and with a book that was a guide to those guns by Charles Chapel: *Guns of the Old West*, Odysseus Editions, Inc., 1995. Every gun used in *McKnight* was a tool used by the men and women of 1874.